THE EVENTS IN THIS BOOK ARE REAL.

NAMES AND PLACES HAVE BEEN CHANGED
TO PROTECT THE LORIEN,
WHO REMAIN IN HIDING.

OTHER CIVILIZATIONS DO EXIST.

SOME OF THEM SEEK TO DESTROY YOU.

THE LORIEN ▭ LEGACIES

BY PITTACUS LORE

Novels

I AM NUMBER FOUR

THE POWER OF SIX

THE RISE OF NINE

THE FALL OF FIVE

Novellas

I AM NUMBER FOUR: THE LOST FILES #1: SIX'S LEGACY

I AM NUMBER FOUR: THE LOST FILES #2: NINE'S LEGACY

I AM NUMBER FOUR: THE LOST FILES #3: THE FALLEN LEGACIES

I AM NUMBER FOUR: THE LOST FILES #4: THE SEARCH FOR SAM

I AM NUMBER FOUR: THE LOST FILES #5: THE LAST DAYS OF LORIEN

I AM NUMBER FOUR: THE LOST FILES #6: THE FORGOTTEN ONES

Novella Collections

I AM NUMBER FOUR: THE LOST FILES: THE LEGACIES

(Contains novellas #1–#3)

I AM NUMBER FOUR: THE LOST FILES: SECRET HISTORIES

(Contains novellas #4–#6)

I AM NUMBER FOUR

THE LOST FILES

SECRET HISTORIES

FOUR

PITTACUS LORE

HARPER
An Imprint of HarperCollinsPublishers

I Am Number Four: The Lost Files: Secret Histories

I Am Number Four: The Lost Files: The Search for Sam,
copyright © 2013 by Pittacus Lore

I Am Number Four: The Lost Files: The Last Days of Lorien,
copyright © 2013 by Pittacus Lore

I Am Number Four: The Lost Files: The Forgotten Ones,
copyright © 2013 by Pittacus Lore

www.epicreads.com

ISBN 978-0-06-222367-8

Typography by Ray Shappell

13 14 15 16 17   CG/RRDH   10 9 8 7 6 5 4 3 2 1

❖

First Edition

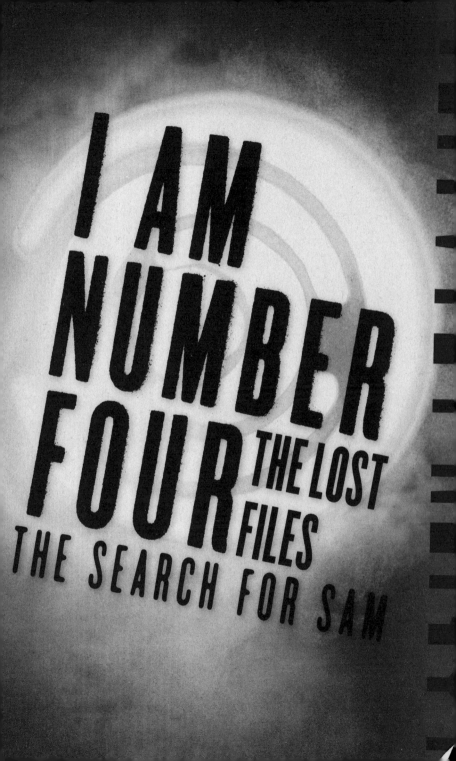

CHAPTER ONE

I DON'T KNOW IF I CAN.

I'm too weak to speak, so I don't say it out loud. I merely think it. But One can hear me. She can always hear me.

"You *have* to," she says. "You have to wake up. You have to fight."

I'm at the bottom of a ravine, my legs twisted beneath me, a boulder pushed uncomfortably between my shoulder blades. A stream laps against my thigh. I can't see anything because my eyes are closed, and I can't open my eyes because I don't have the strength.

But to be honest, I don't want to open my eyes. I want to give up, to let go.

Opening my eyes means facing the truth.

It means realizing that I have been washed onto a dry riverbank. That the wet I feel on my legs is no river.

It's blood, from a compound fracture of my right leg, the bone now jutting out of my shin.

It means knowing that I've been left for dead by my own father, some seven thousand miles from home. That the closest thing I have to a brother, Ivanick, is the one who nearly killed me, pushing me brutally off the edge of the steep ravine.

It means facing the fact that I am a Mogadorian, a member of an alien race bent on the extermination of the Loric people and the eventual domination of Earth.

I clench my eyes shut, desperately trying to hide from the truth.

With my eyes still closed, I can drift off to a sweeter place: a California beach, my bare feet digging into the sand. One sits beside me, looking at me with a smile. This is One's memory of California, a place I've never been. But we've shared the memory for so long during that three-year twilight that it feels as much mine as hers.

"I could stay here all day," I say, the sun warm on my skin.

She looks at me with a soft smile, like she couldn't agree more. But when she opens her mouth to speak, her words don't match her expression: they're harsh, stern, commanding.

"You can't stay," she says. "You have to get up. *Now*."

My eyes open. I'm in my bed in the volunteers' sleeping quarters at the aid camp. One stands at the end of the bed.

As in my dream, she's smiling, but now it isn't a sweet smile. It's a teasing smirk.

"God," she says, rolling her eyes. "You sleep a lot."

I laugh, sitting up in bed. I *do* sleep a lot lately. It's been seven weeks since I pulled myself out of the ravine and other than some residual weakness in my right leg, I've made a full recovery. But my sleep schedule hasn't adjusted: I'm still sleeping ten hours a night.

I look around the hut and see that all the other beds are empty. My fellow aid-workers have already risen for morning chores. I get to my feet, wobbling briefly on my right leg. One smirks again at my clumsiness.

Ignoring her, I slip into my sandals, throw on a shirt, and exit the hut.

Outside, the sun and humidity hit me like a wall. I'm still sticky from sleep and I'd kill for a shower, but Marco and the other workers are already elbow-deep in morning chores. I missed my chance.

The first hour of the day is devoted to housekeeping around camp: cooking breakfast, doing laundry, cleaning dishes. After that, a jeep will pick some of us up and take us deeper into the village. We're currently working on a water project there, modernizing the town's antiquated well. The others will stay behind in the classroom next to camp, teaching the village children. I've been trying to learn Swahili, but I've got a ways to go before I'll be ready to teach.

I bust my ass at the camp. It gives me great pleasure to help the villagers. But mostly I work as hard as I do out of gratitude.

After dragging my busted body out of the ravine and a quarter mile through the jungle, I was eventually discovered by an elderly villager. She mistook me for an aid-worker, my cover while tracking down Hannu, Number Three. She went to the camp and returned an hour later with Marco and a visiting doctor. I was brought back to camp on a makeshift stretcher; the doctor reset my leg, stitched it up, and put me in a cast I've only recently shed.

Marco gave me a place here, first to recover and now to volunteer, without asking any questions. All he expects in return is that I do my chores and that I fulfill the same labor requirements as the other aid-workers.

I have no idea what story he's constructed in his head to account for my condition. I can only figure that Marco must have guessed correctly that Ivan was the one who did this to me, based on the fact that Ivan disappeared on the day of my accident without a word to anybody at camp. Perhaps Marco's generosity is motivated by pity. He may not know exactly what happened, but he knows I was forsaken by family. And since Marco is more or less right, I don't mind him pitying me.

Besides, the funny thing about being forsaken by my family, by my entire race?

I've never been happier.

Renovating the village's well is sweaty, tedious work, but I have an advantage the other workers don't. I have One. I talk to her throughout my work, and though my muscles get sore and my back aches, the hours fly.

Mostly, she motivates me by teasing me. "You're doing that wrong." "You call *that* trowelling?" "If I had a body, I'd be done with that by now." She mocks my efforts, reclining like a sunbathing lady of leisure at the edge of the work site.

You wanna try this? I bark back in my mind.

"Couldn't," she'll say. "Don't want to break a nail."

Of course I have to be careful not to actually *speak* to her while I work, not in front of the others. I'd developed a reputation as a bit of a weirdo, for talking to myself in my first few weeks here. Then I learned to silence my side of the conversation with One, to merely think *at* her, instead of actually speaking. Thankfully my reputation has recovered, and the others no longer look at me like I might be a total lunatic.

That night I have kitchen duty with Elswit, the camp's most recent addition. We cook *githeri*, a simple dish of corn and beans. Elswit shucks and scrapes the cobs of corn while I soak and rinse the beans.

I like Elswit. He asks a lot of questions about where I come from and what brought me here, questions I know better than to answer with the truth. Fortunately he doesn't seem to mind that my replies are either vague or nonexistent. He's a big talker, always racing ahead to the next question without noticing my silence, always interjecting tidbits about his own life and upbringing instead. From what I've gathered, he's the son of a very wealthy American banker, a man who does not approve of Elswit's humanitarian pursuits.

Living up to my father's standards was difficult enough when I was a child, but after my experiences in One's mind, it became impossible. I had grown soft, had developed sympathies and concerns that I knew would be impossible for my father to understand, let alone tolerate. Elswit and I have a certain amount in common. We're both disappointments to our fathers.

But I quickly realized the similarities between us don't stretch that far. Despite Elswit's claims of "estrangement" from his family, he's still in touch with his wealthy parents, and still has unlimited access to their wealth. Apparently his father has even arranged for a private plane to pick him up in Nairobi in a few weeks just so Elswit can be back home for his birthday. Meanwhile my dad thinks I'm dead and I can only guess he's happy about it.

After dinner I have a well-earned shower and get into bed. One's curled up in a rattan chair in the corner. "Bed? *Already?*" she teases.

I give the room a once-over. No one's around, so it's safe to talk out loud, as long as I keep my voice down. Talking out loud feels more natural than communicating silently.

"I want to get up with the others from here on out."

One shoots me a look.

"What? My cast's off, my limp's almost gone . . . I'm recovered. It's time for me to pull equal weight around here."

One frowns and picks at her shirt. Of course I know what's bothering her.

Her people are out there, earmarked for extinction by my race. And here she is, stuck in Kenya. Moreover, she's stuck inside my consciousness, disembodied, with no will or agency of her own. If she had her wish, I know she'd be somewhere else—*anywhere* else—taking up the fight.

"How long are we going to stay here?" she asks, somberly.

I play dumb, pretending I don't know how she feels,

and shrug as I pull up the covers and turn over on my side. "I don't have anywhere else to be."

I'm dreaming.

It's the night I tried to save Hannu. I'm running from the aid camp into the jungle, towards Hannu's hut, desperate to get there before Ivan and my father do. I know how this ends—Hannu killed, me left for dead—but in this dream all of the naïve urgency of that night comes back to me, propelling me forward through the vines and brush, the shadows, the animal sounds.

The communicator I swiped from the hut crackles at my hip, an ominous sound. I know the other Mogadorians are closing in.

I have to get there first. I *have* to.

I arrive at a clearing in the jungle. The hut where Hannu and his Cêpan lived stands right where I remembered it. My eyes struggle to adjust to the darkness.

Then I see the difference.

The hut and the clearing itself are completely overgrown with vines and foliage. Half of the hut's façade has been blown out, and the roof sags heavily over the missing section of wall. The obstacle course at the edge of the grounds that Hannu must have used for training is so overgrown I can barely tell what it is anymore.

"I'm sorry," comes a voice from the jungle.

I whip around. "Who's there?"

One emerges from the trees.

"You're sorry for what?" I'm confused, out of breath. And my feet hurt from running.

That's when it clicks. "I'm not dreaming," I say.

One shakes her head. "Nope."

"You took over." The words escape my lips before I even understand what I'm saying. But I can tell from her face I'm right: she took over my consciousness while I slept, leading me out here to the site of Hannu's death. She's never done this before. I had no idea she even *could* do this. But her being is so intimately enmeshed with my own at this point, I shouldn't be surprised. "You hijacked me."

"I'm sorry, Adam," she says. "But I needed you to come here, to remind you . . ."

"Well, it didn't work!" I'm confused, angered by One's manipulation of my will.

But as soon as I say it, I know it's a lie. It *did* work.

My adrenaline's up, my heart is racing, and I feel it: the crushing importance of what I tried and failed to do months ago. The threat my people still pose to the Garde and to the rest of the world.

They must be stopped.

I turn away, so One can't see the doubt on my face.

But we share a mind. There's no hiding from her.

"I know you feel it too," she says.

She's right, but I push it away, that nagging sense

that I have a calling I'm ignoring out here in Kenya. Things were just starting to get good again. I like my life in Kenya, I like that I'm making a difference, and until One dragged me out here to rub my nose in the site of Hannu's murder, it had gotten easy for me to forget about the coming war.

I shake my head. "I'm doing good work, One. I'm helping people."

"Yeah," she says. "What about doing *great*? You could be helping the Garde to save the planet! Besides, do you really think the Mogadorians will spare this place when their ultimate plan takes form? Don't you realize that any work you do in the village is just building on quicksand unless you join the fight to stop your people?"

Sensing that she's getting through to me, she steps closer. "Adam, you could be so much more."

"I'm not a hero!" I cry, my voice catching in my throat. "I'm a weakling. A defector!"

"Adam," she begs, her voice catching now too. "You know I like to tease you, and I'd really hate for you to get a big head or something. But you are one in a million. One in *ten* million. You are the only Mogadorian who has ever defied Mogadorian authority. You have no idea how special you are, how useful to the cause you could be!"

All I've ever wanted is for One to see me as special,

as a hero. I wish I could believe her now. But I know she's wrong.

"No. The only thing that's special about me is you. If Dr. Anu hadn't hooked me up to your brain, if I hadn't spent three years living inside your memories . . . I'd have been the one who killed Hannu. And I'd probably have been proud of it."

I see One flinch.

Good, I think. I'm getting through to her.

"You were a member of the Garde. You had powers," I say. "I'm just a skinny, powerless ex-Mogadorian. The best I can do is survive. I'm sorry."

I turn around and begin my long walk back to camp.

One doesn't follow.

CHAPTER TWO

DESPITE MY EXHAUSTING MIDDLE-OF-THE-NIGHT run to Hannu's hut, I manage to wake up with the other aid-workers the following morning.

"Look at you, getting up early," jokes Elswit. "Sure you want to cut into your beauty sleep?"

I almost retaliate by teasing Elswit, calling him the prince like the other workers sometimes do. He earned the nickname when he arrived here with a bunch of expensive nonessentials, none more ridiculous than a luxurious pair of shiny silk pajamas. Nobody makes fun of him to his face, though: he also brought a top-of-the-line laptop with high-tech global wireless, a device he lets us all use and that no one wants to jeopardize their access to.

As I get dressed, I notice that One is nowhere to be seen. She's usually up before I am, hanging around. I figure she's sulking from our fight in the jungle.

That, or she's just disappeared for a while. She does that sometimes. Once I asked her about it. "Where do you go when you're not here?" She gave me a cryptic look. "Nowhere" was all she said.

We step outside to begin our chores, only to find a light rain is starting. It's good for the village, but it means the water project will be suspended for the day: the soil is too difficult to work with when it's raining. So after our chores, me, Marco, and Elswit are free to loaf around, and to read or write letters.

I ask Elswit if I can have an hour with his computer. He's quick to say yes. Elswit might be a spoiled prince, but he's a generous one.

I take the laptop to the hut and begin poking around on news sites. When I get time with Elswit's laptop, I always research possible Loric or Mogadorian activities. I may have removed myself from the battle, but I'm still curious about the fate of the Garde.

It's a slow news day. I double-check to make sure that I'm alone, then open up a program I've created and installed on Elswit's laptop. I've hacked into the wireless signals from Ashwood Estates, my former home, and created a shadow directory that caches Ashwood IM and email chatter.

I wish I could claim I was motivated by some heroic agenda. But the truth is my motive is so pathetic I'd rather die than discuss it with One: I just want to find out if my family misses me.

My family. They think I'm dead. The truth is, they're probably happy about it.

I spent most of my life on earth in a gated community in Virginia called Ashwood Estates, where trueborn Mogadorians live in normal suburban houses, wearing normal American clothes, living under normal American names, hiding in plain sight. But below the granite countertops and walk-in closets and faux-marble flooring, unseen by the mortals of earth, spreads a massive network of laboratories and training facilities where trueborns and vatborn Mogs work and plot together to bring about the destruction and subjugation of the entire universe.

As the son of the legendary Mogadorian warrior Andrakkus Sutekh, I was expected to be a faithful soldier in this shadowy war. I was enlisted as a subject in an experiment to extract the memories of the first fallen Loric, the girl known as One. The plan was to use the information from those memories against her people, to help us track and exterminate the rest of her kind.

The mind-transfer experiment worked only too well: I spent three years in a coma, locked inside the memories of the dead Loric, living through her happiest and most painful moments as if they were my own.

Eventually I woke from the coma. But I came back to

my Mogadorian life different, with an abiding distaste for bloodshed, a queasy but consuming sympathy for the hunted Loric, and with the ghost of One as my constant companion.

In the first of my betrayals, I lied to my people, claiming the experiment had failed and that I had no memory of my encounter with One's consciousness. I tried to change back, to be a normal, bloodthirsty Mogadorian. But with One always around me, whether as a voice in my head or a vision at my side, it became impossible to assist my people in their attacks on the Loric.

As if led by some inexorable force, I became a traitor, working against my people's efforts. I attempted to save the third Loric marked for death.

This Loric died anyway, gleefully murdered by my father right before my eyes. Despite my pathetic efforts, I failed to save him. Exposed as a traitor, I was thrown from a ravine by Ivanick, and left for dead.

In all of my electronic snooping, I haven't been able to pinpoint any communication from my family. Maybe that's a good thing. Something tells me that it would probably just hurt my feelings.

Obviously all official communication from the underground Mogadorian facilities are firewalled well beyond my ability to hack, but the Ashwood Estates signals weren't too difficult to break into. One chink in the Mogadorian armor is their expectation of total obedience. But as a former suburban Mog kid I know that Mogadorian teenagers often flout their parents' rules and use the aboveground wireless to talk about things they're not technically supposed to.

Not that they're *that* loose lipped. The cache I've created is mostly filled with tedious emails and chats that have nothing to do with Mogadorian secrets. But the last time I logged on, I did manage to decrypt the IM chatter of a particularly bigmouthed trueborn Mog, Arsis. Apparently, this Arsis kid was demoted from combat training to a job working as an assistant technician in the labs. Arsis is so eager for information about combat ops that all he does is whine and blab to some friend from his former unit about everything he sees and does in the lab, all in the hopes that his friend will reciprocate.

So far his friend has been mum, but I've managed to learn a good deal about what's going on below Ashwood.

> **Arsis: It's so borrrring. Another hole day guarding the door to Dr. Zakos lab. Apperently they've got humans in their plugged into machines. I dont know if they are being tortured or what, cuz Im not even allowed inside . . .**

Whatever sympathy I feel for Arsis is obliterated by his atrocious spelling and grammar. It's worse than Ivan's. I didn't think such a thing was even possible.

Farther down in the transcript, I discover another detail.

> Arsis: . . . there's only one left, and I guess he's not even awake, just plugged into machines that drege their brains for info. Doctor Zakos thinks tech will imrpove in the next few years and they will get decent intel from their brains. Whatever. It's been a hole week and all I get to do is clean the lab equipment.

I've never even heard of Dr. Zakos. I wonder if he is Dr. Anu's successor. I wonder if there's some connection between this "dreging" they are doing to the captive humans and the technology they used to hook me into One's memories. I wonder—

"What you doing?"

Startled, I realize that One has curled up beside me on the bed, a cheshire grin on her face. As nonchalantly as I can manage, I click out of my program and close the laptop.

Her grin curls into a frown. "Keeping secrets now, are we?"

"We share a brain," I say. "It's not like I can hide

anything from you, even if I want to."

She's quiet for a moment, no doubt processing everything I've just learned from my snooping.

"Answer me this," she says.

I put my hands up. Shoot.

"If you're so determined not to get involved, why bother digging around at all?"

It's a good question, but I brush it off.

"Just because I'm curious doesn't mean I can do anything." I pick up the laptop and get off the bed. "I have to get this back to Elswit."

I pause in the doorway. One has a pensive, inscrutable look on her face. The only thing I can read is her continued disappointment in me.

"Sorry, One," I say, turning to go. "My answer's still no."

CHAPTER THREE

THE RAIN FINALLY STOPS IN THE MIDDLE OF the night, so the following morning after chores, Marco, Elswit, and I head back into the village on the jeep and resume our work on the well. It's muddy, which slows us down and complicates our work. As a result, I'm so involved in my job I don't even notice One's absence until I'm halfway done with the day.

I don't have her usual chatter to help pass the rest of the time, but I'm kind of relieved she's not around. I'm still haunted by the disappointed look on her face yesterday, and I could use a little time off from her judgment.

After work, me and Elswit make a yam mash for dinner, and then join a few of the other workers for a game of cards in the recreation tent. Around ten, I return to the hut. Marco's already under the covers, asleep. I undress quietly and slip into my bed, conscious of

One's continued absence. It's unlike her to disappear for so long.

I scan the room, looking to see if she's tucked into some corner, hiding, but she's nowhere to be seen.

"One?" I whisper, as quietly as I can. "You there?"

No answer.

"Come on, One." A little louder this time.

"*Dude*." It's Marco. "I'm trying to sleep."

Hearing Marco say "dude" with his funny Italian accent is usually a highlight of my time at the camp. But getting caught talking to my invisible friend, I'm mortified.

"Sorry, man," I say, blushing, annoyed with One for making me raise my voice.

I still expect to see her emerge from a doorway or closet any minute, laughing at me for getting busted talking to "myself."

But she's nowhere to be seen.

I try to sleep, tossing and turning as the room fills up with the other aid-workers, one by one. But sleep doesn't come.

For all of One's comings and goings I've never gone a whole day without seeing her—not since those three years I spent plugged into her memories. She's just always been there.

Eventually I give up trying to sleep. I half dress, put on my sandals, and shuffle out to the compound's backyard. It's surprisingly cold and I clutch my arms to my chest for warmth. It's dark outside, barely illuminated by moonlight and the dim lamp next to the latrine, and it takes me a minute for my eyes to adjust.

That's when I see her, a faint outline crouched beside the baobab tree at the center of the yard.

I approach slowly. "One?"

She looks up at me. I can't tell if it's a trick of the moonlight, but there's something strange about the way she looks: it's like she's both luminescent and too dark to see.

She remains silent. I stop in my tracks.

"Come on. This isn't funny."

"Oh," she says, laughing bitterly. "I agree. This isn't funny at all." I can tell from her voice that she's been crying. "I didn't want you to see me like this," she says.

Now I'm spooked. "See you like *what*?"

But up close I understand what she means. Her skin, her whole *being*, is strangely milky, almost translucent. I can look right through her.

"I keep disappearing," she says. "Lately it's been taking all my strength to keep myself visible."

I'm quiet, afraid to speak. But I'm also afraid to listen, afraid of what she'll say next.

She turns to me, staring right into my eyes. "Remember when I told you I went 'nowhere' when I was gone from you?"

"Yeah," I say. "I thought you were just being mysterious. . . ."

She shakes her head, tears welling in her eyes. "I was being literal, actually. I really do go nowhere. I disappear completely." Now she's crying freely. "Each time, I can feel myself getting weaker. Less *real*. It keeps happening. I can still fight it, but it's getting harder. It feels like I'm dying all over again."

She closes her eyes. As she does, she flickers in and out of visibility. I can intermittently see the bark of the tree behind her.

"Well," she says, opening her eyes again. "Dr. Anu never promised this would last."

"One," I begin. "What are you saying?" I ask the question even though a part of me—the One part of me—already knows the answer.

"My existence . . . us . . . this . . ." She gestures to the empty space between us. "You're forgetting me, Adam."

"That's impossible, One. I'll never forget you."

She smiles sadly. "I know you'll always *remember* me. That's not what I'm talking about. It's one thing to remember I existed, it's another for me to stay alive inside of you."

I shake my head and turn away, not following, not willing to listen.

"It's been a while since we were connected in Anu's lab. Too long, I guess. I'm fading. The way we are, the way we talk to each other, the way you can see me, the way I feel alive even though I died years ago. Maybe *forgetting* is the wrong way of putting it. But whatever you want to call it, this wasn't built to last. It's breaking down."

Seeing how upset I'm getting, she shrugs, trying to seem casual. "We're both going to have to accept it. My time is running out."

"No," I say, refusing to believe it.

But when I turn back to her, she's already gone.

After a restless night, searching for One and eventually making my way back to the cabin alone, I drag myself out of bed. I brush my teeth, get dressed, finish my morning chores. I work in the village under the baking sun.

What choice do I have? It's not like I can ask Marco for time off. "Hey Marco, a few months ago I emerged from a three-year coma, during which I lived inside the memories of a dead alien girl, and she's been my constant companion ever since. But now she's dying, this time for good. . . . Any chance you could cover for me at the well today?" Wouldn't really fly. So I grit my teeth and keep working.

One is not as scarce today as she was yesterday. I saw her briefly when I woke up but she stayed far away, and she's hanging out at the edge of camp when I return from the village, sitting against the same tree as last night.

"Don't," she says, as I walk over to join her. "No puppy-dog eyes, please."

"One . . ." I start.

"I'm fine," she says, interrupting me. "Yesterday was just a bad day. I'm sure I've got a few more weeks."

I'm speechless, heartbroken.

"You've got dinner to cook."

I balk. Dinner? Who cares about dinner when I have so little time left with her?

"You have to leave. Elswit's giving you funny looks for talking to a tree." She laughs, waving me off. "Go."

I head to the kitchen. As we cook, Elswit tells me stories about his rich-kid misadventures, before he got his shit together and dedicated himself to service. Usually I find Elswit's stories amusing, but my mind keeps drifting back to One, sitting under the tree.

This camp, the village . . . these have been my sanctuary the past couple months, and it has gotten so easy to imagine a happy future for myself here. But when I look across camp to see One, flickering in and out of sight, leaning wearily against the tree, I imagine what this place feels like to her.

While her people are out there, fighting for survival, she's stuck here for her last hours, simply because I've found a place where I feel safe.

I realize that to her this place isn't a home. It's a grave.

CHAPTER FOUR

I LEAN BACK IN MY AIRPLANE SEAT, STARING at the passport in my hand as the jet hums somewhere over the Atlantic: adam sutton. In the photo, I'm beaming, the tooth I lost in battle with Ivan a small black gap in my smile. Looking at Adam Sutton's smiling face no one would ever know how afraid I am, what an insane risk I'm taking right now.

Elswit sits next to me, headphones on, watching some first-run blockbuster on his tablet computer while joggling his knees. The joggling is annoying, but I'm in no position to complain: Elswit came through for me big-time.

I didn't even have to come up with a grand lie for him. I just told him I had a family crisis and needed to get back to the United States. He said that was all he needed to know: he took me to the American embassy in Nairobi, paid for my new passport, and arranged for

me to join him on his father's private jet, already sched-
uled to bring him home to Northern California for his
birthday.

If I didn't already have an active American identity,
none of this would've worked. Fortunately my father,
"Andrew Sutton," never bothered to report me missing. I wonder what alarms my passport replacement
might have set off at the Mogadorian headquarters, but
I guess it doesn't make any difference. When I show up
at Ashwood Estates, either they'll kill me or they won't.
Knowing I'm coming shouldn't make a difference.

We touched down in London to refuel, our second
refueling stop. Now we're back in the air, next stop Virginia, where I'll part ways with Elswit. At that point
nothing besides a cab ride to Ashwood will stand
between me and my upcoming confrontation with my
family.

I sink even deeper into my seat, dreading my arrival.

"Must be scary." I turn to see One, sitting in the seat
next to mine. She's been gone for most of the twenty-
hour trip, off to her own private purgatory. "I can't even
imagine."

Yeah, I say. I don't need to say any more: One knows
what I'm thinking.

I'm about to see my family again for the first time
in months. I expect to be greeted as a traitor. Maybe
I'll be executed for treason: killed where I stand, or fed

to a piken. Mogadorians have no particular history or protocol for handling treason; dissent is not a problem they have much, if any, experience with.

I know my only hope is to convince the General that I'm worth more to him alive than dead.

"You don't have to do this," she says, a guilty, worried expression on her face. "It's dangerous. When I talked about taking up the cause, I didn't mean this. . . ."

This is what we have to do, I say. I sound way more certain than I feel. But I have no choice: I can't lose her.

"Once we land, we don't need to go to Ashwood. We can go anywhere, try to find the other Loric . . ."

Screw the others, I say. Though my plan is vague, I know that my only hope of saving One, of keeping her by my side, lies somewhere in the laboratory beneath Ashwood Estates. *I'm not doing this for them.*

"I know," she says. "You're doing this to try and save me, to find some way to keep me alive. You think if you go back, you can *maybe* find some way into the labs. And *maybe* my body's still there, *maybe* you can reengage the mind transfer, restore me, buy me a few more years." She bites her lip, worried about the risk I'm taking. "Seems like a lot of maybes to risk your life over."

She's right. But I don't have a choice: without One, I'm nothing. Even a 1 percent chance of succeeding is worth pursuing.

In the cab on the way to Ashwood Estates, my fear is like a fist in my stomach, pushing upwards. We're getting close, maybe ten minutes away.

Nine minutes. Eight minutes.

I feel bile churning. I ask the driver to pull over to the side of the road and I rush out to the tall grass at the edge of the highway and throw up what little I've eaten since leaving Kenya.

I take a moment. To breathe, to look out over the grass to the open fields beyond. I know this is it: my last chance to run.

Then I wipe my mouth and return to the cab, grateful that One isn't around to see me like this.

"You okay, kid?" the driver asks.

I nod. "Yeah."

The driver just shakes his head and gets us back on the road.

Six minutes. Five minutes.

We enter the suburbs surrounding Ashwood Estates. Fast-food-glutted intersections give way to middle-class townships, then to upscale gated communities indistinguishable from Ashwood. The perfect hiding place.

From above we're just another suburb: no one would imagine the strange culture inside those tastefully bland McMansions, the world-destroying plans being hatched below. In all my years living at Ashwood we'd never fallen under even a moment's suspicion from the government or the local police.

As Ashwood's imposing gates loom into view up the road, I find myself darkly amused by the irony that a walled fortress has been such an effective way to deflect suspicion in suburban America.

I tell the driver to let me off across the street, passing him the last of the money that Elswit was kind enough to give me to get home.

I approach the front gate's intercom system, glad I threw up back on the highway: if I hadn't then, I would now.

There's no point being coy. I step right in front of the security camera and press the buzzer for my house and look right into the camera. Every house has a direct feed to it. I will be identified immediately.

"Adamus?" It's my mother. Her voice cracks on the second syllable, and at the sound of it my legs almost give out.

I know she's a monster. She wants nothing more than the destruction of the entire Loric race and domination of this entire planet. But the sound of her voice hits me hard: I've missed her. More than I realized.

"Mom," I say, struggling to keep my voice from breaking.

But the intercom line has gone dead.

She's probably pulled an alarm. Notified the General.

Within minutes I'll be on a rack, or thrown into a piken's feeding pen . . .

"Adamus?!"

Her voice again. It's not coming from the intercom.

I step around the intercom panel to see my mother in the distance through the gate. She's run out of our house at the top of the hill. She's in a sundress, the kind she wears when she's baking, running down the hill barefoot. Running towards me.

In rage? In confusion? I steel myself for her approach.

"Adam!" she cries, getting closer and closer, her bare feet slapping against the asphalt. Before I know it she's swung open the pedestrian access gate and has pulled me into her arms, hugging me, crying.

"My sweet boy, my fallen hero . . . you're alive."

I'm stunned. She's not greeting me with anger. She's greeting me with love.

CHAPTER FIVE

I SIT ON OUR LIVING-ROOM COUCH, SIPPING the lemonade my mother brought me. She's talking up a storm, and I'm careful not to interrupt: I need to tread carefully, to figure out what happened here before I commit to a particular story.

"I didn't believe them," she says, sitting next to me and putting a hand on my knee. "I couldn't believe them."

I take another sip, buying myself some time. *Didn't believe them about what?*

"They told me everything and I knew it had happened, but I didn't believe it . . . I knew you couldn't really be dead."

Oh. She couldn't believe *that* part.

"I've always known physical combat wasn't your gift. I told your father a thousand times you'd be better suited to a tactical role, but he was determined not to break with custom, and insisted we make no distinction between combat and strategy. Everyone must fight in the war. But when he told me you'd been killed, that that disgusting Loric had thrown you off a cliff . . . it felt like my worst fears had come true."

My mind reels. It was my adopted brother Ivan who threw me into the ravine, under my father's approving gaze. I hadn't been killed by a Loric: I'd joined the Loric cause.

"They said they searched high and low for you . . ."

A lie. They left me for dead.

". . . that they were as heartbroken as I was . . ."

More lies.

"But they didn't find your body, and that gave me some hope. I knew in my heart that somehow you had managed to survive."

She hugs me again. It takes all of my effort to receive her hug without betraying the revolution going on inside me. I expected to return home to a Mogadorian firing squad, but instead I've come back as a fallen soldier.

"No." His voice. My mother and I turn at once to see my father in the doorway, his mouth open in shock.

"He's come back to us," my mother exclaims. "Our boy's alive!"

I have never in my entire life seen the General at a loss for words, but there he is, too stunned to speak.

In a flash I understand everything. My father lied to my mother. My father lied to the rest of the Mogadorians. Whether to protect his ego from disgrace or to maintain his authority as a general, or both, he fabricated an honorable death for me. No one here except my father—and Ivan, wherever he is—knows that I turned against the Mogadorian cause.

I only have a moment to act, to interpret my father's stunned silence and play it to my advantage.

I leap off the couch and embrace him.

"I'm alive, Father." I feel all six and a half feet of his body stiffen in disgust, but I forge ahead with my ruse. "I've come home."

I tell them a story of my return to Ashwood. Washing up on the shore at the bottom of the ravine, being rescued by a local, recovering at the aid camp. I adjust the truth slightly, characterizing my human friends as fools, claiming that I deliberately manipulated Elswit for his assistance in order to get back here, painting myself as the Mogadorian loyalist I no longer am—but this version is close enough to the truth. And I know it's what they need to hear.

"I had to get back here to see you," I conclude. "To keep serving the cause."

I force myself to stare right into my father's eyes. It takes all of my effort not to flinch from his gaze, just as

I know it's taking all of his will not to lunge across the coffee table and strangle me where I stand.

In the kitchen, the oven timer dings. My mother, clucking over my heroic and daring escape, excuses herself to check on whatever is in the oven.

"So . . ." I say to my father, waiting for his reaction.

He says nothing but jumps at me, gathering my shirt in his fist and lifting me off the ground. I hover inches from the floor, held tight by his grip.

His face, getting redder every second, glowers before mine. "Tell me why I shouldn't break your neck right this instant."

"If you wanted the truth to come out, wanted people to know how I failed you, you wouldn't have bothered to lie to everyone." My twisted collar is beginning to cut off my oxygen. I force myself to keep talking. "How'd you convince Ivan to keep your secret?"

He ignores my question. "If you think having this over me will keep you safe, you are sorely mistaken. If I killed you now, the only person I'd have to tell the truth to is your mother." He gives me a violent shake. "She'd learn to accept it. She'd have no choice."

My heart seizes: I know he's serious. He could kill me. He *wants* to kill me.

I quickly switch tacks, hoping I'm not too late.

"I'm sorry, General." Channeling my own mortal terror, I will repentant tears to my eyes. "I'm so sorry."

He looks at me with renewed contempt: the sight of his son groveling for his life is probably as hard for him as the sight of me turning against the cause. I know my new tactic is as risky as my old one: he could just as easily kill me out of disgust as out of anger.

But I keep going. This is the only gambit I have.

"I failed you and I failed my people. I'm a coward. I don't have what it takes to kill. On the field of battle I . . . I couldn't stand to see bloodshed."

My father releases my shirt and I drop hard to the floor.

"I knew coming back was a risk. That I might be justifiably executed for treason. But I thought it was worth it."

"Why?"

"Because," I say, pausing for dramatic effect, scrambling back onto my feet. "I hoped you would give me a chance to make up for my failure."

"And how do you propose to do that?"

I fix my shirt and give him the most unblinking stare I can muster. "Clearly, I don't have what it takes to be a warrior. I'm not like Ivan."

At that, my father lets out a derisive snort. "Son, you are unworthy of even an unflattering comparison to Ivanick."

"But I am a better tactician. Ivan never would've gotten through his early studies if I hadn't been there to do his work for him, every step of the way."

The General's not even looking at me anymore: he's staring towards the kitchen, no doubt preparing himself for the explanation he'll have to give my mother once he's killed me. I can see I'm losing him. Yet I press on, trying not to let my desperation show.

"I found Number Two first. Back in London, well before your entire team of surveyors managed to pinpoint her location. And in Kenya I got to Number Three ahead of Ivan. I didn't have the will to kill them myself, but I found them first. I could be one of the best trackers you have if you just give me a chance—"

My father lunges at me again, grabbing me by the throat this time. I can't breathe.

This is it, I think. *This is the end.*

"One week," he says. "I'll give you one week to show me what you can do."

He releases me.

"And if you fail to produce a miracle for me in that time . . ." He trails off. I can tell from his look he expects me to finish his statement.

"You'll kill me."

His level stare confirms that I've guessed right.

I nod, accepting his terms.

CHAPTER SIX

I LIE IN MY OLD BED, IN MY OLD BEDROOM, staring at the wall. I was surprised to find everything just as I left it, half-expecting it to be stripped bare following my supposed "death." I guess my mother won *that* battle with the General.

I try to get comfortable. After months on a bare cot at the aid camp, my expensive pillow-top mattress should feel unbelievably fluffy and soft. But it feels like a bed of nails.

After a strained dinner, during which my father and I both pretended to be happy I was home, alone in my room I can finally let my guard down and drop the fake smile. I'm exhausted and scared. Even if I somehow manage to avoid being executed within the trial week the General has granted me, that's no guarantee I'll manage to break into the labs. And even if I do, that's no guarantee I'll find a successful means of reviving

One, of keeping her imminent disappearance at bay. And even if I manage to save her, I have no plan for how to save myself, for how to escape this place once I'm done.

I'll need to figure that out, because right now death doesn't even feel like the worst-case scenario. Passing my father's test and being "allowed" to remain in this place, having to indefinitely maintain the pretense of being a loyal Mogadorian, feels like the grimmest fate of all.

"That was hard to watch." One appears, standing in the doorway.

I sigh, grateful for her presence.

"Didn't realize you were there."

She ambles towards me and sits at the foot of the bed. "I hung back. Tried to stay out of your line of sight. Figured you needed to focus." She gives me an affectionate look. "Performance of a lifetime, huh?"

"You said it."

She looks guilty, worried for my safety. "You sure I'm worth it?"

I manage to fake a confident smile. "Definitely."

My bedroom door opens and my sister Kelly swings in.

Surprised, I hop off the bed.

"So you're back," she says bluntly, sizing me up.

"Yeah," I say. I'm not sure if I should rush up and embrace her.

I decide to wait and follow her lead.

"Well, that's good, I guess." She fiddles with the doorknob hesitantly.

"You weren't at dinner." Over dinner my father explained that Ivan had been promoted to a new position somewhere in the Southwest—news that filled me with such relief I had to cover my mouth so the General wouldn't see how happy I was—but I hadn't been given a reason for Kelly's absence.

"Ran late. I'm doing an afterschool program at the Nursery now." The Nursery is what some of us call the piken pens in the underground complex. Pikens are bred in the labs down there and conditioned for combat. "I think I'm going to be a trainer when I graduate. They say I have what it takes."

"Oh," I reply. "That's great."

I can't believe how dumb I sound, how tentative. Back in the hornets' nest of Ashwood, and I'm scared of my own kid sister. It's pathetic.

"Whatever," she says. "So listen. Congratulations on surviving and stuff, and for coming back here. But, you know, having you dead was embarrassing enough. Now I have to explain to my friends that my loser brother is back. You're basically ruining my life."

I'm stunned by her callousness, but I understand. In Mogadorian society, dying in combat is not afforded the prestige it is among most human cultures. And *failing* in combat and surviving is hardly better than being a traitor. My mother's relief at my survival won't be shared by my sister . . . or anyone else at Ashwood.

"I'm just telling you this so when I ignore you in front of the others, you don't freak out, okay?"

"Fair enough," I say.

"Okay," she says.

She leaves, without a good night, much less that hug.

I shoot One a despairing look.

She quickly covers her expression of pity with one of her best, most sarcastic grins. "Welcome home, Adamus," she says.

CHAPTER SEVEN

A KID A LITTLE OLDER THAN ME NAMED SERKOVA
comes to get me in the morning. According to the General, he's a promising young surveyor in the Media Surveillance division. My father assigned him to bring me up to speed and put me to work.

We ride the elevator down to the underground complex together. He gives me a sidelong glance. "Heard you bit it in Kenya."

"Yeah," I concede, feigning sheepishness.

"And now you're angling for a position as a surveyor?"

"That's the idea," I say.

He snorts. Serkova has a generic trueborn face, but there is something gross and oddly piggish about his nose that's even grosser when he snorts.

"I didn't know we were in the business of giving failed soldiers second chances." He turns his stare on me. "Guess there's an exception for the General's son."

The elevator doors open and we stride into the hub at the center of the underground complex. The domed ceiling and orb-like fluorescent light fixture give it the feel of a massive—and massively ugly—atrium.

Trueborns and vatborns stride in every direction in and out of the various tunnels radiating out from the hub. I feel them react to my presence: the trueborns avoid my gaze, while the vatborns sneer at me with naked contempt. Word sure traveled fast, even down here.

We make our way past the entrances to the Southeast and Northeast tunnels on our way to the Northwest tunnel. With the exception of the General's briefing room, I've never been granted access to any of the tunnels off the hub before. But it's fairly common knowledge that the tunnels lead in one direction to combat training facilities, and in the other direction to weapons stores and bunkers for the vatborn. We're heading down a third tunnel, to the R+D laboratories and the media and surveillance compounds.

I struggle to keep pace with Serkova. It's obvious he doesn't like me and resents being saddled with the job of babysitting me.

"What's your problem with me?" I genuinely want to know: the Mogadorian worldview has become foreign to me so quickly. "So I'm being given a second chance. Why should you care?"

Serkova turns to me, a contemptuous sneer on his lips. "You think I don't get enough shit as it is from the combat Mogs for being a surveyor? They already call us tech wienies. Now we're being forced to take on a *proven* loser in combat. So the next time they say we're only surveyors because we're not good enough for combat, they'll be *right*. All thanks to you."

Great.

I follow him into the Media Surveillance facility, a large room lit only by the screens of the twenty or so computer monitors throughout the room. No one looks up as Serkova leads me to my monitor. Thanks to his outburst, I don't have to wonder why.

He explains to me what our job is, then sits down at the console next to mine. "Good luck, Adamus," he says, with evident sarcasm, then gets to work.

I turn to my monitor.

A steady stream of links scrolls across my screen, in color-coded text. The Mogadorian mainframe scours satellite and cable TV, radio transmissions, and every last corner of the internet, 24/7. A certain amount of automated culling occurs before these links reach our screens: most human interest stories are weeded out in advance, as are most articles or news segments devoted to U.S. or international politics. But a significant major-ity of what remains—weather reports, natural-disaster coverage, police blotters—makes it to our screens as a veritable geyser of hyperlinks.

Our job is to sift through the links on our respective screens and sort them, moving material that is clearly of no pertinence to the Mogadorian cause to the "Discard" directory, while kicking material that *might* have some bearing on our interests up to the "Investigate" directory, where it will be assessed personally by the lead surveyor before being dismissed or moved up the chain to Command HQ. We are also supposed to tag and grade the material we move to the "Investigate" directory according to our judgment of its possible relevance: "PV" for Possible Value, "HP" for High Priority, and "EHP" for Extremely High Priority. Items we flag with an "EHP" rating are simultaneously routed to the lead surveyor and to a small cadre of analysts over at command HQ for immediate review.

Ultimately, if Command HQ is persuaded a news item is a legitimate sign of Garde activity, reconnaissance teams are dispatched.

All three eliminated Garde members were located with some degree of surveyor assistance. But despite our importance, we're really just data monkeys. Exciting stuff like reconnaissance and combat occur outside our purview as surveyors.

Not that it's easy work. Within minutes of struggling through this endlessly updating data stream, I miss the clarity and simplicity of my physical labor back in Kenya. Jumping all over the place on the internet—from a story about the birth of quintuplets in Winnetka, Illinois, to a grainy web-video from a Syrian insurgent—without getting involved in what I'm reading or seeing is a challenge, and after just twenty minutes of wide-eyed staring at the monitor, my eyes feel like they're going to bleed.

Then it gets worse.

At the end of the first hour, a little digital bell sounds and a tab pops up on the upper right-hand corner of my screen. My heart sinks.

"Oh yeah," says Serkova, managing to smirk at me without looking up from his monitor. "I forgot to mention. We get ranked hourly."

Our individual results are tabulated at the end of every hour and broadcast to all the terminals. Number of Discards, number of Investigates, as well as a provisional computer-graded percentage score for accuracy.

There I am, all the way at the bottom, in last place: twenty-seven Discards, six Investigates, and a provisional accuracy ranking of 71 percent. I scan up the list to see Serkova in second place, with a whopping eighty-two discards, thirteen Investigates, and a provisional accuracy ranking of 91 percent. I'm going to have to go *a lot* faster.

"What was that you were telling your father?" Serkova cracks.

I'm too distracted to respond. I need to improve my score, and I resent Serkova's ability to work and needle me at the same time.

"Something 'bout what a great tracker you are, how much better you'll be at surveying than we are?"

Ugh. Not only has the General given me an impossible task, in which failure will result in my *death*, he's also poisoned the well with my new coworkers by reporting what I said about my superior tracking skills.

But I don't bother to respond: I don't have time.

I get back to work, fighting against my own dismay. One reason I manipulated the General into placing me in the Media and Surveillance facility was because I thought I might have enough downtime to use my console to hack into the servers of the adjacent laboratories, do some digging into Dr. Zakos's research. I know that One's only hope lies in those files. But if I don't pull my ranking up soon, my father could justifiably terminate our agreement: I'd be killed before I even got a chance to help One.

I need to improve my score.

I manage to go faster. The trick, I learn, is not to process any of the information I encounter. Instead I let my consciousness skim just above the text or video, then let my judgment occur without thought or reasoning.

Basically the trick is to accept that I am just a cog in a data-combing machine.

Finally, I feel myself getting into a groove. In the next hourly ranking, I've climbed two positions. In the one after that, I'm position thirteen out of twenty.

"Luck." Serkova sniffs.

I glare at him. I know I'm not here to compete with this jerk, but I can't help it: wanting to knock him down a peg drives me on. By late afternoon, I've climbed up to position eleven.

I figure I've bought myself enough of a cushion to give myself five minutes of snoop time. I quickly page away from the hyperlinks and try to access the hub's central servers.

But doing research with a ticking clock hanging over my head proves disastrous. I enter in searches for phrases like "mind transfer," "Dr. Anu," and "Dr. Zakos," but they all lead me to restricted areas on the server, and I don't have time to hack into them. I try to be more general. Remembering what Arsis said about humans in the lab, I do a search for "human captives." Instead of directing me to anything about Anu or Zakos's research subjects, I'm led to some internal, hub-wide memo about a broad new policy regarding human captives. "Whenever possible, humans suspected of aiding and abetting the Garde shall henceforth be held at the government base in Dulce, New Mexico."

A government base? Why would the U.S. government have anything to do with the Mogadorians?

I put it aside for now. It's an interesting—and unsettling—tidbit, but it's not going to help me save One. Before I even have a chance to enter a new search, my five minutes is up.

I turn back to my work. Predictably, that short diversion cost me, and my hourly rank plummets. Regretfully, I accept that I can't afford any more "independent research" today.

We finish at seven p.m., replaced by the night shift, who we'll relieve at seven tomorrow morning. My body aches from remaining hunched and sedentary, and my eyes feel like they've been blasted with sand. I've finished the day back in the middle, at position eleven.

"Not bad," admits Serkova, getting up from his chair. "But hardly what you promised the General."

He's right. Landing right in the middle of a group of twenty can hardly qualify me as a master tracker. I can only hope my ranking is enough to let me live another day.

I walk the tunnel alone, heading back to the hub.

I'm too tired to even consider sneaking off and snooping around the other tunnels: I'd definitely blow my cover.

"Arsis, you flaming moron!"

Arsis! The idiot assistant technician in the labs.
Advancing my secret agenda was the last thing on my
mind until I heard that name.

"Sorry, Doctor."

I round the corner to see an open doorway leading
into one of the laboratories. Inside the gleaming white
lab, an incredibly tall and spindly doctor has a young
guard backed up against a wall, prodding him with an
angry index finger.

"These samples were supposed to be refrigerated
at *subzero* temperatures. You put them in the regular
freezer."

"Sorry, sir." The boy is docile, subservient, nothing
like the sullen brat I'd imagined from his IM transcripts.

The doctor commands him sternly. "Revial the
samples from our remaining cultures, and get it right
this time. You asked to be trusted with more important
work; now show that you can do it properly."

"Yes, Doctor." Arsis scrambles off to redo his work.

I stand gaping at Dr. Zakos, at his massive laboratory. This is the man who might be able to save my only
friend.

He catches me looking.

Shit.

He glares at me. I either have to turn around and
walk away, or think of something fast.

"Doctor Zakos?" I say, deciding to wing it.

"Yes?" He looks puzzled.

I step forward into the lab.

"I'm Adamus Sutekh. Son of General Sutekh."

He looks at me, evidently suspicious.

"I wanted to meet you," I go on, "because my father has spoken so highly of your work."

My ruse pays off: I watch Dr. Zakos flush with pride. Even Mogadorians have their vanity. An exploitable weakness.

"I'm glad the General is satisfied," says the doctor, giving a little involuntary bow.

"I was actually a subject in your predecessor's experiments," I continue. "The work he did with the first fallen member of the Garde . . . the memory transfer . . ."

"Ah, of course." He shakes his head. "Dr. Anu's work was a deplorable failure. I'm certain the mind-transfer technology I have been developing since is much improved, if I could ever get clearance to actually use it."

I'm confused. Zakos keeps talking, looking at me with much more interest now. I struggle to maintain a neutral expression. "You're saying the procedure could be done more successfully now?"

He nods. "That's my theory."

"How is that possible? I thought the procedure needed to be done soon after a subject's death."

He cocks his head curiously and ignores my question. "Where have you been since the experiment?"

"In Africa," I tell him. I don't want to get into too much detail about my activities since I was last with the Mogadorians. But the doctor seems to accept my answer without question.

"And did you suffer any . . . side effects due to the procedure you underwent?"

I'm tempted to be sarcastic. *Only that little coma.* But I hold back. "Nothing other than those that you already know about."

The wheels seem to be turning in his head as he looks me up and down.

"It's a possibility," he muses, almost as if to himself. "The neural pathways of the Garde have been dormant far too long to attempt the transfer again with a new host. But with the original subject, from the original experiment—"

I can't help interjecting. "What are you talking about? What Garde? You can't mean *her*."

Dr. Zakos just grins and struts over to the laboratory's wall, which is covered with ten or so off-white square tiles. He places his hand over a small steel control panel next to the wall and performs an elegant sequence of hand gestures across the panel's surface. With a sudden and jarring hydraulic whoosh, one of the tiles slides out of the wall, opening like a drawer, spewing cryogenic vapors.

It's like a mortuary slab.

He stares down proudly at what's lying on it.

"Have a look," he says.

I step deeper into the lab, peering over the edge of the tile.

"Perfectly preserved."

I can't believe my eyes. She doesn't even look dead: she looks like she's sleeping.

My best friend in the world.

One.

CHAPTER
EIGHT

ONE KEEPS ME UP HALF THE NIGHT, BOMBARDING me with questions I can't answer: about Doctor Zakos's experiments, about what he meant when he said he could successfully download the entirety of One's memories, about what it meant that her body had been so thoroughly well preserved.

"Well, you're still dead," I say.

"Uh? A little tact, please," she says, laughing.

I'm in bed. She's sitting on the floor in the corner of my bedroom.

"Sorry," I say. I'm a bit rattled. Seeing her in the flesh like that, a corpse on a cold steel slab, has upset me more than I'd like her to know. She's been my constant companion for years now, but the sight of her body brought home to me how tenuous her current existence is.

"Did you notice?" asks One, jumping right back into

her excited speculation. "There were at least ten tiles on that wall. Remember what that Arsis kid said in those chats? About humans being dredged for intel? You think they're being kept preserved on those slabs too?"

I marvel at One's mind. She wasn't even present until I finished reading Arsis's IM transcripts, and she was definitely gone when I was in Zakos's lab.

She clocks my amazed look. "What?" she says. "You already know your mind's an open book to me. Just because I'm gone when stuff happens doesn't mean I can't see it once I come back."

And without skipping a beat, she returns to her obsession. "Anyhow, if I've been so well preserved, that means we can probably jack into each other again somehow and kick-start my memories inside you. I mean, I know I'm pretty, but I don't think Dr. Zakos has been preserving me for my *looks*. He must've been doing it to keep the stuff inside my brain, like, fresh." She nods, pleased with her reasoning. "We need to get back into that lab."

I look away from her. "One, what I need is to get some sleep." It's the middle of the night, and I have to be at the media facility in four hours.

One is silent.

"If I screw up at work, I'm as good as dead. And if I'm dead, you're dead, and this whole lab plan will be moot anyway. Okay?"

I turn back to One. But she's gone.

It occurs to me that I'll never know when one of her disappearances is her last. One day she'll blink out, just like this, and I'll wait for her to reappear . . . but she won't.

For all I know I just saw her for the last time.

I force my face deep into my pillow and try to sleep.

I arrive at my console the next morning groggy and bleary-eyed, dreading the next twelve hours. I take my seat next to Serkova and dive into the data stream.

Despite my fuzzy head, I pull a decent rank after my first hour. But with exhaustion creeping up on me, I can feel my productivity beginning to slip. By the fifteen-minute mark of the next hour, I know I'm headed back to the bottom of the pack.

So I come up with a little trick.

For every five or so sources I legitimately review, I automatically throw another one in the Discard directory. I know my provisional accuracy percentage will take a hit, but from what I can tell it carries a relatively low weight on overall ranking compared to Discard and Investigate totals.

Using this technique I've climbed all the way to number six by the next hourly rankings, with seventy-three Discards and seventeen Investigates. My provisional accuracy is 73 percent, lower than the hour before but not bad enough to raise any red flags.

I can feel Serkova sneering at me. I don't bother to hide my smile.

I pass the day like this, racing against Serkova. Giving up on finding time for research, I use the task in front of me to distract myself from everything: from One's perilous condition, from Zakos's strange work in the lab, from my hateful father, from what the work I'm doing even means. My only goal is to get ahead of Serkova in at least one hourly ranking.

My last rank of the day is number two. Right ahead of Serkova at three.

"Better luck tomorrow, Serkova," I say, wearing a bright, fake-friendly smile.

He curses me and heads out of the lab.

After work, I head upstairs to my room to wash up before dinner. My mother told me Kelly's skipping dinner again for her afterschool program in the Nursery. Yeah, right. I know the real reason: she doesn't want to share a table with me.

But not even that can get me down: beating Serkova, even just the once, was too big a victory. I find myself racing up the stairs to my room, three steps at a time.

I open the door to my room, hoping to find One. I can't wait to crow to her about kicking Serkova's ass.

When I enter, I see her feet peeking out from behind the corner of the bed.

"One?"

I step closer.

She's flat on her back on the carpet. Mouth and eyes open. She looks glazed, and her skin is doing that milky flickering thing that it did back under the baobab tree. Only much, much worse.

"What happened?" I crouch beside her on the floor. She's silent. "One?"

After a moment's silence, she speaks. "Nothing." Her lips barely move and her voice is raspy. "It's just that each time it's darker than the last time. It hurts more, it's more . . . obliterating." Her eyes swim around in her head, searching for me.

Her gaze finally finds mine. "It's like, what's blacker than black, you know?"

"Yeah," I say.

But I *don't* know. She's going through something I have no experience with. She's going through the End.

I hear my mother call me for dinner.

I turn back to One. "I'm going to stay with you."

She shakes her head, almost imperceptibly.

"No," she says. "You should go." Her eyes drift back to the ceiling as she lies there, flickering in and out of view.

Heartbroken, I leave.

My father joins my mother and me for dinner. He barely speaks, except to ask my mother for seconds—he has a true warrior's appetite—and to give us an update on Ivan. "His superior officer says Ivan is doing excellent work. Says he has the makings of a general, himself."

"That's wonderful," says my mother, beaming approvingly. "Does he know the good news about Adamus?"

My father and I exchange a quick, uneasy glance.

The General wipes his mouth with a napkin. "No."

"Why not?" she says, looking back and forth between the two of us. "I think he'd be happy to hear his brother is alive."

"Adamus is *not* Ivanick's brother," my father says, silencing her.

Technically that's true—I'm their biological son and Ivanick was adopted, raised by my parents—but I catch the General's subtext. Saying I am not Ivanick's brother is my father's way of saying that I am unworthy of being honored that way, that I am less their son than even Ivan. My father steps into the kitchen, leaving me and my mother alone in awkward silence.

The truth is, I'm too upset about One's worsening fades to even care about the hateful soap opera of my family life.

"You've barely touched your plate, Adamus." My

mother looks at me with concern. "Is something upset-ting you?"

The question is so ridiculous, given the circum-stances, I almost laugh. I almost say, "Yes, Mother. Everything is upsetting me." But I bite my tongue.

I hear One's voice from last night. *"We need to get back in that lab."*

She's right. She's fading so fast I need to convince Dr. Zakos to try the procedure again if she's going to have any hope of living. But how can I convince my father to let me go, to grant me leave of my temporary position in the surveillance facility?

"Adamus?"

"I'm just afraid," I say. I don't know where I'm going with this, but I see it, the dim outline of a new card to play.

"Afraid?" my mother asks. "Afraid of what?"

"Of Father. I'm afraid he'll make me . . ." My voice trails off dramatically. I force myself to look as stricken, as ghostly with fear, as I can.

"What are you saying—"

And then I blurt it out. I explain to my mother that I ran into Dr. Anu's replacement in the Northwest tunnel the other day and he said that he could do the mind-transfer procedure again.

"He says it'll work this time. That they can't do it to just anyone, it has to be me. And I'm afraid, I don't want to go back into the labs and be hooked up to machines. I'm afraid I'll go into another coma or—or . . . worse!" I will tears to my eyes. "He says he can dig up real information about the Garde if they do it, and I think the General will make me . . ."

"Oh Adamus, I doubt that—"

I interrupt her, louder than before. "But he will! If the General finds out, I'm sure he will!"

Then I hear his low deep voice, coming from behind me.

"If he finds out what, exactly?"

It's the General. Taking my bait.

CHAPTER NINE

"HAVE A SEAT, GET COMFORTABLE." DR. ZAKOS has positioned a large curved chair in the center of the room and gestures for me to get in. Nervously I take a seat.

"I was delighted to hear from your father last night," he says, flitting around the laboratory, putting monitors in place, booting up scary-looking medical equipment. "But with the short notice, it might take me a while to get this equipment up and running."

I can tell he's ecstatic to use the equipment on me. Adamus, the Mogadorian lab rat.

I sink into the chair, trying to get comfortable while Zakos sets up. I should be happy: my ruse worked. I deliberately let my father overhear that I didn't want to be used in Zakos's mind-transfer experiments, and he had Zakos on the phone within minutes, giving him the go ahead to plug my brain into One's corpse.

The General still hates me, and seeing me weak and afraid, as I'd pretended to be at the dinner table, gave his meager conscience whatever license it needed to risk my life again in the lab.

The General is free to hate me. I hate him too. And now that I've succeeded in tricking him again, my hatred has a new depth, a new dimension: contempt. I fooled him.

The machines begin to whir.

I'm afraid of what will happen while I'm under, but push that aside. More than anything else, I'm relieved to know that One may have a chance of survival. If the technology has improved, maybe I can get through the procedure unharmed, rescuing One in the process.

"The transfer rig will take about twenty minutes to warm up," Zakos announces.

I nod as I watch the doctor approach the steel console beside the tile containing One's body. He presses a few buttons and the slab comes out with the same hydraulic whoosh as before.

From where I'm sitting I can't see One's body. Zakos presses a few buttons on the edge of One's slab, then presses the console again. The slab whooshes shut.

"You don't need . . ." I start, then catch myself before I call her One. "You don't need to connect the body to me?"

"No," he says, with professional pride. "All of the

containment pods are linked to this mainframe terminal," he says, pointing at the largest monitor. "Everything besides the pods' hydraulics are controlled through here: brain scans, vitals, preservation protocols . . ."

"Do you have other bodies in there?" I ask.

"Yes," he says. "Quite a few. Some of them are unaffiliated mortals I've used for experimentation. The rest of them are Greeters."

Zakos, oblivious to the fact that I'm a traitor to the Mogadorian cause, explains to me that when the Loric were first scouting for a planet where they could hide from the Mogadorians, they made contact with a few scattered mortals. The Mogadorians captured these humans almost ten years ago and subjected them to a series of interrogations. However, Mogadorians knew next to nothing about earthling psychology or behavior back then, and at that point our interrogation techniques were quite crude. Some of these "Greeters" caved to Mogadorian interrogation, but it was quickly discovered the intel they gave—about the Loric's locations, what they told the Greeters upon contact—was often faulty. Because of this, my people began an ongoing research endeavor that used complex brain-mapping technology to find a more accurate means of extracting information. In other words, rather than asking for it, we tried to find a way to take it.

"And, as a matter of fact, Anu's experiment with you was an offshoot of that research. Unfortunately it failed, but I was intrigued. The procedure you are about to undergo represents a massive refinement of his work."

I can tell that Zakos thinks this little history lesson is complete, but I want to know more.

"And you've kept these Greeters alive this whole time?"

Zakos gives a breezy laugh. "Not exactly. We've raked their brains so thoroughly trying to extract information about the Garde that all but one of them have perished. Of course we're keeping the others preserved, should our technology advance to the point—"

"Who lived?" I ask, interrupting him, steering him back to information I know One will want, should both of us survive the procedure.

Dr. Zakos looks at me silently for a moment. For a second, I worry that I've raised his suspicions.

Instead, he impishly raises an eyebrow. "Want to see?"

He dashes over to a panel next to another tile and opens the containment pod. After the mist clears, I crane my neck to get a better look.

I see a handsome, solidly built middle-aged man. His skin is shockingly white from being in containment for so long: it's practically the color of vatborn skin. But otherwise he looks healthy. His eyes are closed.

"Just one moment," Zakos says, pressing a few buttons inside the pod. Then Zakos leans over the man.

"Malcolm Goode?" he says, addressing him gently, like a normal human doctor addressing a normal human patient. "How's it going in there?"

Malcolm Goode opens his eyes.

I feel a chill, a wave of nauseating pity for this poor human, trapped in a cold box for years on end.

"Hello," he says, looking up at Dr. Zakos with an expression of utter guilelessness and trust. It's like he has no idea how much time has passed, or what he's been subjected to. "I seem to have forgotten where I am," he says, smiling innocently. "Could you tell me where I am?"

Dr. Zakos only chuckles in response. "Well," he says, addressing me. "You get the idea."

And with that he reaches over to the panel, presses a few more buttons, and Malcolm is prompted—whether by wire or chemical—to return to sleep. But not before he fixes me with a haunted, quizzical look.

I'm under. At first it's just a void, a black so black I wonder for a moment if this is what One experiences when she disappears. Then come blasts of light and crackling static, as I find myself plunged into One's memories.

I look around, getting my bearings. I'm in a wooden

shack, in bed, my head hanging over the side of the mattress. Through the cracks in the floorboards, I see rushing water: a river.

The Rajang River.

"They're coming."

I turn to see Hilde, One's Cêpan. She's staring through a slat in the door, ready to fight. She rushes to me, shaking me, pulling me out of bed.

That's when I realize I'm not just a spectator to One's final memories, as I was during most of my time in her consciousness. I've been plugged *directly* into her experience. Ghost-One is nowhere to be seen. I'm completely fused with her: every thought, every feeling. The humidity inside the shack. The sweat trickling down my back. I can feel Hilde's eyes on me, inspecting my readiness for combat.

I'm not ready, I think. *I'm just scared.*

The Mogadorian assault team kicks in the door and Hilde leaps into action. She dodges a Mog's knife, and as the Mog spins around to recover his balance she crushes his windpipe with a single strike. As he collapses, she whirls to another Mog, swiftly snapping his neck.

I'm too paralyzed with fear to move. I know what's coming. Hilde is about to die.

My heart screams. I love this woman with all of One's love.

Another Mogadorian attacks. Hilde flips him onto his back.

But this Mog is quicker than the others. He unholsters his blaster and shoots Hilde right in her chest.

Everything goes red. All of One's anger, shock, and rage at the loss of her Cêpan—*my* Cêpan—floods my system. *No, she can't, they couldn't. It's my fault, I failed, how could I?* These are One's thoughts but I feel them, hear them, as my own. *I want her back. I want her back. No no no! Must pay, someone must pay, they must pay.* Our combined fury rises. *They will pay, yes they will pay, we will make them pay.*

And that's when I feel it. Something ripping open inside of me, something so entirely new yet so strangely familiar that it's almost funny I never noticed it before, that it took this crisis for me to notice it. The floors start to shake, a massive rumble coming from beneath my feet but also coming from inside me. And as my heart sings—*yes, they will pay, they will pay*—everything goes black and—

␥

Shadows. Hands waving in front of my face, fluorescent light burning through the dark.

I am back in Zakos's lab. He's cursing, ripping electrodes from my head, adjusting the console I'm plugged into.

"What happened?" I ask.

I'm still buzzing from what I've just experienced. As chaotic as the memory transfer was, as turbulent as it felt, there was something I was on the verge of understanding inside it, a promise of something great.

But now that I'm back, it's gone.

"Your vitals were spiking faster than I'd anticipated. If I'd kept going . . ." He lets out another string of curses.

I sit up in my chair.

He stares at me. "Are you able to recall anything? Do you have any usable intel I can send up the chain?"

I shake my head.

Of course I'm lying. Beyond what I just experienced, I already have an intimate knowledge of Loric psychology, the relationship between the Garde and their Cêpan. I have the entirety of One's history burned into my brain. I've had that ever since the first transfer.

He levels me with his stare. He's evidently flustered, his hair damp with sweat, but that doesn't make him any less scary.

"I know it's in there," he says.

I feel a chill at his words.

"You may not remember it consciously, but I know it's in there, in your brain. And I know that I could get it," he says.

The way he speaks, it's like he's talking to himself. "Our understanding of Mogadorian physiology is well beyond what we understand about Loric or mortals.

With my neurological mapping techniques, I could do what Anu couldn't. Run those currents three times as hard, and rip that intel straight from your brain and onto my hard drive."

He stares at me. I feel weirdly exposed, objectified, like a slab of meat at a butcher shop.

"But for that," he says, chuckling bitterly, "I'd need your father's permission to kill you."

CHAPTER
TEN

I'M DISMISSED TO FINISH OUT MY DAY AT THE surveillance facility. I have no fight left in me, and my rankings take a nosedive. Sixteen, eighteen, eighteen, twenty. Last place.

I know Dr. Zakos immediately reported the experiment's failure to my father, but I doubt he took the risk of pitching his idea of mentally vivisecting me to the General. I have two more days left in the lab before my father decides if my results qualify me for survival. Either he will have me executed, or he will deem me an asset to the cause and allow me to continue working as a surveyor. *Oh joy.*

After the lab it's another miserable dinner. The General is busy down in his briefing room, so it's just my mother and Kelly. Kelly refuses to even look at me. When my mother goes to the kitchen, I turn to her, try to start a conversation. We haven't been close since before the mind transfer, almost five years ago. I wonder if she can even remember back then, when she hated Ivan for teasing her and roughhousing with her, and seemed to adore me, her gentle older brother.

"Haven't seen you in the tunnels," I say. "How are things going in the Nursery?"

She is silent, slowly chewing her food and staring straight ahead. It's hard to believe a fourteen-year-old girl could be so full of such a steely hatred.

"Kelly, I'm sorry if it's embarrassing that I survived, that you have to explain that your loser brother has come back—"

"Ivanick told me," she says, hissing at me suddenly. "He told me the truth about you. I know what Mom doesn't. You're a traitor."

My stomach does a somersault. I feel like I could throw up my entire dinner.

"So you can pretty much stop trying to make up with me. It's not going to happen." She gets up from the table.

"I wish you were dead," she says, before running up the stairs to her room and slamming the door shut.

"Good night to you too," I say, laughing miserably to myself.

⌐⌐

After dinner I go up to my room. One isn't there. I haven't seen her since last night.

Somehow, this doesn't surprise me. The mind transfer was so fast, and so quickly aborted that I doubt it did
much to reestablish her foothold in my consciousness.
Perhaps that's the thing I felt like I was on the verge of
understanding—how to keep her alive inside of me.

It's funny to think Zakos thought he was covering
his ass with the General by protecting my life. If Zakos
had killed me, my father probably would've given him
a medal.

I have nothing to stay up for. I go to bed early.

Sleepless in bed, I consider the pitiful irony of my
current situation. I came back here to rescue my one
and only friend in the world, yet I fail to save her, just
as I failed to save Hannu. If she isn't gone for good, she
will be soon enough. And now I'm stuck here, trapped.

Alone.

A desultory day at work. I'm pulling in rankings in the
thirteen-to-fifteen range. Pathetic.

I've scaled back on my "Discard" trick. Why bother
trying to impress anyone with my rankings, anyway?
So I actually investigate each link that's fed to my
monitor, even though it damages my productivity. At
least it's more interesting than mindlessly shuttling the
leads into one folder or another.

I click on a link.

This one leads to a forum dedicated to readers of

some publication called "They Walk Among Us." The
Mogadorian mainframe has isolated a thread titled
"NEXT ISSUE?" posted by a user TWAUFAN182. A
threaded dialogue unfolds when I click on it.

> Please I've read TWAU no. 3 so many times.
> Please tell me when next ish will come out?
> Thanks! ✒
> —TWAUFAN182
> Sorry TWAUFAN. No plans for issue #4 yet, but
> be assured we have plenty material for one.
> Thanks for reading.—admin
> What? What material? U can't leave us hanging
> like that! Spill it!—TWAUFAN182
> Come on man, give us a hint!!!—TWAUFAN182
> It's been weeks with no updates. This forum is
> dead, RIP. LOL.—TWAUFAN182

That exchange was dated a year ago. Then, this morning . . .

> Sorry. Been busy. We've made contact, definitely
> extraterrestrial. True MOG in captivity. —admin

I almost gasp. There are humans out there who have
captured a Mogadorian? Or who at least *think* they've
captured a Mogadorian?

I know at once that this is the first link that's passed through my monitor that's truly worthy of an "EHP" ranking. I click on the hyperlink and drag it over to the "Investigate" directory . . . but then I stop.

Why would I alert the Mogadorians to the location of these humans? Humans the Mogs will undoubtedly capture and kill? I might get in trouble if I discard the link—surely there are failsafes built into the system for erroneous Discards—but why should I make it easier for these Mogadorian bastards? By discarding this link, I will save a human life . . . or at least slow down the Mogadorian hunting machine for a few minutes.

It's worth it.

I don't care if I live or die. If One is gone and I'm stuck in this vile society, why should I fight to live? The pleasure of outperforming Serkova has faded; besides, with rankings like my current ones, that ship has sailed.

I click Discard.

They'll come for you.

In my bones, I know I'm going to reap hell for what I've done. And I don't care.

Fuck the Mogadorians.

I start dumping every link on my monitor into the Discard directory, as fast as I can. There's no upper limit on the number of links that can get routed to a single monitor—the more links you process, the more get routed your way—so before I know it I've chucked

PITTACUS LORE

upwards of three hundred links into the Discard directory.

I'm making a spectacular mess of their system. The
clock counts down to the end of the hour. How many
unevaluated Discards can I cram into the directory
before my fellow surveyors catch on? For that matter,
how long until my treasonous evidence-burying gets
discovered?

I'm exhilarated.

The hourly rankings come in. I've discarded 611
links. Investigated 0. My provisional accuracy ranking is a hilarious 11 percent. Better yet, as if to make
a mockery of their entire ranking algorithm, I come in
first place.

"What the hell, Adamus!" Serkova snarls at me. The
others turn around to face me, all the work in the surveyor facility grinding to a halt. No one knows how to
react to my total breakdown. "Are you fricking nuts?"

I smile at Serkova, dizzy from my own outlandish
behavior. "Yeah, I think I might be."

Then an alarm goes off.

I hear the heavy march of footsteps coming down
the hall: soldiers dispatched from HQ.

"You deserve whatever you get," says Serkova, spit-
ting at me.

I run.

I dodge out into the Northwest tunnel to see the

77

soldiers coming, fronted by the General. They look *pissed*.

If I'm going out, I'm going out with a bang. I run *towards* the marching guards . . . then pull to a stop in front of Zakos's lab.

"Hey Pops," I say, taunting the General. "Did I do something wrong?"

"You know what you've done," he sneers at me. He gestures to the guards to seize me.

I resist, swinging my arms wildly, shouting as loud as I can. The Mogadorians hardly know how to react to such an undignified resistance. I can feel my father cringing in embarrassment.

The guards manage to subdue me, but the ruckus has attracted Dr. Zakos's attention. He steps out into the hall, as the guards begin dragging me away, probably to feed me to some hungry piken.

For a moment I worry my plan has failed, but then I hear Zakos's voice, calling from down the hall.

"General! Wait!"

My father halts our progress to listen to what Zakos has to say.

"If I may be so bold . . . I may be able to put your son's life to some use."

CHAPTER ELEVEN

I'M BACK IN THE CHAIR.

Zakos has convinced my father to allow him to perform an accelerated mind transfer between me and One. The process will be so intense it will kill me, literally frying my brain. But Zakos has guaranteed the General that he will be able to download the contents of One's transferred memories from *my* brain after my death. "If your son has been such a disappointment in life, at least allow him to be of service in death."

Zakos assured the General that even if the intelligence he extracts from my brain is of little consequence, the results of the experiment will represent a tremendous leap forward for Mogadorian technology.

"You don't need to make a hard sell, Zakos," I said, still trapped in the guards' grip. I turned to my father, an impudent smile on my lips. "Isn't that right, Pops? He had you on board at 'Kill Adamus,' didn't he?"

The General didn't even look at me. He nodded at his guards, who released me, then turned to the doctor. "Have the results on my desk by tomorrow morning," he said.

I've been in the lab since.

Guards monitor the door, but I'm not bound or watched by anyone but Zakos. Where am I going to go? How can I possibly escape? As my little demonstration in the hallway proved, I'm no match against Mogadorian soldiers.

Neither my father nor my sister has seen fit to visit me in my final hours. But my mother ventured down to deliver me a last meal. She entered the lab a few hours ago, carrying a couple slices of fresh-baked bread wrapped in a napkin and a plastic container filled with soup. She hesitated for a moment, looking for a suitable place to lay the meal. Then, realizing there was no good place for it, she wordlessly put the bread and soup on a laboratory counter. Then she turned her back to me, her hand on the door.

"Is it true?" she asked.

"Is what true?" I asked, a bit spitefully. I wanted to make her spell it out.

"That you've betrayed the Mogadorian cause."

I guess my father figured we were past sugarcoating things and had told her everything.

"Yes," I said.

Without another word, she left.

Moments later, as I held the still-warm bread in my hand, I realized that final home-cooked meal would be the last kind and motherly thing she would ever do for me.

I threw it in the trash.

Now Zakos is prepping me for the procedure. He's filled a syringe with some kind of anesthetic, explaining that this time he will render me unconscious before the procedure begins, which should give him greater precision over the neurological mapping. Soon I will be put under, then I will join One in her memories, and then I will be dead.

Zakos opens One's pod, to make a couple of adjustments before the procedure begins. I think of One and all the Greeters in their pods.

"Does it hurt?" I ask.

"Excuse me?" He's absorbed in his preparations.

"What you did to all the Greeters, keeping them alive, raking their brains for intel all those years."

"Oh, I never really thought about it," he says. "Yes, I would guess it's quite excruciating."

Just then I hear her voice. "You're not *really* going to let him get away with that, are you?" I turn to see One, flickering beside my chair. I had wondered if I would get to see her again before going under, if she hadn't already flickered out of existence.

I don't really have a choice, I say. *I'm trapped here.*

She leans against the counter. "You always have a choice. You had a choice to screw up today on the job, to bait your father into sentencing you to death, to do it in Zakos's earshot so you'd end up here. . . ."

I was afraid you were already gone. I couldn't think of anything else. I ran out of hope, figured I was going to lose you anyway, and we could at least—

"See each other one last time?" she says, finishing my thought. She gives me a flirty, cockeyed grin.

"That's sweet," she says. "But that wasn't the real reason you went haywire today."

She's right. That isn't how all this started. In the moment, I just couldn't bring myself to rat out those humans to my people. That was the first time the work I was doing as a surveyor was clearly going to help the Mogs and hurt others, and I couldn't do it. Over the past week I've had to take some crazy, on-the-fly risks, but that was the first time I acted completely without a plan, without any clear sense of what the consequences would be.

One, I say. *I don't even really understand why I did what I did.*

She doesn't answer me immediately, but instead turns back to the tiled wall, crossing her arms. I can see an idea brewing in her head. After a moment, she turns back to me and fixes me with a cryptic stare.

"Don't worry, Adam," she says. "You will. Seeing as you're going out anyway," she says, leaning close to my ear. "Don't you want to go out swinging?"

I look at her, confused.

"A giant leap for Mogadorian technology," she whispers, casting a glance over at the tiles where the Greeters' bodies are kept. "Is that what you really want your legacy to be?"

It's time.

I'm in the chair, connected to Zakos's console by a bunch of wires and cables. The machine that will plug me back into One's consciousness is already humming. "The parameters are in place," Zakos says. "It will just take a moment after we administer the anesthetic to begin working." He gestures to a syringe on a tray of tools next to me. The syringe hasn't escaped my attention either, though.

He approaches, towering above me in my reclined seat. As he holds my left hand against the arm of the chair and begins to pull the strap over my wrist, I know I only have a second to act.

I jerk my hand loose from Zakos's grip and leap up, grabbing the syringe and stabbing it into Zakos's throat before he can make another move. He punches me desperately, making contact with my face, but it's too late: I've already depressed the plunger.

He staggers back in a woozy daze, the drugs already making their way into his system, and falls to the floor.

I rip the strap off my left hand and stand up.

"Why . . ." he says, puzzled at what I've done. "What could you possibly hope to accomplish . . ."

Then he's out.

I rush to the lab's door and, as quietly as possible, lock it from the inside. I'm lucky that Dr. Zakos didn't knock anything over on his way to the ground: any noise would've attracted the attention of the guards on the other side of the door. But I know that once I do what I'm about to, alarms will sound, getting their attention. It won't take them long to override the lock.

But that's okay. I only need a little time.

I run to the steel panel controlling the containment pods. There are no buttons, no instructions. I have no idea how to imitate Doctor Zakos's complex gestures.

"Let me," I hear. One's voice.

She takes over my movements, just as she did when she hijacked my body in the jungle. I'm a spectator to my own body, watching as my hand dances elegantly across the surface of the panel.

An alarm goes off. I feel One vacating my body, ceding control back to me.

I get back in the chair, reattach a couple of electrodes and grip the arms of the seat.

I turn for one last look at the wall behind me, as all of the containment pods open noisily at once, a hydraulic chorus, disgorging their captive corpses. All except One's pod, which is still linked to me through the mainframe.

Exposed to open air, the corpses will be rendered useless to further Mogadorian experimentation within minutes.

It's hardly an elegant sabotage. But it will keep the Mogadorians from getting any intel from the dead Greeters, and should set Zakos's research back a few years.

The machine connecting me to One begins to thrum louder. I used up all the anesthetic to knock Zakos out, so I expect this will hurt. But I know that One has a plan for me, and it doesn't involve dying.

That's when I see Malcolm Goode, waking up on his slab.

"One?" I ask, nervously.

In the heat of the moment, I hadn't even considered what would happen to Malcolm, the sole surviving Greeter. I watch as he pulls himself loose from his connecting cables and steps off his slab. His legs, unused for years, instantly give out on him.

He locks eyes with me. He's almost three times my age, but he looks as lost and confused as a child.

One's voice in my ear: "Don't worry about him. He's going to be fine."

That's when the pain hits.

I'm plunged back into the moment of Hilde's death, the blast of the Mogadorian's gun opening up her chest right in front of my eyes. Hilde falls to her knees before me.

Red, orange, and purple swarms my vision. Everything's faster, louder than before, pulsing and buzzing. One's thoughts are screaming in my head again: *No, she can't, they couldn't. It's my fault, I failed. How could I? They will pay, we'll make them pay*. I feel it again, that ripping sensation inside me. *Oh right, that's right, that's how, so simple*. The floors start to shake, a massive rumble coming from beneath my feet but also coming from inside me and as my heart sings *yes, they will pay, they WILL pay*, the walls of the shack begin to shake and I stomp my foot. A wave of energy shoots through the floor. It's a power greater than any I've ever wielded, and it's coursing through us and rippling outwards.

Through the orangey blur of my vision I see the walls of the shack explode, I see four Mogadorian warriors flung out of sight by the force that's come from within me.

As the dust settles, I look down at my hands, at my

legs. I expect to see One's body as the source of this power.

But I don't see One's body. I see only my own.

"That's it," I hear. One's voice.

I turn around, surprised to discover I am no longer in the Malaysian shack. I am on that beautiful California beach. Our place.

One sits on the sand, waiting for me. "Pretty cool, huh?"

I nod, flabbergasted at the sheer power of One's Legacy. I'm dizzy from wielding it.

"Come sit with me. We don't have much time."

I collapse beside her, still breathless.

It's perfect: the sun is warm on my skin, the sand cool on my feet. And best of all, One's here, right by my side.

Across the sea, there's a roiling storm, the clouds as black as ink. But we're still in the sun.

One touches me.

In this place, I can feel it. I reach out and touch her too. We're shoulder to shoulder, staring forward at the approaching storm.

"We got what we came for," she says. "It's time for me to go."

I turn to her. *What is she saying?*

She bites her lip, looking at me apologetically. "You realize this was never about saving my life, right?"

My heart sinks into my stomach, but I don't know why.

"Of course it was," I say. "You think I came back and faced my family, went through all that for no reason? I was trying to save you."

"There was never any way to save me. A part of you knew that."

"I don't understand."

"We needed to help the Garde." She looks away from me, like this is as hard for her to say as it is for me to hear. "But after your defeat at Ivan's hands, you felt you had nothing to offer the cause. You said you were too weak, too skinny, that you weren't the hero I am. That you didn't have any power.

"But now you do."

Her Legacy. She's . . . *given* it to me? I get to keep it?

"I'm sorry for tricking you, Adam. But you needed to get to this point. If you hadn't come back here, a part of you still would've been attached to your family, to your people. You've seen how little they value you, how little they value anything but bloodshed and war. Now you're ready to walk with the Garde, to truly fight against your own people."

No. I pull away, my mind reeling.

"Please Adam. Use my Legacy well."

Across the sea, shadows dance and crackle and writhe in the clouds. Out there I can see her moving in slow-motion combat. Her last seconds, playing out in front of us.

"One," I plead. "Please stop."

"This is how it has to be. Deep down you knew it all along, Adam. I'm not real. I was *never* real." She turns to the roiling storm, to the tragic movie of her death playing in the clouds. The blade of some faceless Mogadorian's sword penetrates her through her back, erupting from her stomach. The killing blow.

"Deep down you knew. I've been dead this whole time."

I look at One. She's my best friend. She's everything to me.

She turns from the scene of her death to look at me. "You created me, made me out of my memories, so you wouldn't have to walk this path alone."

"That's not possible. You're all I have."

She smiles. "No. You have *you*. The courage it took to turn against your people, the courage it took to come back here, to risk your life to get the power you'd need to walk a hero's path . . . that was always *all you*."

One has never spoken so highly of me. I should be flattered, but all I am is scared. I'm going to lose her.

"I can't be alone." I feel pathetic, exposing my fears and weakness so totally to One. But I'm desperate. I've lost too much already to lose her too.

"Adam, the alone part is over. I promise you."

"One," I say, my eyes filling with tears. "I love you."

She nods, smiling, then reaches forward to touch my cheek. She's crying now too. "If I'd lived, I think . . ." she says, "I think you really would have."

She kisses me and says good-bye.

And then she's gone forever.

CHAPTER TWELVE

THERE'S A SHAPE IN THE DARK, MOVING AROUND me.

I see the sky. Stars above.

The shape is moving my limbs. Resting my head on a soft mound of earth. Pouring water over my wounds. Forcing me to drink.

The shape's skin is as white as the moon.

"Malcolm," I say.

"Yes," he says. He laughs, crouching beside me. "I'm Malcolm. I remember that now."

I sit up, half expecting to find myself still trapped in the lab, despite the sky. Despite the stars. But we're in the wilderness, in a field at the edge of a forest.

"I carried you as far as I could. Then I needed to rest." He sighs, taking a sip of water. "But we have to keep moving soon."

I'm baffled, utterly confused. *How did we escape?*

Malcolm senses my confusion. "I woke up in the lab. Mogadorians were at the doors, trying to break in. That doctor was on the floor. And you . . . you were convulsing. And then, just as the Mogadorians came through the door, there was . . ."

He trails off, laughing with amazement. "There was an earthquake."

As soon as I regain my strength, we begin to make our way on foot through forests, pastures, and farmland, traveling mostly at night to escape detection. We're headed west, trying to put as much space between us and what remains of Ashwood Estates as we can.

Outside of Ashwood, with only the sky to measure time, days and nights pass without comment. I lose track of the hour, the day of the week, how long we've been on the road. *Ten days? Twelve days?* I cease to measure time in numbers, counting instead the shifting landscapes, the changing scenery.

Malcolm eventually explains that the earthquake seriously damaged the underground facilities. He says it was a miracle he was able to get us both out through the collapsing structure without being apprehended. He says it was as if the entire structure was collapsing around us, but never *on* us—almost like it was creating an escape for us with every step he took. He figures the Mogs have their hands full rebuilding, that there's a good chance they haven't yet realized we even survived the devastation.

But he thinks we need to keep moving to be safe.

I agree.

We've camped out for the day in an unused shed at the edge of a tobacco farm. My limbs are tired from our constant trekking, but my cuts and scrapes are starting to heal.

Malcolm sees me mopping down the worst of my remaining cuts. "It's a miracle you weren't hurt worse." He shakes his head in wonderment. "It's a miracle we weren't both killed. And it's an even bigger miracle the earthquake happened in the first place. If not, there would've been no escape."

Now's as good a time as any to tell him.

"It was no miracle."

He stops what he's doing, looks at me curiously.

I haven't used One's Legacy on my own since the day I used it to destroy the Mogadorian lab. But I know the ability is still inside me. I can feel it there, nestled, pulsing, waiting for me to pick it up. To play.

I close my eyes and concentrate. The ground beneath us heaves and ripples, the walls of the shed quake. A few rusted tools, hung by hooks, clatter off the wall to the ground.

It's nothing major, barely a tremor: I only wanted to test myself, and to show Malcolm my gift.

Malcolm's stunned, eyes bulging. "That was amazing."

"It's a Legacy. A gift from the Loric."

Malcolm looks at me with one of his befuddled expressions.

"Do you know about the Loric?" I ask. I still don't really know what Malcolm remembers, how much is left of his brain.

"I know a little," he says. "My memory, it has . . . patches." He sighs heavily, clearly frustrated. "I've been working on it. Trying to remember everything. But mostly I remember the darkness."

"The darkness?" I ask, but as soon as the words are out of my mouth I realize what he means. The darkness of the containment pod. All those years in an induced coma, hooked up to machines, having his brain dredged for information. I shudder.

"When I try to summon a memory, it's like I have to go back into the darkness to find it. I have to go back through years of nothing to remember any one thing." He laughs, with a note of bitterness I've never heard in his voice before. "But there *are* a few things I remember that I don't have to fight to recall. Important things."

Malcolm goes quiet, lost in thought. Before I can press him to explain, he changes the subject.

"You said you were given a Loric's power." He leans forward. "So you're not a Loric?"

I grin. "You thought I was Loric?"

He nods. "Yeah. That or a high-priority human captive like me."

"No," I say, a bit nervously. "I'm not human. And I'm not Loric." I've been dreading telling him the truth. How will he react if he knows I belong to the same breed that held him in captivity and tortured him for years? But I knew I'd have to come clean eventually. I figure now's as good a time as any.

"I'm a Mogadorian."

That befuddled look again. "If I'd known that," he says, "I probably would've left you in the lab."

Uh-oh.

But then he begins to laugh..

Before I know it, I'm laughing too, and starting to tell him my story.

Malcolm and I develop a routine, sleeping by day and walking by night. We graze farmland and forests and roadside Dumpsters for sustenance. We cross hills, streams, and highways. We spend weeks—months?—like this. I begin to lose track of time.

When we're in remote fields, far from roads and houses, we train. Malcolm has no experience with Legacies, but then neither do I. Brute force with my newfound power is no problem: I was able to nearly decimate Ashwood Estates—quite literally—in my sleep. But my precision and control need work. So we focus on that.

In today's training session Malcolm takes a position on the other side of a field. I stand, getting ready to wield my power. When we're both ready, we signal each other with our arms. Training time.

I stare across the field at Malcolm, mentally mapping the distance between us. Malcolm has set pebbles on top of the fence posts running the distance between us; for every pebble I knock off its post, he will deduct a few points. It's easy to send out my seismic force in an indiscriminate wave, knocking everything in its path, but he wants me to hit the area right beneath him, and *only* that area. He says this practice will increase my precision.

I focus hard on where he is, until everything else disappears. Then I unleash my power.

There are days when I can't even reach Malcolm, when the farthest I can send my power is ten yards in front of me. There are other days when distance comes too easy, and I wildly overshoot, felling trees fifty yards past Malcolm's position. Sometimes I hit him with pinpoint accuracy, and the ground trembles delicately below him. When this happens he calls out, telling me to sustain that gentle force. But sometimes the intensity of my seismic power slips outside of my control, and the ground will erupt beneath him, sending him ten feet in the air.

He's always patient, gracious, and kind about my misfires. Which only makes me happier when I manage a perfect score at this game we've created, rumbling the earth immediately beneath his feet without sending him flying. It takes extraordinary control, and so much mental effort I usually wind up with a minor migraine, but it's worth it to see his proud face.

My parents disowned me. I don't think my father *ever* loved me. I was never going to have the kind of unconditional love from a parent I saw on television or read about in human literature.

During the three years I spent in One's mind, I saw her close relationship with Hilde, and I was jealous. They fought all the time, but on some deep level they trusted and loved each other. Hilde trained and cultivated One's talents, encouraged her when she succeeded. Ever since I witnessed that, I've craved something like it. A mentor. And now I have one.

One promised me I wouldn't be alone. She was right.

Our route through the country becomes a zigzagging path, designed to escape Mogadorian detection. It's so roundabout that I never even consider we're heading somewhere specific, that Malcolm has a destination in mind.

I enjoy the aimlessness. I feel safer off the grid, like

I did back at the aid camp. But I know that eventually we're going to need a plan, some way to reconnect with the scattered Garde. I may cringe at bloodshed, and I may fear that they will reject me for being a Mogadorian, but I can't help being excited by the prospect of meeting my new allies.

After a long night's trek, we camp out in a small grove at the edge of the woods in rural Ohio. Malcolm devotes so much time and energy to training me that I've been repaying the favor, usually as we're settling down for a day's sleep.

I train *him*. I ask him questions about his past, trying to jog his memory. I know his patchy memory is frustrating, but he will never recover his memories unless he works at it. So I grill him, pressing him for details.

"What happened before the darkness?" I ask tonight.

He's clearing some brush on the ground, making a smooth surface to sleep on. "I hate this."

"I know," I say. We're both exhausted and mental training is the last thing either of us wants to do right now.

But I keep going. "What happened before the darkness?"

"I'm tired," he says, stretching out on the dirt. "And I can't really remember."

"Come on. One thing," I say. "Just tell me one thing you remember from before the Mogs took you."

He's quiet.

"Malcolm. You already told me there's one important thing you remember from before, one thing you didn't even have to try to remember." I figure I can at least get that out of him. "Just tell me that."

He turns to me, suddenly serious. "My son. I remember my son."

Whoa. I had no idea he had a son.

"The details of how I made contact with the Loric, how I was captured by the Mogs . . . those things are starting to come back to me, though they're still fuzzy. But I remember *everything* about my life back in Paradise." He smiles. "I remember everything about Sam."

"Don't you want to see him?" I ask.

"Of course I do. That's why I've been leading us back towards my old hometown." He looks at me, clearly concerned about how I will react.

I'm stunned. "That's where he is?"

"Well, I can't be sure he's still there, but it's my only guess. It's only a day or two days' trek from here."

I'm confused. I thought we were just running from the Mogadorians, but this whole time Malcolm's been leading us to his home. "But our path, it's been so random."

"I'm still trying to keep the Mogadorians off our tail. That we continue to evade detection is even more important, the closer we get to Sam." He sits up, giving me a solemn look. "You don't have to come into town with me. It could be dangerous. For all I know the Mogadorians are waiting for me there."

Malcolm looks at me, waiting to see how I'll react. Under his gaze, I feel it: that familiar twinge of fear in my gut. My typical reluctance to enter the fray.

But there's something different about me now. I have One's Legacy—my Legacy. I don't feel as powerless as I used to.

If anything, I feel a strange itch to see what I can do with my new ability. Months ago, One tried to rouse me back to the Loric cause and I balked. It took her creating an epically complex psychological trick to get me to leave the aid camp.

But I don't need much persuading from Malcolm.

"Let's go," I say.

Paradise, Ohio, is a classic small town. A harmonious blend of farmland and suburbia, a far cry from the tacky faux-luxe of Ashwood's McMansions. Walking with Malcolm along the road leading through the town, sticking to the other side of the tree line to stay out of view, I take a deep breath.

Yeah. I like it here.

Just as Paradise's main drag comes into view down the road, Malcolm starts leading us away, deeper into the woods. We walk for a mile through the trees. We pass houses out here in the woods—some prosper-ous-looking farmhouses, some busted-down-looking shacks. We avoid all of them, beelining through the woods to avoid being seen by anyone.

"What's he like?" I ask. As we've been traveling, I've told Malcolm almost everything there is to know about me—about how the son of a respected Mogador-ian leader came to be the traitor that I am now. But there's so much about Malcolm that's still a mystery to me. Sometimes I wonder if it's because he doesn't like to think about it himself.

Still walking and staring straight ahead, Malcolm smiles sadly. "I don't know," he says.

"You mean you can't remember?"

"No, not that. My memories of Sam haven't faded at all. It's just—" He stops. "I can't say what he's like now, not when I haven't seen him in all this time. I've missed everything. He was just a kid when I got taken. He was smart, and he was kind. A great kid." He laughs. "He was Sam."

"What happens when we find him?" I ask.

Malcolm's expression darkens.

"I just need to see him. To know he's okay. You and I, we're marked for death by the Mogadorians. I know I can't exactly be a father to him under those conditions, but I need to see him at least once. After that . . ." he says, his voice trailing off.

I finish his thought. "After that we go back on the run."

Malcolm nods. "It won't be safe for us to stick around."

I feel a strange twinge of relief at that thought.

"We're close," he says, quickening his stride.

I see a house up ahead, through the trees.

"That's it," he says.

As we walk, the texture of the dirt beneath our feet begins to shift. I look down: it's burned. Scarred. My antennae go up, preparing for a possible attack.

The closer we get, the worse it is. More scorched earth, more fallen trees. There's been a battle here.

"Malcolm," I say. "The Mogadorians have been here."

But of course he's already noticed. He's speeding up, racing towards the house. I keep pace behind him, worried what we're running into.

But when he runs up to the house's side door and bangs on it, and a shocked-looking woman steps outside, eyes bulging at Malcolm, I stop running. Malcolm's given me no instruction; I have no idea what's going on.

I hang back.

Malcolm holds the woman by the shoulders, talking to her, asking her questions. The woman's expression of shock and wonderment begins to melt, giving way to something else.

Anger.

She slaps him. Then slaps him again. Soon she's unleashed a barrage, and Malcolm just stands there, absorbing each and every blow. I can't hear her from where I stand, but I know what she's saying. "Where were you? Where were you? Where were you?"

She falls to her knees on the porch and begins to sob. Moments later, Malcolm joins her.

I wait. Malcolm has been inside with the woman for an hour now. We exchanged a look before he headed inside with her. I nodded, giving him the sign that I'd be fine out here on my own.

Kicking the scorched dirt, I'm anxious, keyed up. To judge by the tracks, by the burned patches of earth, there was some kind of conflict here not long ago. Mogadorians could be close.

I have One's Legacy now, I remind myself. Even if I come face-to-face with a Mog force, I'm not powerless anymore. I can fight back.

The more time passes, the more I worry about Malcolm. To come all this way and discover that something has happened to his son would be devastating.

Malcolm finally emerges from the house. He walks with a hard-nosed determination, strutting right past me and back into the woods.

All he says is "Come."

I follow him across the backyard to a large stone well.

"It's open," he says, shaking his head.

"So?" I ask. "Malcolm, you have to tell me what's going on."

Without answering, Malcolm climbs into the well and disappears.

Again, I follow.

I make my way down a long, narrow ladder and finally arrive at the bottom of the well.

"Malcolm?" I ask. No response. I feel my way along the walls down a narrow passageway, which slowly gives way into a room.

A large halogen lamp lights up, illuminating the space. Malcolm holds it, and swings it around the room.

I follow the arc of the beam. Bare walls, some computer equipment in the corner. A shelf with supplies: water bottles, canned food—

Startled by what I see, I gasp. Against the wall, close enough for me to touch, is a massive skeleton.

The skeleton's head is tipped downwards in an angle of dignified, almost lordly resignation. But it's still a skull, with deep hollow sockets pointing right at me. I yelp, backing against the opposite wall.

"The Mogadorians didn't find this place," says Malcolm. "If they had, they wouldn't have left it like this. They would have destroyed this skeleton, or taken it.

But the well was open. Someone's been here." Malcolm resumes poking around in the chamber. "The tablet's gone. He must have come here, and then after . . ."

"Malcolm," I whisper, hoping he will calm down and explain himself. "I'm in the dark here," I say. "Quite literally."

He ignores my joke.

"My wife saw Sam with some other kids; she said there was a battle. By what she described, those other kids had to be members of the Garde. Sam was with them, fighting by their side."

I experience a brief chill of excitement at the thought that the Garde was here only a short time ago. The Garde. My people. My *new* people.

"In my absence, I guess he took up my cause, and wound up in battle with Mogs and . . . now he's gone."

Malcolm stares at me, a haunted look on his face.

"My son Sam is gone."

Malcolm's wife won't let him in the house again. She's too angry.

As a result, we've camped out in his underground bunker, stretching out on the bare stone floor. I've slept in some pretty rough quarters since going on the run with Malcolm, but I've never faced a challenge quite like trying to fall sleep under the hollow nose of an eight-foot-tall skeleton.

Malcolm explains that she is crushed by grief for her missing son. That as angry as she is with Malcolm for disappearing, the worst part is him finally reappearing only weeks after Sam disappeared—too late to save him.

She blames Malcolm for whatever's happened to Sam. And Malcolm says she's *right* to blame him.

"It was my fault. I was so excited to make contact with the Loric, I didn't even consider the consequences. Once I saw what the Mogadorians were capable of, I realized my role as a Greeter might be a danger to my family, but it was too late. Before I could do anything to protect them, I was taken."

Malcolm theorizes that, haunted by his disappearance, Sam began to unravel some of the mysteries of the Mogadorian invasion. That he somehow forged an alliance with members of the Garde.

And that at some point in the past few weeks, in battle near his house, he was captured by the Mogs, and either killed or detained.

When Malcolm says this, my mind races back to the memo I encountered while snooping around the underground server in the Media Surveillance facility. The memo was already a year old when it declared all future detainees and captives were to be routed to the Dulce base in New Mexico. If Sam was captured weeks ago, there's a good chance he's being kept there.

I stare at Malcolm, stretched out on the floor, his back to me.

"Malcolm," I say.

He rolls over and turns to me. I can see from his gaze that he's lost in doubt and guilt and grief. Clearly the search for his son is what's been driving him since we escaped from Ashwood.

"I think I know where your son is."

CHAPTER
THIRTEEN

I STAND BACK AS MALCOLM OPENS THE GARAGE door. Inside, covered in dust, is an old Chevy Rambler. "I can't believe it's still here," he says, diving towards the passenger door.

We are at a storage facility on the outskirts of Paradise. Malcolm explains that he paid for this garage space many years in advance, keeping the car fueled up and ready should he ever need to skip town on short notice. In fact, he was headed for this garage when he was abducted by the Mogadorians years ago.

I'm impressed with his recall. "Your memory's improving."

"Yeah," he says, smiling slyly. "It seems to be. Must be all of your annoying quizzes." I laugh as he turns to the car's glove compartment, pulling something out. He holds it out of the car door for me to see.

A spare pair of prescription glasses.

"Jackpot," he says, triumphantly. He wipes the lenses with the tail of his shirt and slips them onto his head.

He sits back in the passenger seat, looking at me through the windshield.

"I can't tell you how amazing it feels to be able to see clearly. It's been so long," he says.

He lets out a contented sigh. "Amazing."

"I didn't even know you needed glasses."

"Big-time," he says. "This is actually the first time I've seen your face as anything but a big smudge." He squints up at me. "I can definitely see the Mogadorian thing, now. Yeah, definitely something evil about your face."

I laugh, giving him the finger. Teasing me for being a Mogadorian has become a running joke between us. Joking about it is really just a testament to how accepting of me Malcolm has been.

"Full tank?" I ask.

He leans over, starts the engine, peering owlishly as the gas gauge whirs up.

"Very nearly."

He slides behind the wheel as I get into the passenger seat. We're traveling light. Heading to New Mexico.

"You ready for this?" he asks.

"Not at all," I reply.

"Yeah," he says. "Me neither."

And we're off.

If we weren't traveling incognito, trying to avoid detection by taking side roads, we could've made the trip to the base in three days. As it is, the trip takes almost a week.

I don't mind the extra time.

Sitting beside Malcolm in the passenger seat, it occurs to me that we may be driving towards our own ends. That just as I had to say good-bye to One, I may have to say good-bye to Malcolm. Right when I thought I'd found a father figure, I now find myself embarking on what could be a suicide mission with him. I can't be Malcolm's son. He already has a son, and—for better or worse—I have a father. But I can help save Sam.

I remember what One said to me, that she'd pegged me for a hero, wanted me to try for "great" things.

Well, it turns out a hero's lot is not glory or reward, but sacrifice. I'm still not sure I'm ready for that. I'd be happy if this car trip lasted forever. But soon enough we'll cross the border into New Mexico and be only hours away from the base.

A big part of me doesn't want to go find Sam. If I can't have a normal life, I want to stay with Malcolm, living on the edges of society and evading the Mogs.

But I know that's not possible.

I know what we're doing is what must be done.

PITTACUS LORE

We're at the fenced edge of the Dulce base. We parked out in the desert at dusk and crossed the still hot sands to the electrified perimeter fence, which is a quarter mile or so from the compound itself. Malcolm explained that he knew how to find the base from his alien-conspiracy days, long before he'd known anything about Mogadorians or Loric, when his awareness of extraterrestrials was limited to conspiracy newsletters and countless viewings of *Close Encounters of the Third Kind*. The Dulce base was a lightning rod for crazed speculation about governmental cover-ups of alien life. The irony, he said, is that all that speculation must have predated any actual human contact with the real extraterrestrials by several years. Until recently, it probably *was* just a military base. "Guess me and my wacko friends were ahead of our time," he joked.

We crouch low to the ground, figuring there are surveillance cameras surrounding the fence. We've approached at the rear edge of the compound, far away from the base's entrance. Malcolm thinks security might be a little more diffuse at this end of the base.

For all of Malcolm's knowledge from old newsletters, not to mention the tiny bit of preparatory research we did at an internet café en route, there's only so much you can find out about a secret government base through public channels. We're mostly going in blind.

Malcolm pulls out a crappy pair of binoculars we

111

bought at a truck stop and scans the facility.

After a moment he taps me, pointing out a watch-tower a few hundred yards down the fence. Squinting through the evening's half-light, I can see a generator a few paces off from the watchtower. We can only hope that generator powers the fence. If I can hit it with my Legacy, it's our one chance of getting inside.

"Tower's got to be three hundred yards . . . no, four hundred yards away."

"Yeah," I say. I start pounding my fist into my hand, a little pre-Legacy ritual I picked up. It doesn't make any sense that warming up my hands would help with my accuracy—the power comes from deep inside me, from my core, not from my hands—but it's become habit by now.

"That's like three regulation football fields, Adam. We never trained for that."

"I got it," I say, confidently.

I don't actually feel confident, but figure acting confident can only help my odds.

I reach deep into myself, eyes focused tight on the area encompassing the watchtower and generator.

The trick, I've discovered, is anger. And it has to be my own. The first few weeks I was able to channel One's rage at losing Hilde to access my Legacy, but its efficacy quickly waned. I needed to find my own rage.

So now I think of Kelly, too ashamed of me to even

speak to me. I think of my mother, leaving me to rot in the Mog lab. I think of Ivanick, his hands at my back, pushing me down the ravine. Mostly, I think of my father: delivering the killing blow to Hannu. Sentencing me to death. And a million other, smaller injustices, perpetrated over my entire life.

I hate them. I hate everything they stand for.

And then I feel it, my power, my rage, coursing below the ground, in search of the watchtower. Like a giant stone hand, its fingers curl upward, fondling the earth, feeling.

There it is.

I let it rip.

The ground beneath me and Malcolm remains still, but I can see the watchtower rumble, erupting with tremendous force. The generator, sundered from the ground, shoots sparks. Then the tower collapses.

Malcolm turns to me, shocked, amazed. Proud.

He smiles. "Touchdown," he says.

CHAPTER FOURTEEN

WE CREEP OVER THE FENCE, NO LONGER ELEC-
trified. We know that the generator's explosion and the
collapse of the watchtower must've attracted the attention of the base's perimeter guards, and in fact we're
banking on that to be able to run aboveground without
interference. If they're too distracted by the explosion
to maintain sufficient ground cover along our path,
we've got a shot.

Our optimism pays off. We make it close to the compound without anyone seeing us. Most of the guards
have been drawn to the watchtower; if they're even
aware of a breach in their perimeter, they probably
think it's all the way over there.

Then I stop. On the other side of the sprawling
compound, over the horizon, there is chaos. Noise.
Explosions. Smoke. Weaponry firing.

I turn to Malcolm. "Weapons testing?" I ask.

Malcolm shakes his head.

Something is going down at the base. Something *big*.

I have a strange hunch. Something inside of me says the Garde is here.

"What do you think it is?" I ask Malcolm, wondering if he has the same feeling I do.

"I don't know. But I'm not looking a gift horse in the mouth. The base is massive. If some kind of battle is going down on the other side of it, that means they might be spreading their resources a bit thin on this end to compensate. We might be able to catch 'em off their game, even once we're inside."

He resumes his march to the rear of the compound. I follow.

We position ourselves behind a parked Humvee at a side entrance. We can still hear the distant sound of chaos, erupting half a mile away at the other side of the compound. We lie in wait as a young soldier flies out of the door, running towards the Humvee. I wonder if he's been dispatched to the other end of the base, like Malcolm guessed.

In a flash, Malcolm ambushes him.

I've never seen Malcolm in combat before. Clearly he's not trained for it, but he has two things going for him. First, the soldier was distracted, in a hurry. But even more important, Malcolm knows he's getting closer to his son, and his determination to save Sam lights him up. Malcolm swings wildly, an uncoordinated assault that nevertheless catches the young soldier off guard.

Malcolm manages to knock him out. We drag the unconscious soldier behind the Humvee. Malcolm rips an access card from his chest, then takes the soldier's gun for good measure.

"Just in case," he says, awkwardly wielding the gun. I can read the hesitation on his face: he doesn't want to kill anyone. I know he's relying on me to use my Legacy skillfully enough that he won't have to.

We creep to the side door. Malcolm swipes the card through the access panel. After a second, a green light flashes and the lock disengages. We take a deep breath and open the door.

It's worse than I'd imagined. A long corridor opens up before us, leading to a small alcove with a desk clerk. There are at least five soldiers in the area and six or seven other military personnel. And they've all turned in unison, seeing us at once.

One of the soldiers shouts. "They're coming from both sides!" They think we're part of the same invading force attacking from the front of the compound.

I have no time to consider that, and send a blast out in front of me, shredding the concrete floor of the hallway. And another one. And another one.

Soldiers and workers are knocked off balance or thrown against walls as we rush forward through the fresh rubble.

I know I'm causing pain and injury; I can only reason that at least I'm saving them from gunfire. More important, I'm keeping Malcolm safe.

We round the corner by the desk alcove, only to be confronted by three more soldiers. I let loose another seismic wave, sending them hard against the walls behind them, knocking the wind out of them, breaking bones.

I cringe inwardly at what I've done, even as I feel a creeping exhilaration at my own power. I didn't realize I was capable of such tremendous force.

Malcolm dives forward to the overturned desk, scrabbling through its scattered contents, all while struggling to keep his gun-wielding arm raised. I circle Malcolm. He searches for a compound map, or something to give us a clue as to where Sam is being held, while I keep an eye on the fallen soldiers, ready to blast anyone who manages to get to their feet.

"Got it," he says, leafing through a large binder. "Compound directory."

"Hurry," I say, still scanning the fallen soldiers, my fists raised.

A soldier clambers to his feet, hugging the wall, out of breath. We lock eyes as his hand drifts to his gun.

I shake my head. *No.*

He looks at me, confused, helpless.

He's seen what I can do. To my own shock and amazement, he puts one hand up and then tosses his weapon aside with the other.

"There's a cell cluster in Wing E, this way," says Malcolm, pointing in one direction. "But there's another cell cluster at the other end of the compound."

Malcolm tosses back and forth through the pages. He's torn, unsure of which way to go. I can see him beginning to melt down, to lose his cool. The closer we get to Sam, the higher the stakes, the more likely it is that one false move could mess everything up.

"There are also interrogation rooms in Wing C. He could be there." Malcolm clutches his forehead. "He could be anywhere."

Watching Malcolm on the verge of a breakdown, I know what I have to do.

I leap at the soldier, grabbing him by the collar. He whimpers at my touch.

"We're looking for a captive. Sam Goode. Where is he?"

The soldier bites his lip, closes his eyes. Surrender is one thing, but to give up information to an invading force is a step farther than he is willing to go.

"Tell me," I say, with menacing calm. He keeps silent.

I will a seismic rumble, right beneath our feet.

He gasps.

"Tell me," I say. I increase the rumble's force as the concrete beneath us goes liquid, waving and rocking and cracking beneath our feet. I maintain an even intensity, but it's a terrifying sensation, for me as well as for him. "Tell me now or I'll make this floor rise up, chew us up, and drag us straight to hell."

He whimpers again, tears streaming down his cheeks.

I increase the intensity.

"Wing C!" he screams, giving up. "He's in Wing C! He was kept away from the others. He's the only prisoner being held in those cells."

I release my grip, and the soldier falls to his knees, crying.

I know I've done a terrible thing, completely humiliating an adversary who had already surrendered. But there's no time for guilt.

I turn to Malcolm. "Wing C," I shout.

Relieved, he tosses the binder aside and races through a door to our right. After doing one last sweep of the fallen soldiers, I join him.

We enter another long hallway.

"Wait!" I yell.

I turn back to the door we've come through. The last thing we need is for any of those soldiers to follow and assault us again. So I target the doorway with my

Legacy, and knock out the stone structure. The door-way collapses in a noisy heap of rubble.

That should keep them.

We race down the passage for what feels like a mile. The tunnel gets narrower and narrower, darker and darker, the farther we get.

We finally arrive at a locked door. Either the soldier whose keycard we swiped didn't have clearance for this area, or some kind of security override has kicked in in the wake of our assault.

"Stand back," I say, an idea quickly forming.

I reach deep into the earth below the compound. I've never had to use this much precision with my legacy, and the amount of focus it requires is going to create an excruciating headache. I force the earth upwards, up against the door frame. The stone floor erupts and the steel door is blown from its hinges.

It's not an ideal entrance—we have to climb up the rubble and then crawl through the half-blocked door-way—but it works.

We get up off our knees on the other side of the door.

We're in the base's armory, a warehouse-like space filled with shipping containers and crates. Judging by the warning signs emblazoned on the crates, they contain powerful explosives. I never would've used my power in such close proximity to explosives if I had known what was on the other side of that door. We are lucky.

Malcolm grabs my arm, leading me forward through the armory. We come to another set of double doors. Malcolm tries the keycard: this time it works. "Lucky swipe," he says. "That soldier must've had access through another route than the one we took."

We step through the doors and enter a massive, multistoried prison-like structure, cold and oddly damp.

Now that we know there's another way in, we're certain that more soldiers will be coming soon. We have to hurry.

We race along the corridors, past rows and rows of empty cells, and start calling out Sam's name at the top of our lungs.

I hear something, a rustle from above, off the second-story gangway.

I run ahead of Malcolm, up a stairwell, and along the gangway, running past cells.

I arrive at Sam's cell. His hands grip the bars of his cage, eyes blinking against the light of the complex. He looks like he's been through hell.

I'm speechless.

"Who are you?" he says, eyeing me suspiciously, backing into his cell. "What do you want?"

He senses it. He knows I'm a Mogadorian.

"We're here to help," I start. But explanations aren't necessary: Malcolm appears behind me and plunges his hands through the bars towards his son.

Sam stares at him, speechless. "Dad?" he says, incredulous.

"I'm here, Sam. I'm back."

This reunion isn't about me: it belongs to Sam and Malcolm.

I slowly back away from the cell. Alone again.

That's when I hear it. Something Malcolm and Sam are too caught up to hear: the sound of marching soldiers.

Staring out over the gangway, I see soldiers pouring in from multiple shadowed doorways, from every corner of the complex.

Worse still, these are not human soldiers. They're Mogs.

"Guys," I say, shaking Malcolm's shoulder. "We have company."

I act without thinking, pulling Malcolm away from the bars and shouting to Sam, "Stand in the center of your cell and cover your head!"

Sam is confused, unsure of what I'm about to do, but he's smart enough to know we don't have time for explanations: he quickly assumes a huddle in the middle of his cell.

I reach my hands through the bars, sending feelers

out to the other side of the cell's wall. I find the wall, the floor, then I sense the entire structure of the wall.

And then I blast.

The wall behind Sam crumbles, seismic shock ripping straight up its seams. But this whole structure is connected, and the impact sends aftershocks through the concrete floor beneath Sam. The floor of the cell juts out against the gangway, banging it so hard it almost buckles.

Sam tumbles forward and Malcolm and I are knocked hard against the gangway's railing.

The Mogadorians are getting closer.

I turn back to the cell, where the dust is beginning to settle. There's now an opening for Sam to get through the wall to the other side.

"Go!" I say. "Run!"

Sam picks himself off the floor, looks at me, then does as I tell him.

I look around. The floor beneath the cell has fissured, warping the cell bars enough that I think we can squeeze through them. I push Malcolm forward, but he struggles to get through the bars.

Mogadorians have completely swarmed the complex now—there must be at least thirty of them, with more coming, and they're already making their way up the stairs to the gangway we're standing on. We have thirty seconds, max.

Malcolm finally squeezes through into the cell, then turns to me.

"Hurry!" he pleads.

I look back at the approaching Mogadorian swarm. In the rear, in commander's attire, I see Ivanick. The only person in this world I fear as much as my father.

The General said he had been promoted, that he was working in the Southwest. And here he is.

My blood runs cold.

I step to the bars, about to squeeze through. Then I stop.

"What are you doing?" Malcolm begs. "Adam?"

I realize I'm not going through those bars. If Malcolm and Sam are going to have a shot of escaping the Mogadorians, one of us is going to have to hold them off. They won't stop chasing Malcolm and Sam unless someone *makes* them stop.

Besides, I don't want to run from my own people anymore. I want to kill them.

"Go," I say.

"What? Adam, no."

"Go with your son. Now."

I can see from Malcolm's eyes, from the dawning horror in his face as he realizes what I'm saying, how much he cares about me.

But I also know he has a greater responsibility to his son than he has to me. After one last moment's hesitation, he turns and disappears through the hole in the cell's wall.

I turn back to the approaching Mogs. They've slowed down, but their swords are raised. They're coming from both ends of the gangway, surrounding me.

I scan the complex. The stairways are full, the first floor is swarming with Mogs, and both routes down the gangway are blocked.

I have a choice: be captured, or go out swinging.

I aim my Legacy at the corner of the room behind one group of Mogadorians, and blast. The entire room shudders, and the gangway breaks free from the wall, knocking several Mogadorians to the ground below.

I grip onto the gangway as tight as I can. Whirling to the other side of the room, I blast again.

This time I almost flip over the gangway myself as the struts supporting it give out completely and it tips out towards the center of the room. There's no way back into the cell now. I'm flat against the railing, but still safe.

The floor below is teeming with Mogadorians. I look both ways down the gangway. Some Mog soldiers are merely struggling to stay on the precarious, creaking structure, but those with a firm grip are still coming, sliding along the railing towards me like acrobats. Getting closer.

I could blast the gangway again to hurt the Mogs

still clinging to it, but that's not nearly enough to get me out of here safely.

My situation is so hopeless I almost laugh.

"Adamus," I hear. I look down to the floor, to the massed Mogadorians, weapons all pointed at me. Among them stands Ivanick, staring up at me.

His expression is cold, mock-pitying. Nothing about his manner betrays any surprise at seeing me here, under these circumstances.

"Long time no see," he says.

I know I've only bought Sam and Malcolm a minute's lead on the Mog scum, but I hope it helps. I'm ready to deal with whatever comes my way next.

"You've got some power, Adam. It's impressive. I'm sure Dr. Zakos or one of our other scientists would love to study you, to learn from your ability. Give up now and maybe we can work something out. You can be a test subject or something. I know how you like that." It's strange to see Ivanick promoted to a leadership role. He doesn't really have the brains for it. But brains never counted for much among the Mogs.

"I mean," he says, letting out a little laugh, "of course we'll still have to kill you when we're done."

I cling to the bars. The Mogadorians are sliding closer, just waiting for the order to take me out.

"You suck at bargaining," I say.

Ivan laughs. "Well, what else are you going to do?

From what I can see, you've run out of options. It's sur-render-or-be-killed time."

There's no way I'm letting myself get captured.

Go out swinging.

I look to the wall perpendicular to the half-fallen gangway. The armory is behind it. I get an idea.

"That's not exactly true, Ivan."

I reach forward with my mind: one hundred yards, two hundred yards, three hundred yards. I stop.

There it is.

I see Ivan, staring up at me. His face has changed from mocking to suspiciously fearful. There's no way he can know exactly what I'm about to do, but he knows me well enough to read my expression: I'm going to wipe us all out.

"That's right," I say. "The armory."

"No way," he says. "You wouldn't. You're Adamus. Son of the great General Andrakkus Sutekh. You can't bring yourself to kill one of us, let alone all of us."

I grin at him. *Watch me.*

I let rip another seismic pulse, aimed at the ground right below the armory.

Only a moment after the impulse leaves my body, my blast triggers a massive explosion.

There is a deafening boom, steel and concrete flying.

All around me I see Mogadorian bodies getting rid-dled with shrapnel.

The whole thing begins falling apart around me. The gangway collapses and I go flying, landing so hard on the ground that I'm almost knocked unconscious.

My ears ringing, my eyes half blinded by dust, I crane my neck to see tumbling concrete knocking out Mogadorian after Mogadorian. The whole cave is coming down around us.

On the ground by the fallen gangway I see Ivanick, his head nearly severed from his neck by the collapsed steel. Dead.

Mogadorians scream all around me.

To my own surprise, I *like* the sound.

Something heavy lands against my shoulder, slamming my head against the floor, pinning me in place. I can't move, and am too stunned to know if it was a minor wound or a fatal blow.

Why keep track now? I think. *There's more where that came from.*

Indeed there is: concrete keeps falling, all around me.

As the entire structure gives out and collapses onto us, I know I only have a few moments of consciousness left. But I'm not afraid.

I survived my fall down the ravine. I survived the implosion of Ashwood Estates. I wasn't even conscious then, and Malcolm said something kept us from being crushed, that it was as if some force kept us safe as the world fell down around us.

Third time's the charm.

It may just be exhaustion, it may just be delirium, but I'm overcome by a deep, sweet certainty that I was meant to survive. That my ultimate purpose lies somewhere beyond these tumbling walls, sometime beyond this frenzied moment. That the best of me is yet to come.

I will live.

I AM NUMBER FOUR

THE LOST FILES

THE LAST DAYS OF LORIEN

CHAPTER ONE

THIS IS LORIEN. IT'S "PERFECT" HERE. THAT'S what they say, at least.

Maybe they're right. Over the years, Lorien's Office for Interplanetary Exploration has sent recon missions to pretty much every inhabitable planet out there, and they all sound terrible.

Take this place called Earth: it's polluted, over-crowded, too hot and getting hotter every day. The way the scouts tell it, everyone there is miserable. The earthlings all spend a lot of time trying to kill each other over nothing; they spend the rest of their time trying not to get killed.

Scan through one of their history books—we've got a bunch of them available in the Great Lorien Information Depository—and you'll see it's all just one pointless war after another. It's like, *Earthlings, you idiots, get it together!*

The thing is, other than Lorien, Earth's about the best place there is out there. I'm not even going to bother mentioning Mogadore. Talk about a dump.

Here on Lorien there's no war. Ever. The weather's always perfect, and there's enough variation in ecosystems that you can find a place with whatever your own version of perfect weather is. Most of the place is pristine forests, perfect beaches, mountains with views you wouldn't believe. Even in the few cities we've got, there's plenty of space to move around and no crime at all.

People don't even argue all that much.

What is there to argue about? The place is perfect, so of course everyone's happy. Like, always. You walk down the street in Capital City and you see everyone smiling like a bunch of happy zombies.

But there's no such thing as perfect, is there? And even if there is, then I have to say: "perfect" is pretty boring.

I hate boring. I always do my best to find the imperfections. That's where the fun usually is.

Although, come to think of it, as far as a lot of people are concerned—my parents chief among them—*I'm* the biggest imperfection of all.

It's positively *un-Loric*.

The Chimæra was packed the night it all finally caught up with me. The music was blaring, the air was full of sweat, and—surprise!—everyone was happy and grinning as they bounced and spun and crashed into each other.

Tonight, I was happy too. I'd been dancing for hours, mostly on my own, but every now and then I'd bump into some girl and we'd end up dancing together for a few minutes, both of us smiling and laughing but not taking any of it too seriously until one of us got caught up in the music and danced away. It was no big deal.

Okay, it was turning out to be a pretty great night.

It was almost dawn before I was out of breath and ready for a break, and after hours of nonstop motion I finally let myself flop up against a bank of columns near the edge of the dance floor. When I looked up, I saw myself standing next to Paxton and Teev. I didn't know them very well, but they were regulars at the Chimæra, and I'd come here enough that we'd been introduced a few times.

"Hey," I said, nodding, not sure if they'd remember me.

"Sandor, my man," Paxton said, thumping me on the shoulder. "Isn't it past your bedtime?"

I should have been annoyed that he was making fun of me, but instead I just felt happy to be recognized. Paxton always thought it was funny that I always found my way into the place even though I was still techni- cally too young.

I didn't see what the big deal about being underage was—the Chimæra was just a place to dance and listen to music. But on Lorien, rules are rules.

Paxton was only a few years older than me and was a student at Lorien University. His girlfriend, Teev, worked at a fashion boutique in East Crescent. From what I could tell, they both had the kind of lives I wouldn't mind having someday. Hanging out at cafes during the day, dancing at places like the Chimæra all night, and no one giving either of them a hard time about any of it.

I didn't have that long to wait anymore. But it felt like I'd already been waiting forever. I was tired of being a teenager, tired of going to school and obeying my teachers and playing by my parents' rules. Soon I wouldn't have to pretend to be an adult. I would just *be* one, and I'd be able to live my life the way I wanted.

For now, the Chimæra was the one place I could actually be myself. Everyone here was a little like me, actually. They wore crazy clothes, had weird hair; they did their own thing. Even on a planet like Lorien, there are people who don't *quite* fit in. Those people came here.

Sometimes—not often, but sometimes—you'd even catch someone cracking a frown. Not because they were unhappy or anything. Just for fun. Just to see how it felt, I guess.

Teev was looking at me with an amused expression, and Paxton pointed at the identity band on my wrist. "Aren't those things supposed to be foolproof?" he asked with a smirk. "Every time I see you, you've figured out another way in that front door."

The gates at the Chimæra scan all patrons upon entry, mostly to prevent underage Loriens like me from getting in. In the past, I'd sometimes snuck in a back entrance or shoved through the doors unnoticed with a big crowd. Tonight, though, I'd gone a step further, modifying my ID band's age signature so the machines would think I'm older than I am. I was actually pretty proud of myself, but I wasn't about to give up all my secrets. I just gave Paxton a sly shrug.

"That's me. Sandor, Technological Wizard and Man of Mystery."

"Forget about the door scan, Paxton," Teev said. "What about the Truancy Register at his school? You *do* still go to school, right? You better hurry or you're going to get busted. It's getting late."

"You mean *early*," I corrected her. The sun would be coming up any minute. But she was right. Or, she *would* have been.

Teev had a mole above her lip and a scarlet-colored birthmark high on her cheek, fading back into her hairline. A thin-line tattoo encircled the mole and then curved up into an arrow, pointing at the birthmark.

She was shortish and kind of cute and there was something offbeat about her. She was who she was, and she wasn't going to hide it. I admired that about her.

I was tempted to tell her how I'd gotten around the problem of the Truancy Register. It had actually been an easier fix than the door-scan problem—or maybe I was just that good. All I did was borrow my friend Rax's ID band and embed a copy of my own digital biosignature inside it. Now whenever I cut class, the class register scans me as "present" as long as Rax is there.

I'd figured the trick out after I'd gotten in trouble a few months ago and had been forced to do some time working in the school's front office. There, I'd discovered the flaw in the Truancy Register's system: it doesn't catch redundancies. So when Rax and I both *do* show up, there are no red flags. It's perfect.

"Can't reveal my secrets," I say, giving a little smirk.

"Cool kid," said Paxton, his admiration curdling slightly into contempt. I flushed.

"Thanks," I said, trying to act like I didn't actually care. But before I could think of anything else to say, I froze. Over by the club's entrance, I spotted someone I knew. And not someone I *wanted* to know.

It was Endym, my interplanetary cultures professor at Lorien Academy.

Okay, Endym was generally a pretty cool guy, probably the only teacher I had that I actually liked. But cool or not, if he saw me out at the club, underage and with no hope of making it to school in time, he'd have no choice but to report me.

I grinned at the couple I was talking to. "Teev, Paxton, it's been a pleasure," I said, easing myself out of Endym's line of sight and into a mass of dancing people with a half wave. Under the cover of the crowd, I peered back towards the entrance and saw Endym as he was approached by one of the club's vendors. He took one of the proffered ampules and popped it into his mouth, his eyes scanning the club, and then he stepped forward, onto the dance floor. I was pretty sure he hadn't seen me—yet—but he was heading right in my direction.

Shit. I ducked behind a column to escape his sight.

The Chimæra's a big place, but not big enough. If I stayed where I was, I was going to spend all my time trying to avoid him—and even then, I didn't like my odds that he wouldn't spot me.

I had to get out, and I had to take my opportunity now, while Endym was distracted. He'd just struck up a conversation with a woman in the middle of the dance floor and was flirting with her shamelessly as she danced. I rolled my eyes. The fact that my teacher was at the Chimæra was suddenly making it seem significantly less cool.

The only way out was to go deeper in. I'd never been

in the dressing room below the stage, but the performers had to come from somewhere. The only problem was that Endym had somehow positioned himself in the worst possible spot for my purposes: I'd have to go past him to make it to the entrance, but he had a direct line of sight to the back stairwell, too.

I cast around the place, trying not to attract attention by seeming frantic, hoping I'd find a solution to my dilemma. Then I realized it as I spotted them, still standing a few paces away: Teev and Paxton. They would help me. At least, I hoped they would.

"What would you say," I said, sidling back over to them with my conspiratorial smile plastered across my face, "if I told you the guy over there is a teacher of mine?"

The couple glanced over at Endym, then back at me.

"I guess I'd say this place is going significantly downhill," Teev said. "They're letting *teachers* in now?"

"Bad luck, dude." Paxton laughed. "All that trouble to get in here and now you're going to get busted."

"Come on man. Don't laugh. How about helping me out?" When they just looked at each other skeptically, I gave a sheepish shrug. "Please?"

Teev tossed her hair and rolled her eyes amiably. "Okay. You got it, little dude," she said, patting my face. It was kind of humiliating, but what could I do? "We'll take care of you," she promised. "Get your ass out of here."

I watched for a second as Teev and Paxton approached Endym and the woman he was dancing with and inserted themselves between the dancing pair. Teev danced off with Endym; Paxton danced off with Endym's partner.

When I was sure they'd reeled Endym in, I took my chance. I slid through the crowd, keeping my head low to avoid being seen.

I was almost home free when someone shouted at me. "Hey!" I looked back, startled, to see an angry face and a guy shoving toward me. I had accidentally knocked the guy's ampule to the floor as I'd pushed past him, and he wasn't happy.

The last thing I needed was to be caught in a fight on the dance floor. I picked up speed and ran for the edge of the stage, where I groped the dark corner and found a small door.

Of course it was locked.

"Hey! You!" shouted the guy whose drink I'd spilled. He was getting closer. "You're gonna replace that!"

I jiggled the handle furiously. When it didn't budge, I gave up on trying to be cool and began throwing myself against the door, hoping that with enough force—and a little luck—it might give.

The dude was getting closer, still shouting. What a jerk—making this kind of scene over one spilled drink? All over the room, heads were turning toward me. I'd be caught any minute.

One last try. With all of my force I threw myself against the small door.

This time, it gave.

CHAPTER TWO

THE FORCE OF MY WEIGHT SENT ME TUMBLING blindly into the room on the other side of the door. I tripped across the floor, crashing through layers and layers of fabric. I tripped and fell, my head hitting the ground with a snap.

Then I heard a voice. A *girl's* voice. "Now *that's* funny."

As I lay there, I realized that what I'd crashed into was a rack of clothes. Women's clothes. Now I was lying in a heap of them on the floor. I looked like I'd gotten caught in an explosion of rhinestones and sequins.

Standing above me, a guy in black metallic pants and a collarless shirt was struggling to lock the door I'd just busted through.

"Yeah, funny," he was saying sarcastically. "I love it when underage pipsqueaks come barging into the dressing room."

I stood up sheepishly and tried to gather up the pile of dresses I had knocked loose. This really was not how I'd imagined my night going.

"So. So. *Funny.*" I spun around to see a girl with electric-white hair sitting on a low stool in the corner of the room. She was wearing a tiny pair of shorts and was in a crouching position. She was drawing on herself with some kind of makeup pen, marking her bare calves with an elaborate pattern of swirls and curlicues.

"No," I said.

I probably should have apologized. Or at least explained myself. But I couldn't. I was too starstruck. All I could say was *no.*

"Oh, *yes,*" she said, still drawing on her leg. She leaned down closer to the serpentine markings, pursed her lips, and blew up and down her calf, drying the ink.

It couldn't be. But it *was.*

It was Devektra.

Most people on Lorien probably would have had no idea who she was. But I'm not most people, and I'd been listening to Devektra's music for months. For people in the know, she was *the* most buzzed about Garde performer on Lorien. With her striking beauty, her wise-beyond-her-years lyrics—because she was practically a kid herself, only a little bit older than me—and her unusual Garde legacy of creating dazzling, hypnotic light displays during her performances, it was all but certain she was going to be a huge star before long. She was already well on her way.

"What, you've never seen a girl putting makeup on her legs before?" she said with a twinkle in her eye.

I tried to regain my composure. "You must be the top-secret performer," I finally managed to say, stumbling over practically every word. "I'm, um, a big fan." I cringed as I said it. I sounded like a total loser.

Devektra appraised her legs, then stood up and looked at me like she didn't know whether to be angry or to laugh. In the end, she split the difference. "Thanks," she said. "But you know, they lock those doors for a reason—to keep big fans *out*."

Stepping forward, she threw her arms theatrically around my shoulders and pulled my ear right up next to her mouth. "You gonna tell me what you're doing in my dressing room?" she whispered. "I don't need to call security, do I?"

"Um," I stuttered. "Well, see, it's like this . . ." I searched my brain for an explanation and couldn't think of one. I guess I'm a lot better at hacking software than I am at talking to girls. Especially hot, famous ones.

Devektra stepped back and looked me up and down with a mischievous twinkle in her eye. "You know what I think, Mirkl?" she asked.

"What?" the guy I'd practically forgotten about asked in a bored voice. Honestly, he sounded like he was kind of sick of Devektra.

"*I think*," she said slowly, "that this little fellow's *way* too young to be here. It looks to *me* like he was about to get kicked out for being underage and snuck in here looking for a place to hide. We've got a law-breaker on our hands. And you know how I feel about lawbreakers . . ."

I looked at the floor. Now I was *definitely* busted. This wouldn't be the first time I was in trouble for something like this. Or the second. This time, though, the consequences would definitely be serious.

But Devektra surprised me.

A grin spread across her face and she began to giggle. This girl was sort of crazy, I was starting to suspect. "I love it!" she said. She narrowed her eyes and wagged a scolding finger at me. Her nails were glittering in every color of the rainbow. "Such a naughty little Cêpan."

For the second time in just a few seconds, she'd caught me by surprise. "How do you know I'm a Cêpan?" I asked.

Like the majority of public figures on Lorien—athletes, performers, soldiers—Devektra was a Garde. I was a Cêpan. An elect group of Cêpans were mentor Cêpans, educators of the Garde, but most of us were bureaucrats, teachers, businesspeople, shopkeepers, farmers. I wasn't sure which kind I'd turn out to be after school was finished, but I didn't think any of my choices seemed too great. Why couldn't I have been born a Garde and get to do something actually *fun* with my time?

Devektra smirked. "My third Legacy. The dull one I don't like to mention. I can *always* tell the difference between Garde and Cêpan."

Like all Garde, Devektra had the power of telekinesis. She also had the ability to bend and manipulate light and sound waves, skills she used in her performances and which had made her the rising star she was. That was a pretty rare power already, but the third Legacy that she'd just mentioned, to be able to sense the difference between Garde and Cêpans, was one I'd never heard of at all.

For some reason, I felt self-conscious. I don't really know why—there's nothing wrong with being a Cêpan, and although I'd often thought it seemed like a lot more *fun* to be a Garde, I'd never felt insecure about who I was before.

For one thing, I'm not usually a very insecure person. For another thing, that's just not how it works around here. Though Garde are revered as a collective—a "treasured gift" to our planet—there was a widespread conviction, shared by Garde and Cêpan alike, that the Garde's amazing abilities belonged not to them alone, but to *all* of us.

But standing there, faced with the most beautiful girl I'd ever seen, a girl who was about to go onstage and demonstrate her amazing talents for everyone at the Chimæra, I suddenly felt so *ordinary*. And she could see it. She was Devektra, *the* Devektra, and I was just some stupid, underage Cêpan with nothing going for him. I didn't even know why she was bothering with me.

I turned to go. This was pointless. But Devektra caught me by the elbow.

"Oh, cheer up," she said. "I don't care if you're a Cêpan. Anyway, I'm just kidding, thank the Elders. What a boring third Legacy *that* would be. My *real* third Legacy is much more exciting."

"What is it?" I asked suspiciously. I was starting to feel like Devektra was messing with my head.

Her eyes glittered. "Isn't it obvious? I make men fall in love with me."

This time, I knew she was pulling my leg. I blushed, suddenly realizing the truth. "You read minds," I said.

Devektra smiled, impressed, as she leaned back against Mirkl, who looked less than amused. "Mirkl," she said. "I think he's starting to get it."

A half hour later, I stood on the second-floor balcony overlooking the club, watching Devektra perform. She was better than I could have imagined. It took my breath away.

She sang passionately, and melodically, but even though Devektra was known for her lyrics, I barely even heard the words she was singing. She was dancing, too, and dancing well, but that wasn't the main attraction either. And even though she was pretty much the most amazing-looking girl I'd ever laid eyes on, that wasn't it either.

All that paled in comparison to what she was doing with her Legacies.

She would wave her hands, modulating the texture of her voice, pitch-shifting it eerily. She could flick her wrist and boost her voice's volume dramatically; she could even target and shape the volume such that listeners in the back of the club would get walloped with sound while the front of the crowd was merely tickled. With her other hand, she manipulated the club's already sophisticated lighting system, bending its multicolored beams in skillful, dazzling counterpoint to the sounds coming out of her mouth.

I was transfixed. I'd heard about her performances, but nothing could have described what she was doing.

Some things you just need to see with your own two eyes.

Now it was almost over. I had been so absorbed in watching Devektra from my exclusive spot in the VIP balcony that the past hour had flown by like minutes, and as the music began to slow, taking on a baleful tone, and the lights shifted from bursts of pink and orange to long, undulating waves of purple and green, I knew it was coming to a close.

She held the song's final notes at a delicate volume. Her left hand twirled gently, caressing the air and twirling the sound out into the crowd.

Then her voice rose to a roar. The sound pummeled my chest, so hard I felt like the noise could hollow me out. Then, suddenly, she slammed her fists together and the club's lights surged into an overwhelming blast just as the noise disappeared, as if sucked out of the room by a vacuum.

I staggered against the railing, blinded.

As my vision slowly came back, I could see the people in the audience below me rocking dizzily on their heels. Like me, they were dazed but satisfied.

"That was incredible," I said, finally capable of speech. But when I turned around, Mirkl, who had been watching the show with me, not saying a word, was already gone.

Turning back to the stage and dance floor, I saw Devektra already halfway to the front door, with Mirkl and the rest of her entourage silent behind her. They were leaving.

She'd mentioned they'd all be going to another club called Kora for an after-performance party. At the time the mention had felt like an invitation, but it looked like Devektra was on her way out without giving me a second thought.

I bolted down the stairs, down the hall, and through the crowd, desperate not to lose her. I forced my way through, squeezing between people. I heard a few people snap at me as I knocked into them, but I no longer cared about anything except finding Devektra.

I finally spotted her as I reached the entrance. She was standing outside the Chimæra with her entourage, and she turned back to the club and saw me, giving me a mysterious smile. I didn't know what it meant, but I knew I had to find out.

"Excuse me," I said, pushing past a couple, making my last dodge for the door.

"Sandor?" My heart sank as I felt someone grab my arm. I knew that voice. There was no point trying to run. It was Endym.

"I *thought* I saw you earlier," he said.

"Some show, right?" I said, praying Endym would let

this slide. After all, he was here too—and he sounded like he'd had more than a few ampules since I'd last seen him.

"Incredible," said Endym. "Best I've ever seen her."

"So," I said, hopefully. "Any chance we could just forget you saw me here today?"

Endym smiled back at me. "None at all."

CHAPTER THREE

"IF I WEREN'T SO DISAPPOINTED, I'D BE impressed." Principal Osaria was flipping through papers on her desk outlining my misdeeds, reading out charges as she went. "Charge: Tampering with the Truancy Register. Suggested punishment: expulsion. Charge: absences more than ten per semester. Suggested punishment: expulsion."

She looked up at me. "Ten's just a provisional figure of course. We've yet to sort through the Register's data logs to get a precise estimate for how many classes you skipped."

"Ten's about right," I admitted.

"That better not be sarcasm," my dad said in a tired voice from the monitor on the wall of Osaria's office, where his face crackled in by remote feed. My mother sat silently beside him. They were at their vacation home on the beaches of Deloon and couldn't be bothered to make the two-hour trip to the capital to witness my expulsion in person.

"What does this mean, exactly?" my mother asked. As if she didn't know. I'd been warned before. Cutting school and sneaking into the Chimæra was one thing— but this went way beyond that.

Osaria swiveled her chair to face the screen. "It means that my hands are tied. If it were just one or the other of these charges, I'd be able to exercise my discretion in meting out punishment." She frowned deeply. "But in addition to the rules he broke at school, he also tampered with the ID scans at the Chimæra. I have no choice."

"Oh no," said my mom. She looked like she was about to cry.

"This is a surprise to you?!" My dad was turning red, nearly as mad at my mother as he was at me. "He's always been like this."

It was true. I'd always been a rule breaker, I'd always had a way of getting myself into trouble. I wasn't ashamed of that; I *liked* that about myself. But it tended to flummox the people around me. Lorien was a happy, prosperous and law-abiding planet. The fact that I was always getting into trouble made me practically a freak of nature.

Principal Osario shifted uncomfortably in her seat, put off by my parents' bickering, and quickly broke in before they could continue. "I must say I'll be sorry to lose Sandor." She turned back to me. "Attendance issues aside, you are one of our very best students—and I have to admit that your tampering with the security systems, while illegal and dangerous, shows a certain amount of"—she paused—"*ingenuity*. Now, as I see it, there are two options available to him. If he elects to stay in the capital—"

"Yes," I said. "I'm not leaving the city."

"—then we can arrange to have him placed as an apprentice with the Munis."

My heart sank. The Munis? The Munis were the custodial corps of the city's workforce. Maintenance work. Most citizens of the capital were conscripted for Munis service by lottery, for year-long terms no more than twice in their lifetimes. There was no shame attached to performing Munis service in Lorien culture, but it was far from my idea of a good time. And entering the Munis as an apprentice was basically signing up to haul trash for the rest of my life. To me, that was a fate worse than death.

I felt myself beginning to panic. "There's got to be something else in the city. Can't I get some kind of job at Kora, or the Chimæra?" I knew it was a reach to ask for a work assignment in one of the very places I'd just gotten in trouble for sneaking into, but I was open to taking *any* job in them, no matter how menial. I'd scrub floors if that's what it came to.

"Yes, surely there are some better options?" my mother spoke up. I was surprised to hear her coming to my defense.

Osaria shook her head with regret. "Unfortunately, all urban job assignments other than apprenticeships are reserved for adults. It's either Munis, or a Kabarak relocation."

I thought my heart had already reached the bottom of my chest, but I felt it plunge deeper, right into the pit of my stomach. A *Kabarak?* Doing time outside of the city on one of Lorien's communal Kabaraks was an important part of Lorien's culture, not to mention essential for keeping the planet running smoothly, but it was definitely not a glamorous experience: loralite mining, Chimæra husbandry, farming. And all of it way out in the country, miles from any excitement. Unless pulling up weeds and digging through dirt all day is your idea of a good time.

I had a bad feeling about this. On the screen, my father was nodding, looking almost satisfied, and I knew that my fate was as good as decided. Having done time on a Kabarak was considered a noble credential, and was a prerequisite for working in government or the Lorien Defense Council, helping to protect Lorien from an attack by one of our nonexistent enemies.

Among a bunch of equally terrible options, the

Kabarak looked like it had managed to win my parents' approval.

"Osaria, I think a few years on a Kabarak is just what my son needs." My dad was smiling as he said it, actually *pleased* with the outcome of the conversation. I looked up at the screen, but he avoided my gaze—he had to know exactly how awful it sounded to my ears.

Even my mother wasn't going to bail me out this time. "I agree," she said, giving me a furtive, apologetic glance. "It really is the best option."

"Well then it's settled," said Osaria.

Right then, I wished again that I'd been born a Garde—one with the Legacy to go back in time and undo all my mistakes of the previous night.

Of course, if I undid the night, it would mean I would have never met Devektra. Which might have almost been worth it. Well, *almost.*

I left the academy, beginning the long walk back home to my parents' empty apartment. The school's shuttles to the city center didn't start running for hours, so I had to walk by myself, on desolate streets. My parents weren't due back from Deloon for weeks, and they'd made no mention of coming back to the capital to see me off. I'd likely spend my last days in the city alone in the apartment, waiting for my Kabarak assignment and transportation details. The transpo details would probably come first, and would offer some clue about my fate: if the state arranged for a terrestrial craft, it meant I'd been assigned a nearby Kabarak colony, like Malka. If they ponied up for air transport, it meant I was being shipped far, far away, to a Kabarak in the Outer Territories, the other side of the planet.

Not that it made any difference. Exile was exile. And even after I did, my future would be forever changed. While I'd always imagined myself going on to a job that was easy and low-key, like Teev and Paxton's, or even working at a place like the Chimæra, most people on Kabaraks ended up going on to a position in Lorien government.

I shuddered at the thought of finding myself spending the rest of my days pushing paper as a bureaucrat at a dull-as-dirt office like the Lorien Defense Council, wasting my life trying to stave off an invasion from an extraplanetary attack that everyone knew was never coming while I tried to cheer myself up by pretending I was actually doing something *important*.

It was hopeless. For now, all I could do was try not to think about it. And keep walking.

My school disappeared behind me as the Spires of Elkin loomed ahead, beckoning me towards the city center.

I'd considered hanging around, waiting for the shuttle. It would've given me a chance to say good-bye to my friends when they got out of class. But the thought depressed me too much to bother. I couldn't stand the thought of them finding out how badly I'd messed up.

Anyhow, I liked Adar and Rax and a few of the other kids at the academy well enough, but I didn't consider them my *real* people. I'd always been different, even from them. Everyone else on Lorien seemed to be content with exactly what they had. They were happy to live on the most perfect little planet in the whole damn universe. Why couldn't I be more like that?

I was still wallowing in my un-Loric pool of self-pity when I heard my name.

"Sandor?" I stopped in my tracks and turned around to see that an unfamiliar man, a few years older than me, was standing next to a parked Muni hovercraft a few paces behind me. "Are you Sandor?"

He wore the distinctive blue tunic of a Mentor Cêpan, the special class of Cêpans who work for the LDC and are charged with training the Garde and monitoring their Legacies as they develop. I had no idea how he knew my name, and I didn't really want to find out. I'd had enough trouble today, and for all I knew, this guy was about to tell me I'd committed some new infraction without even realizing it.

"Yeah," I said, "that's my name all right." Without waiting for a response, I turned again and resumed my walk.

Without asking permission, he kept pace beside me.

"My apologies. I'd meant to catch you at your meeting with Osaria but I got there too late."

I was silent.

"I'm Brandon. I'm a Mentor Cêpan at the Lorien Defense Academy—"

"Sorry, dude," I said. "I'm not a Garde. Just your typical, boring Cêpan—no need for a mentor. And I flunked the LDA aptitude test years ago."

"Yeah," said Brandon. "I've seen your scores." He waggled his eyebrows suggestively, like he *knew* I had tanked the exam on purpose to avoid being sent off to the prestigious academy.

Of course compared to a Kabarak, mentorship training sounded pretty good at this point. If I'd known what was in store for me, maybe I would have thought twice about bombing that test all those years ago.

"We got word of your little hijinks over at the academy," Brandon said. I looked at him in surprise. How in the world would they have heard about one underage Cêpan's misadventures at the Chimæra?

But Brandon was talking like that was the most normal thing in the world. "We were impressed," he said. "That kind of technological work is quite unusual for someone your age—especially someone without academy training. If you put your talents to work in a more serious way, you could really make a difference in the

Lorien security efforts."

I was reminded why I didn't care for LDA types. They took themselves *way* too seriously. Lorien had never had a war. We had never been attacked. And yet these people acted like we were living under constant threat. It was like they just told themselves that so they could feel important.

I waved Brandon off. "Yeah, well," I said. "I'm off to a Kabarak. Hopefully they'll appreciate my skills there."

"They won't," he replied with a shrug. "Listen. The LDA could use some fresh blood and some new hands. We have some decent engineers and techs, but no one with your gift for problem solving."

I rolled my eyes. An engineer at the LDA? That was almost as bad as joining Munis.

"Sorry, man. Not interested." I kept walking.

"Our reputation is not what it used to be, I see." Brandon gave me a wry smile. I could tell he was amused by my snottiness. "And it's true that many Loric question the need for a defense at all during such a time of peace. Their mistake. But we have resources, Sandor. You'd have full access to our engineering and computer laboratories. Plus after six months you'd have weekend privileges. And I've been given authority to invite you to join the academy despite your, ah, *uncharacteristically* poor performance on the aptitude exam."

I stopped in my tracks.

"You'd be close to the city," he added. "Who knows? Maybe eventually, when you're a little older, you'd be able to get some time off to visit the Chimæra."

Clearly Brandon had more information on me than could be gleaned from security bulletins about my stunt at the Chimæra. He was pushing my buttons a little *too* precisely.

"You got a psych profile on me, Brandon?"

He only smiled. "Just decide if you'd rather spend the last few years of your adolescence playing with defense tech near the city, using your actual skills, or out in the Outer Terrritories shoveling Chimæra shit."

"Outer Territories?" I felt my mouth go dry. Why had he said that? Had he heard something about my likely assignment?

"What do you know?" I asked.

"It's not what I know, Sandor. It's what I can make happen."

And with that, he turned around and walked away.

CHAPTER
FOUR

EXITING THE TRANSPORT VAN A FEW WEEKS later, I approached the front entrance of the Lorien Defense Academy warily, my bags over my shoulder. The school was a windowless gray cube plopped on a grassy stretch of land at the edge of Capital City. Somehow, for such a prestigious place, I was expecting something a little more lavish. Instead, the only thing that set it apart from any other Loric government building was a single statue of the Elder Pittacus.

Near the entrance, a few feet away from the statue, a few young Mentor Cêpans in shapeless blue tunics and loose black pants were talking in low tones with a Lorien councilmember, who I identified immediately from his tan robe. They had as little style or flair as the building itself. As I passed, the councilmember and the Cêpans looked up in neutral acknowledgment. I waved at them and then felt stupid.

It was practically a relief when I entered the building. The lobby was as sparsely decorated as the building's outside, but at least it was busy. Young Mentor trainees, about my age, single-file marching off to class. There were a few adult Mentor Cêpans, and even a couple of Garde kids laughing and chasing after each other in their tiny blue suits.

"Kloutus!" a Mentor shouted. With a sheepish look on his face, one of the young Garde slowed down.

Recognizing the Mentor as Brandon, I walked up to him. He'd been nice to me when he'd recruited me on the street, and the sight of a familiar face was suddenly welcome.

But if I was expecting him to be a new friend, I shouldn't have. Brandon gave me a cursory up-and-down look like he barely knew me, and then was all business.

"What are these?" Without a word of greeting, Brandon plucked the bags off my shoulders.

"They're my things from home," I said, struggling to hold on to them.

"We're going to have to confiscate them," he said. "You'll be issued everything you need in processing."

"Those are my clothes!" I don't know why I cared— of course I'd have to wear the LDA uniform now, so I don't know what good my clothes would do me. Still, the thought of having them *confiscated* depressed me. My clothes were part of what made me *me.* Now I'd just look like everyone else.

Brandon shook his head at my foolishness. "You can arrange to have those shipped back to your parents' place. They'll be waiting for you when you graduate." With a curt nod, he pointed towards the processing office and disappeared down a hallway.

Feeling worse than ever, I trudged to processing, where an LDA administrator curtly issued me three identical green tunics, wrapped in paper. After handing them to me, he stood there expectantly, and I realized I was expected to change right in front of him so that he could collect the clothes I was already wearing. Probably so he could take them off to whatever storage locker or incinerator the rest of my clothes were destined for.

"A little privacy?" I asked.

He turned around. I seized the opportunity to undress quickly, throw on the tunic, and hide my favorite Kalvaka T-shirt inside the folds of my scratchy new garment. One piece of real clothing was better than none.

"All done," I said, shoving the rest of my clothes in the administrator's hands, hoping that if I bunched them all up in a wad the guy wouldn't notice he'd been shorted.

It worked. He gave me my dormitory assignment and told me to go there and await instructions for the rest of my orientation.

After being stripped of nearly all my worldly possessions, I made my way deeper into the building, trying to get a feel for the place. I walked past open seminar rooms, administrative offices, gymnasiums, labs, even a glass-walled Chimæra observatory where a clutch of Lorien's legendary beasts chased after each other in circles, growling and snorting as they changed from one form to another, the shapes of their bodies shifting with liquid ease.

At least *they* were allowed to look how they wanted. I stood and watched them for a few minutes before moving on.

Finally I reached the long corridor of the dormitory section and arrived at my dorm, 219. This was my room.

I hadn't been issued a key, so I took a deep breath, knocked, and waited.

A moment later the door opened and a guy with small, nervous eyes, a wide mouth and a bulbous nose greeted me. His green tunic was identical to mine, and I stupidly wondered how we were going to remember whose was whose.

"You must be Sandor," the guy said stiffly. "I'm Rapp. Come in."

I entered the room, doing my best to conceal my horror as I appraised the spartan bunk beds, the bare stone floors, the curtainless window staring out onto a sparse and underlit courtyard.

"How minimalist," I said.

"Yeah," Rapp said. "The LDA keeps it pretty simple. We're here to defend Lorien, not to sleep comfortably, I guess." At least he didn't sound any happier about it than I was.

I flopped on the bottom bunk. The mattress was thin and hard.

"So we're roommates, huh?" I asked. "Are you training for the tech department too?"

"Yep. We'll be seeing a lot of each other, I guess. Between the two of us, you're looking at the whole program."

"What?"

"We're it. There's a corps of about twenty active engineers and fifteen active techs on the whole planet, but only two trainees at a time."

Oh, man. This guy seemed nice enough, I guess, but if it was just us, he could be the coolest guy on all of Lorien and we'd *still* get sick of each other.

"It's not so bad, though," he went on, not registering my disappointment. "Even though we're just trainees, the corps is so short staffed lately that they send us out on grid surveys, repair work on the electronic perimeters, stuff like that."

"Exciting." I didn't mean to sound so sarcastic, but I couldn't help it. This would be my new life for *at least* the next two years, and it was already a total bore.

Fortunately, Rapp was immune to irony. "It is. To know that I'm playing a small but significant role in keeping Lorien safe . . . I feel really blessed."

I couldn't take it. I lurched up from the bed.

"Safe from what?" I asked.

Rapp stared at me, dumbly. "What do you mean?"

"Keeping Lorien safe from *what?* There hasn't been an attack on this planet for aeons. For all our explorations and recon missions, we haven't even had direct communication of any kind with another planet for hundreds of years. What are we afraid of? A *civil* war? Loriens are all pacifists, even in the sketchiest part of City Center or the most backward parts of the Outer Territories, nothing bad ever happens. I mean, *I'm* considered a hardened criminal around here. And all I did was get caught at a Devektra show!"

Rapp looked taken aback, but I didn't care. "Do you *really* think you're making a difference?" I spat. "Please. All this stuff about ancient prophecies and attacks that will probably never come—it's superstition."

Rapp didn't take my bait. Instead of answering, he solemnly walked to the door.

"I'll come back in a little while to give you a tour of the grounds. But I gotta say if this is your attitude on day one, you're going to have a pretty miserable time here."

Yeah, I thought. *No shit.*

CHAPTER
FIVE

IT WOULD'VE BEEN NICE IF I COULD SAY MY first week at the LDA passed by in a blur. Actually, it dragged on even more endlessly than I'd anticipated.

Rapp, it turned out, was still learning things in class that I had taught myself ages ago, so I couldn't even count on my schoolwork to keep me interested. Sure, I could have told Professor Orkun that I already knew all this stuff, but I kept it to myself. Instead, I just kept my head down in three-person seminars, nodding along with the lesson and trying to pretend like it was all new to me.

I knew I was being stupid. If I had to be here, I might as well have tried to learn something. But, in a weird way, it felt like that would be letting *them* win. If I wasted my time, I was still getting away with something, right?

Things weren't much more interesting in the

170

commissary than they were in class. I kept pretty much to myself and so did all the other students at the academy. As for the Mentor Cêpans who'd been assigned their own Garde to train, they were pretty scarce around campus, and the ones who did eat in the commissary usually had their hands too full with their young Garde charges to mix with engineering trainees like me and Rapp.

The only people at the academy who interested me at all were the Garde kids, who were just coming into their powers and gave the school what little sense of life it had. On Lorien, Garde children are raised by their grandparents until their eleventh year, when they're sent away to a place like the LDA to train with their assigned Mentor Cêpan. There are training academies for them all over Lorien, but LDA is considered one of the best—the Garde who wind up here are the ones who are expected to have some serious power going on.

Some of these kids racing the halls of the LDA had only started to manifest the very beginnings of their gifts, while others were already onto their second and third Legacies, but almost all of them were lit up, charged by the excitement of coming into their powers, not to mention living away from home for the first time. They had their whole future to look forward to.

Pretty much the only exciting thing that happened in my entire first week was that one of the youngest

Garde, a dark-haired, mischievous-looking kid named Samil, almost destroyed the whole school. That was actually kind of fun—I guess Samil'd been showing off his emerging pyrokinetic Legacy to some older kids in an empty classroom, when things had started to get out of control. Before long, the fire was raging. The halls of the school filled with smoke as sirens blared and Cêpan raced to evacuate the students and staff while the older, more experienced Garde headed toward the fire in an attempt to contain it.

The rest of us were gathered on the lawn, waiting for it all to get sorted out and, for a few minutes at least, as black smoke curled from the building into the sky, it looked like maybe my stay at the Lorien Defense Academy would be a short one.

"So if this place burns to the ground they'll send me home, right?" I asked Rapp.

"Don't sound too disappointed, or anything," he said disdainfully. When I didn't reply, he just snorted. "Dude. You think this doesn't happen all the time? The walls here are fireproof. Not to mention everything-else-proof. This school's built to withstand just about anything. It's what's *inside* that room that you should be worried about. Like the poor kid who just found out being able to generate giant fireballs might not be as cool as it sounds."

I felt instantly guilty that I hadn't even considered

that. Every year on Lorien there were stories about young Garde perishing in grisly accidents, killed by powers that they didn't know how to control or, in some cases, didn't yet know they even *had*. There had been the girl with the ability to manipulate temperature who'd accidentally frozen herself to death in the bathtub, and a boy with sonic flight who'd overshot Lorien's gravitational pull and found himself caught in the unbreathable atmosphere many miles above the ground. It was the purpose of Mentor Cêpans to prevent such incidents. But accidents still happened.

"Sorry," I mumbled to Rapp. "I guess I wasn't thinking."

He shrugged, and his expression softened. "Yeah," he said. "I know. Don't worry about it."

I glanced over at Vatan, the Cêpan of the kid who'd started the fire. His face was pale and anguished, and I knew that if anything had happened to his charge, he'd never be able to forgive himself. But a few minutes later, a tiny figure crept from the smoke and flame. It was Samil, completely unscathed. He had an expression on his face that was equal parts shame, terror and exhilarated pride.

Everyone whooped with joy and relief, and, in the first show of real emotion that I'd seen since I'd gotten to the academy, Vatan ran across the field and wrapped Samil in a huge hug. The boy's skin—just as fireproof

as the walls of the school, it turned out—was still burning with heat. Vatan didn't let go even as it charred the
fabric of his blue tunic.

I was relieved too. I mean, of course I was relieved.
I didn't want anyone to die, much less an eleven-year-
old kid. But at least the fire had been *something*. Once
it was over, everything was just back to normal. And
by now, I'd had enough normal to last me the rest of
my life.

The nights at LDA weren't much different from the
days. At least I had Rapp to keep me company. Yeah,
he took himself way too seriously, but at least he was
someone to talk to. And he wasn't quite as lame as I'd
thought he was at first. He had no idea who Devektra
was, but ever since I'd told him my story about meeting her, he'd wanted to hear all about it. Not just about
Devektra, but about the Chimæra, and about how I'd
managed to sneak in, and had I *really* been a regular
there?

Plus, he let me copy his homework, which was nice
because even though it was mostly easy, there was a
lot of it.

Maybe if I'd thought there was a point to doing it
myself, I would have been more interested. Back at
home, I'd taught myself to tinker with machinery and
electronics as a means to an end. It was a way to get
out of class, to get into places like the Chimæra. To

be whoever I wanted to be. It was a way to trick the system.

Here, it *was* the system. And it was a system I didn't have faith in.

According to legend—or *history*, depending on who you listened to—the original Nine Elders had brought forth the Great Loric Age aeons ago when they'd discovered the Phoenix Stones. It was this ancient event that had supposedly awakened the Legacies of the Garde and called the shape-changing Chimæra out of hiding, making Lorien a place of prosperity and peace that was unprecedented throughout the known universe.

From that time on, Lorien's ecosystem flourished. Where food and resources had once been scarce, there was now more than enough for everyone. What the planet itself didn't offer up in excess could easily be provided by the strange, amazing, and endlessly varied powers of the Garde. On other planets, this was the stuff people fought tooth and nail over. Not here. Here on Lorien, we could just *live*.

But the Elders had also set forth a prophecy: that one day, when we were least prepared for it, a threat would come to test us—and destroy us. We wouldn't know when that threat was coming, but it *would* come, and when it did, we would have to be ready for it.

That was why the LDA existed. That's why I was learning to create and maintain ever more elaborate systems of defense against an enemy that I was pretty sure was mostly fantasy. Just in case tomorrow was the day we all woke up and found ourselves under attack.

Back home, everyone knew the deal, but no one seemed to pay much attention to it. The discovery of the Phoenix Stones was just a story, something that had happened so long ago it barely seemed real. And the ancient Elders' prophecy—well, even if it did come true someday, it sure didn't seem like it was going to happen anytime soon. While most good Loric paid lip service to the *good work* that people were doing at places like the LDA, ensuring that Lorien "stayed safe for generations to come," even the most Loric among them didn't seem to take any of it too seriously.

Things were perfect, after all. Why worry about what might happen someday?

Here at the academy, it was a totally different story. Everyone walked around acting like the prophecy was about five minutes away from coming to pass—like we were going to be under attack at any minute. When I'd told Rapp I didn't really think it much mattered whether the grid, the vast defense system that scanned Capital City's airways for potential intruders, was perfectly maintained at all times, it was like I'd insulted him personally.

"Some of us actually care about what we do here," he said. He spoke slowly and carefully as he said it, but his voice was shaking. I could tell I'd really gotten to him. "While everyone else on Lorien is living in their little utopia, congratulating themselves for how perfect the place is, it's people like me who are busting our asses to keep it that way. Without the grid, we'd be sitting ducks. And people just laugh at us."

"Calm down," I said, taken aback by how angry he'd gotten. "You're acting like I just said Pittacus Lore's a big loser or something."

He scowled. "Yeah, well," he said. "You probably think *that* too, don't you?"

I paused. "No," I said. "I mean, not exactly."

Actually, I had no idea what the famous Pittacus Lore was like at all. I'd never seen him—even the statue of Pittacus outside the school wasn't of the current Pittacus, but of one of the old ones, probably from like a thousand years ago or something.

The current Elders had the same names as the original nine who had supposedly discovered the Phoenix Stones all those years ago, but they were otherwise many times removed from the Elders of legend. The names were passed along like titles, along with the Elders' special abilities, to specially picked successors who took on their forebearers' role of watching over Lorien, of safeguarding our environment, and of protecting our traditions and way of life. I knew that they made occasional trips to the LDA to consult with the

Mentor Cêpan and the instructors, but I had never seen them.

Aside from these brief interactions with the world, the Elders had long ago removed themselves from the day-to-day activities of life on Lorien. Even their exact whereabouts were unknown: some Loric said they lived deep in the mountains of Feldsmore, while others claimed they lived in a giant glass fortress deep at the bottom of the Terrax Ocean. Those were just some of the more plausible theories.

The only thing I knew was that it didn't seem like the Elders did very much at all, and that most people at the LDA, along with the rest of the Lorien defense operation, were telling themselves stories about prophecies that would never come true.

CHAPTER SIX

ON MY ELEVENTH DAY AT THE LDA, I WAS WOKEN by Rapp tugging on my arm.

"Come on, Sandor," he said. "We're going to be late."

"Your mom's a chimæra's butt," I mumbled irritably, shoving him away and pulling my thin, scratchy sheet over my head.

This had become a morning ritual between us. He'd try to wake me up, reminding me that it was my Solemn Loric Duty to rise and shine, and I'd come up with more and more colorful ways to tell him to leave me the hell alone. We were both getting sick of the routine.

"Fine," said Rapp, turning to go. "I'll just go to City Center by myself."

I opened my eyes and sat up in bed. "City Center?"

"Yeah," he said. "I saw Orkun at the commissary, she said class was cancelled and that we're supposed to report to transport immediately. She wants us to use the time to do grid maintenance."

"Why didn't you just say that?" I was already out of bed, hurriedly throwing on my tunic, excited by the chance to go into the city.

He just snorted as I checked myself out in the dull, tiny mirror over my dresser, trying in vain to flatten the irregular ridges of my cowlicked hair with spit.

"Dude," he said. "You think a little primping's gonna make any difference? All the girls in the city just stare right through us. Our tunics may as well be invisibility cloaks."

I knew he was right, but I groaned anyway, turned from my reflection and headed out the door as he followed behind me. It was hard to be too upset. No, grid maintenance wasn't all that exciting or anything, but still. We were going to the city.

We arrived at the transport hangar and got into the academy's only available two-seater, a teardrop-shaped vehicle some of the other students referred to as the Egg. I watched from the passenger seat as Rapp spoke into a receiver on the dashboard, programming our journey into City Center according to the assignment that Orkun had given him. "Sector Three twenty-nine, Security nodule H, Patch Three." He flipped through a binder, pulling up additional coordinates. "Sector Two ninety-seven, nodule J, Patch Seven." He had a cocky little smile as he said it, like this stuff made him feel really important or something.

I didn't get Rapp at all. How could anyone get excited about grid maintenance? It was like getting excited about brushing your teeth, except that brushing your teeth only takes two minutes, and *that's* if you do a really good job.

At the same time, I felt sort of bad that I was always giving him a hard time. Rapp was like me, in his own weird way. I was in the LDA's engineering program because I'd been forced to be here, but he actually *wanted* to be here. Considering there were only two of us in the whole class, that sort of made him an even bigger freak than me. And he didn't care. Most of the time, he hardly even seemed to notice when I made fun of him. I almost had to admire the guy.

Obviously I would never tell him that, but at least, I figured, I could tell him I didn't really think his mom looked like a chimæra's butt, and that she was probably actually pretty hot.

But before I could even formulate my apology, he'd entered our last coordinate and the Egg took off, shooting us out of the hangar, past the cube of the academy building, and then through the pastures and mud huts and Chimæra pens of the Alwon Kabarak.

Alwon was the only Kabarak on Lorien within city limits, and thus would've been my first choice had I been assigned to one. I watched the early-rising

Kabarakians, dressed in their red silks and ceremonial charms, busily tending to their land as our Egg whizzed past them and around them, unfazed by another routine intrusion of LDA speedcraft.

It was funny to think, only weeks ago I was in a depressed panic at the idea of working on a Kabarak. After my time at the academy, it no longer looked like such a bad way to live. Then again, maybe I was just jealous of their outfits—I looked better in red than in green.

The Egg crossed the western edge of Alwon and gained speed through the depopulated outer industrial zones of the city's east side on its course to City Center, miles ahead. The Spires of Elkin glinted brightly from the morning suns. I realized I had never seen City Center from this particular distance and angle. Perhaps it was nostalgia, or homesickness, but it looked more beautiful than ever.

Then, beyond the spires, I saw something strange.

Off in the distance, sprouting between the spires on the horizon, was a massive column of violet light, stabbing upwards into the clouds. It was a bright morning, and yet the rays of the suns did nothing to diminish the hard-edged, almost tactile thickness of the light. It was astonishing.

"Quartermoon's in three days," said Rapp, barely even looking at the light.

According to our collective legend, a quartermoon hung in the sky the day the First Elders discovered the Phoenix Stones, and over the years a holiday had developed around the regular appearance of the quartermoon in the sky. In the city and out on the settlements and Kabaraks, people party into the wee hours, dancing, gathering around campfires and lighting fireworks, celebrating the miracle of our planet's rebirth. Temporary monuments and light displays, called Heralds, were often arranged for by city government or by the Elder Council, to commemorate our history and to celebrate the quartermoon's approach.

This was a much bigger and more elaborate Herald than I'd ever seen before, so tall and majestic it was probably visible far outside the city—if it was even coming from the city at all. It was a little weird, but I brushed it off. If there's one thing we Loric, not to mention our Elders, are good at, it's thinking up new ways to celebrate how great we are.

Personally, it seemed to me like the Elders could think of better ways to use their time and powers, but who was I to question their ancient wisdom?

When the Egg finally whirred to a stop at a corner on the edge of Eilon Park, I felt a pang of surprise.

"Wait a minute," I said, turning slowly to Rapp. "*This* is where we're doing our grid maintenance?"

Rapp looked at me like I was crazy. "Yeah, sure," he said. "I told you we were going to City Center. Why?"

"Because," I said. "This is Kora." I pointed to a nondescript door on the side of a big nondescript building. "That's the rear entrance."

"That's the club you've been talking about all this time?" Rapp pushed the door open and climbed out of the Egg, his feet hitting the pavement with a thud. "I have to say, man, I was picturing something—I don't know—like, fancier or whatever. That just looks like a big, dirty warehouse."

I frowned as I climbed out after him. "It's the *back* door," I said. "Anyway, it's not supposed to look like anything on the outside. That makes it seem special when you see the *inside*."

Rapp cocked his head curiously and gave me a shrug like, *whatever you say*, and headed to a pole towering above the bottom slope of Eilon's Hill.

In the days before I'd learned how to manipulate my ID band, it was practically the only place in town where I could go to dance and hang out at night when my parents were out of town. It wasn't anywhere near as cool as the Chimæra, and the music was actually pretty bad most of the time, plus it always sort of smelled. But because they didn't serve ampules, there was no age restriction for getting in. I took what I could get.

Now, though, I would have given just about anything

to be back at Kora, even with the bad music and the awful smell. Suddenly I missed that smell.

Now I was standing outside, in a wrinkled, ugly green tunic, and well, there was nothing I could do about it. I shuffled over to Rapp, who had already used a harness to elevate himself a third of the way up the pole towards the grid point's control panel, and prepared to hoist myself up with him. At least up there, no one would recognize me in my tunic.

Before I could begin my ascent, Rapp called down at me. "This one's actually not in such bad shape—looks like a one-man job. I *told* Orkun I'd be able to handle it on my own, but she still doesn't trust me."

I was annoyed. It wasn't like I was that into the idea of hauling myself all the way up there just to fiddle with a bunch of wires for hours, but at least it was something to do. "So what? I'm just supposed to stand here and watch you work?"

Rapp, already engrossed in running diagnostics on the control panel, sighed and looked back at me. "If you want to help, go check on the next patch on our list. Sector Two ninety-seven's walkable, but if you're feeling lazy you can program the Egg and I can meet you there." Rapp turned back to his work.

It was like Rapp was *trying* to get to me. He knew I had never done a maintenance run before and wouldn't have a clue how to start. He was forcing me to ask for help. Maybe he knew me better than I'd figured—if there's one thing I hate, it's asking for help.

"Rapp. You know I've never done it before."

"Orkun ran through every last step just two days ago in class."

Had she? I honestly had no recollection of it. "Guess I missed that," I said.

"It was on the homework too. Oh, wait . . . you never do the homework."

For a second I thought he was actually mad, but then he started to chuckle, and tossed the key to the Egg down to me. "The spare kit's behind the passenger seat. The equipment is mostly self-explanatory, and if you get confused you can always hit the Prompt button for an explanation."

He turned back to his work. "Trust me, it's not that hard. If you can trick the door scanners at the Chimæra, you'll be able to figure it out in no time."

I walked up Eilon's Hill with my kit on my back and an info-mod in my hand—it was a small square device that could pinpoint my exact location in the city, and would also allow me to communicate with Rapp, or even with the other Cêpan back at the academy if necessary.

Even though I knew this area like the back of my hand, I'd never bothered to learn the city's official coordinate system. As I crossed over the hill and entered the commercial district north of Eilon Park, the info-mod indicated I had entered Sector 302, which most people called the Crescent because of the way the main street curved in on itself like a sliver of a moon.

I watched the module with strange fascination as all my old favorite neighborhood haunts—the Pit, Arcadia—were converted to their Munis numbers on my tab. 282, 304, 299.

I finally arrived at 297. Looking up from the locator, I realized with a start that I was standing just outside the Chimæra. I sighed to myself, trying not to think too much about it. It didn't matter what building I was outside. I wasn't here to go inside—I *couldn't* go inside.

I was here to climb a pole.

So I threw the harness on and made my way up. When I reached the top, I looked out onto the horizon. From up here, the column of light Rapp and I had seen earlier looked even more impressive. Well, maybe *impressive* is the wrong word. Actually, it was sort of creepy. It was vibrating and pulsing in a way that was almost otherworldly. And it was hard to tell where it was coming from—it could have been a few blocks away, or a hundred miles. It wasn't like anything I'd ever seen for a Quartermoon celebration before.

It wasn't my business though. I was here to work on the grid. So I unlocked the front of the control panel and flipped it open to find the keypad tucked within a dense nest of overlapping multicolored wires.

I sighed again, a longer, deeper sigh than before.

This was going to take a while.

It was still the tail end of the morning, pretty much the only time of day the club wasn't hopping. The entrance to the Chimæra was still quiet. But I knew the crowd would pick up within a few hours. I wondered for a second what my old friends would think if any of them stumbled by. Then I realized that they probably wouldn't even recognize me. To them, now, I was just another guy in a green tunic.

The work was surprisingly absorbing. I started running automated diagnostics on individual wires to determine if they were in need of replacement. The only tricky part was figuring out which wires were which. They were all numbered, and the degraded wires had to be removed and replaced within a correct sequence lest I damage this entire piece of the grid. But as Rapp had promised, the Prompt system that came with the kit provided pretty helpful instructions when I got confused or when I had trouble identifying one of the degraded wires by sight.

It had been weeks since I'd messed around with my ID band tech, and I had forgotten how much I missed this kind of tinkering. In my brief time at the LDA, I'd already forgotten that I was actually pretty good at it. I liked the way you could take it one step at a time, the way all the different pieces fit together like a puzzle. How even if you had no idea what you were doing, you could pretty much figure it out as long as you had a handle on the basic principles of it.

Before too long I'd stopped relying on the Prompt module at all. I was identifying the wire sequences with no trouble and was adjusting them easily, going mostly on instinct.

I had never really given much thought to the grid, or what a vital function it provided to the city. In addition to using sophisticated sensors to monitor and register the goings-on of Capital City, compiling information for Munis about the flow of people and goods—keeping everything running smoothly, *perfectly*—the grid's lesser-known function was a protective one. The nondescript poles that were so omnipresent that I barely noticed them actually stretched an invisible latticework of defensive shields and counterattack systems above the skyline. The reasoning behind the installation of the grid some hundreds of years ago was that the city had by far the highest population density of any part of the planet and was home to most of the important members of the Lorien government, along with being the central hub for our most important information and communications systems. Any enemy planning an attack on Lorien would likely strike the city first.

I still didn't believe that was going to happen, but I also had to grudgingly admit that the whole thing was pretty cool. Too bad it was also basically useless.

As I worked with almost unconscious ease, I contemplated the grid with new interest. One out of every four wires I ran diagnostics on needed replacement, which seemed strange. I reached back into my kit to check the date of this pole's last maintenance check, and was surprised to discover it was only a couple weeks ago. These wires were burning out at a pretty fast clip.

Of all the wires I was servicing there were very few backups or redundancies—almost every wire served a unique function—and a bunch of them were messed up, which meant that this pole was probably pretty much broken. If I understood the nature of the grid's defense shield well enough, that meant the entire area around here was vulnerable to attack. Why would that be, if it had just been repaired? I wondered if the control panel had a special glitch that was shorting out wires at a faster rate.

My curiosity stoked, I hurried through my work, eager to get back to Rapp and ask him if he'd seen anything similar in the poles he'd serviced. I wanted to know if this one was a fluke or if there was a bigger problem.

Not that I cared.

"What *is it* about a man in a dress?"

I had become so absorbed in my work that the unexpected voice sent my heart leaping into my throat. I knew exactly who it was without even looking down.

I looked down anyway.

The electric-white wig had been replaced by a brunette pageboy; she was now wearing a simple red dress with a short flared skirt. The dress, along with the hair, was covered in white, irregular polka dots.

I don't even know how you get polka dots in your hair. Was that another of Devektra's Legacies? Honestly, with her, nothing would surprise me.

"Hey," I said, the word coming out of my throat in an awkward croak.

She looked up at me with a pursed-lip smile, shielding her eyes from the suns. "Never figured you for the Munis apprentice-type."

"LDA, actually," I said, determined to hide my embarrassment. "Engineering trainee." Then, realizing what a dork I sounded like, I added, "I'm just in it for the tunic."

She let out a lilting, genuine laugh. "You actually don't look bad in it," she said. "I just don't see why you guys wear those dumb pajama pants underneath. What's the point of wearing a dress unless it's to show off your legs?"

"You wouldn't say that if you'd ever seen my legs," I said, and then turned back to my work. Today was not the day that I was in the mood to be made fun of by the world's hottest girl.

To my surprise, though, Devektra didn't leave. "What exactly are you doing up there anyway?" she asked. "I've always wondered what those poles were for."

"It's the grid." I didn't want to humor her ditzy act. Everyone knew what the grid was. Most of them chose not to care.

"The grid," she said. "So I guess you're one of those people who believes in all that stuff?"

"What do you mean by 'that stuff'?"

"Great Elder Prophecy, threat to Lorien, eternal vigilance, blah blah blah. Aliens are going to land tomorrow and take us all back to their home planet to clean their toilets unless you fix that box up there right this second!"

I thought for a second. No, I wasn't one of *those people.* Obviously. Considering that it was basically what I'd been saying to Rapp all week, I was surprised to find myself resisting her interpretation. Instead of laughing along with her, I bit my tongue, replaced the last of the faulty wires and closed the front of the control panel before gearing up to make my descent back to the ground.

Devektra made no motion to leave.

"Don't you have a show to prepare for?" I asked.

"Nah," she said, leaning against the entrance and

staring at me with a tough, inscrutable smile. "I just came here for a fitting. I'm not playing again 'til the Quartermoon."

"Ah," I said, throwing the kit over my shoulder.

"You should come," she said.

I looked up, surprised by the offer and wondered if she was pulling my leg. She *had* been making fun of me this whole time, right?

Her smile widened. It was like she knew the effect she had on me.

Of course she knows, I remembered, kicking myself. *She can read my mind.*

She winked, turned, and walked away without another word. I just dangled there, hanging dumbly from my dumb pole.

Even if she'd been serious, which I wasn't so sure about—being a mind reader must have its perks—there was no way I'd ever be able to take her up on the invitation. I wasn't allowed to leave the LDA campus after dark, for one, and plus, I'd never be able to get into the Chimæra after the debacle of last time.

Of course, Devektra knew all those things. I'd *almost* let myself believe she was for real.

CHAPTER SEVEN

WHEN I REACHED THE BOTTOM OF EILON'S HILL, I found Rapp locked in serious-looking conversation with a Mentor Cêpan I'd never met before.

"This is Daxin." Rapp introduced me as I approached. The guy didn't seem all that interested in meeting me, but I waved a halfhearted greeting anyway. He ignored it.

"I need to commandeer your transport for the rest of the day," said Daxin. "Something's come up and I don't have time to get back to LDA."

"Sure," I said, shrugging. "Take it. We'll just finish our grid maintenance on foot and then walk back after." I was annoyed by the prospect of the long walk back to the academy, but wasn't going to let them see it.

"He can't take the Egg without one of us," explained Rapp. "We're the ones programmed on today's manifest; the ignition won't start unless one of us is at the wheel."

Apparently feeling the situation had been sufficiently explained, Daxin made his way to the Egg and hopped into the passenger seat. Rapp seemed to sense my confusion. "I volunteered you to accompany him."

"Why me and not you?" I wouldn't admit it to Rapp, but I was bummed. I had actually been starting to enjoy my grid repair work.

"Because we've still got five sectors and eight patches to cover, and my completion rate is faster than yours."

I balked. "No, I did one and you did one—"

Rapp interrupted me. "I've done *three*. I just came back to retrieve the Egg and that's when I saw Daxin."

He'd finished *three*? Had I really been that slow? I was going to have to start actually paying attention in my classes if I didn't want to look like an idiot.

"This way we may still stand a chance of getting through our list by day's end."

"Okay," I said, feeling strangely disappointed.

"There'll be other grid maintenance days," said Rapp.

"Yeah," I said. "I know. Next time I'll be faster."

I left him and climbed into the Egg. I'd driven it around the LDA's campus before, but this was my first time piloting it for real, and I felt a funny surge of excitement. I mean, it's not the biggest thing to pilot it since it does most of the work on its own, but still. It's a big flying egg, what's not fun about that?

The doors closed behind me with a whoosh.

It was only once I took my seat that I became aware of the weird vibe Daxin was giving off. He was urgent and fidgety, and I was pretty sure I saw a line of sweat forming on his brow.

"Where to?" I asked.

"We're going out west of the Malkan Kabarak," he said. "You can just tell the Egg to stop there. We'll cover the rest of the distance on foot."

I spoke our coordinates into the receiver and the Egg took off, out of the city. It picked up speed once it breeched the city limits.

Unnerved by the way Daxin was drumming his leg and glancing around nervously, I stared straight ahead at the scenery whizzing by without speaking. The dusty plains ringing the city gave way to the increasingly lush vegetation of the rest of Lorien. I'd spent so little time outside the city it was a shock to be reminded how *green* the vast majority of our planet was.

The slab of violet light kept coming into view over the tops of the trees. "Elders went all out this year," I said, idly trying to make conversation with Daxin.

He didn't respond.

"The Herald?" I said, pointing out the window. "Must have taken them at least a month to cook that one up."

Daxin shifted uneasily in his seat, avoiding my gaze.

"Yeah," he said.

"What?" I asked. I didn't like the vibe I was picking up from him. And I'd never even seen him before. But Rapp knew who he was, so I had no reason not to trust the guy.

"Nothing," he said. "We just don't know that it *is* a Herald."

Mysteriousness *and* ominousness. Great.

"What are you saying?" I pressed.

"The Elders have been off-planet for a while, and they've been out of communication the past few days."

I couldn't figure out what he was getting at. "Yeah, but that's nothing, right? I thought they were off-planet a lot. Don't they spend a lot of time doing all kinds of Elder stuff that we could never understand?"

"Sure," he said. But he sounded skeptical. Then something occurred to me.

"Does this have anything to do with why my engineering class was cancelled today?"

Daxin did a double take. I had clearly guessed right.

"Orkun and a few councilmembers made a trip to the column," he admitted. "To scope it out, investigate. It's probably nothing."

"Why are you so concerned? If the light isn't a Herald, what do you think it is?"

"Look, don't worry about it, all right? I've just had a long day."

I sunk back into my seat, slightly annoyed. Just days ago I hadn't cared one way or another about the backstage goings-on among the council, the Mentor Cêpans and the other figures of the LDA, but now that I was actually showing some curiosity I was being told to mind my own business. It was frustrating.

The Egg cleared a few particularly dense acres of forest and came to a stop at the edge of the Malkan Kabarak. Daxin jumped out and immediately turned away from the perimeter fence, heading away from the settlement.

I jogged to keep up.

"Why are we walking? Why didn't we just enter the coordinates in the first place, if you knew where we were going?"

Daxin answered without slowing down. "I'm here to meet a Garde. My Garde."

Ah. If Daxin had only recently been promoted to a Mentor Cêpan, then maybe his testiness could be written off as mere nerves. A Mentor Cêpan's first meeting with his Garde is a pretty big deal. The bond between a Mentor Cêpan and his Garde mentee is considered almost sacred—almost as strong as the bond between a parent and child. And it lasted for life, even after the Garde was grown up and no longer under the Cêpan's direct tutelage. I could see how meeting someone you're going to have that kind of relationship with could freak a person out.

Daxin kept talking as we made our way up the path. "Garde's raised by his grandfather, and the grandfather lives this far out of the city for a reason. Hates technology, speedcraft. You know, still likes to do things the old way. I didn't want to surprise him with the sound of the engine."

Gradually, a small hut came into view up ahead, followed by a quickly approaching shape. It was racing right at us.

A Chimæra.

Before I knew what was happening, the Chimæra leapt off the ground and right into me, knocking me off my feet and onto my back.

The Chimæra had taken the form of some kind of grinning, oversized canine. Out came its huge dog tongue, scratchily enveloping my entire face. Within seconds, I was drenched.

Chimæra are pretty common on most of Lorien, but they mostly keep away from the city. I hadn't been licked by one of the creatures since I was little, and I hadn't enjoyed it even then.

"Byscoe! Byscoe! Down!" The animal immediately responded to the sound of its owner's voice and obediently jumped off of me, then scooted down the road toward where the voice was coming from.

Daxin gave me a wry look as I stood and dusted myself off. A moment later, Byscoe had returned to us with his master, a grinning little boy dressed in a Garde's distinctively fitted suit.

The boy's skin and hair were messy, caked in red dust, the whites of his eyes and teeth blazing through the dirty mask of his face. He grabbed a tuft of Byscoe's shag and swung himself up on top of the Chimæra with no fear at all. Lots of people out in the country were like this with the animals; they'd been raised with them. I still thought it was weird. Even when they took on cute, cuddly forms, it was hard to forget exactly how powerful they really were.

"Hi," the kid said.

"Hi," Daxin said awkwardly. I could tell he was unsure of what he was supposed to do next.

Just then, a burly man emerged from the hut down the road and walked towards us, in no hurry. Not quite as dirt-caked as the boy, he was roughly dressed in only loose canvas pants and a few strands of ceremonial necklaces. His skin was weathered, whipped dry and cracked by the outer winds.

"Hello," he called out to us from a few paces away. "Is there something I can do for you?"

Daxin spoke. "Yes. We are from the Lorien Defense Council. I've been selected as your grandson's Mentor."

The man cocked his head. "A bit early. Boy's got a few years left before LDA stewardship."

"Grandpa?" asked the boy, still astride his Chimæra. His grandfather kept his eyes on Daxin, ignoring the boy.

Daxin seemed nervous, fumbling for something within the folds of his tunic.

"We need nothing from you at the present moment except your consent to give this to your boy." He pulled out bracelet from within his tunic, pretty much the same as the government ID band I'd hacked a few weeks ago, but bigger. "A new security protocol, nothing more."

I had no idea what he was talking about—the protocols for Garde and their Mentors weren't something I'd studied at all—but I figured the LDC was doing some kind of tracking of young Garde.

The boy's grandfather seemed reluctant, but the kid charged forward on Byscoe and snatched the band right from Daxin's hand. He whooped triumphantly from the top of his Chimæra and slid the band up his wrist all the way to his elbow, then raced off down the road, kicking up a cloud of red dust in his wake.

"He's a spirited child," the boy's grandfather said. There was something a little sad about the way he said it, something I couldn't quite put my finger on.

"He needs to keep the band on at all times." Daxin

seemed anxious about this point. I could read his worry. It was one thing for the boy to wear the band for fun, as part of a game, another thing altogether to ensure that he *continue* to wear it. Daxin needed the grandfather behind this. "It's imperative."

"I understand," the man said. But it sort of sounded like he didn't.

A few minutes later, we were back in the Egg, back in our seats. I waited for Daxin to give me our next set of coordinates. This whole day had been way too long already, not to mention way too weird. I found myself actually *wanting* to go back to the academy.

But for the moment, Daxin was quiet.

"Well?" I asked, finally. "Are we going home or what?"

Before he could answer, Daxin's module beeped, and he looked down to read what it said. He grimaced and turned to me.

"Do me a favor," he said, holding his wrist out. "Last step. I need to sync my band to the one we just gave the kid."

I took Daxin's wrist in his hand and looked down at the brass band encircling it. Most ID bands were just that—plain bands with all the circuitry inside, so they looked almost like regular jewelry. Daxin's was different. It had a small digital interface and a couple of buttons on it. "Just hold the black button down while I start the sync." As I held the button down, he started entering commands on his communication module, which were presumably being relayed to the ID band.

"Pretty unwieldy," I said.

"Seriously," said Daxin, still typing into his tab. "Since I got this upgraded ID band and locator I've had to take it off every night. It's too big and heavy to sleep in."

I stared down at the band on Daxin's wrist, looking at it in a new light. It was no longer just an ID, or a locator.

It was a key.

That night I lay on my bunk before dinner, processing the events of the day. There was no denying that the place was starting to get under my skin. A month ago I wouldn't have cared that the grid was in sorry shape. A month ago, I barely knew what the grid *was,* for that matter.

But this morning, when Devektra had come along and had called me one of "those people," I hadn't corrected her. I'd actually felt almost insulted. I guess this place was rubbing off on me.

I can't say I liked it. I was supposed to be the kind of

guy who did my own thing and had my own opinions. I wasn't a joiner. Things weren't supposed to just *rub off* on me.

"Good work today," Rapp said, popping by the room to grab a couple of books from his desk just before dinner.

"I was slow," I said. "Next time I'll do better."

Rapp shook his head like he couldn't believe me. "Oh, whatever," he said. "You act like you don't care, and then you go and get all competitive. How'd things go with Daxin?"

"Fine," I said. A part of me wanted to unload on Rapp, to talk about how weird the afternoon had been, but something made me hold back. "How was the rest of your grid maintenance?"

"One out of every three patches I serviced was broken. I've never seen it so bad before."

I perked up at this. He had noticed the conspicuous failure rate too.

"You going to do anything about it?" I asked, trying to sound more neutral than I felt.

"Like what? I put it in my work report. The academy knows, the council knows. It's the rest of the planet that's determined to do nothing. The Kabarakians don't see the value in a defense system that only covers the city and leaves them exposed. And half the city thinks we're all just doing this to amuse ourselves. I seem to remember that *you're* one of those people. Right?"

I brushed him off. "If we're going to do it, we might as well do it right. Right? Otherwise the whole thing really *is* a waste."

Rapp left the room for dinner but I stayed behind, thinking about the Quartermoon concert at the Chimæra, and about Daxin's ID band on his bedside, poised and ripe for the taking.

I thought about Devektra. And I knew what I needed to get my head straight. A party.

CHAPTER EIGHT

AS QUARTERMOON DREW CLOSER, I WAS ALMOST starting to enjoy myself at the academy. It still wouldn't have been my first choice of a home, but at least I was settling in. Once I'd stopped playing stupid in my engineering classes, they were actually sort of fun. And although I wasn't quite sure when it had happened, I was realizing that Rapp and I were something like friends.

I still hated the tunics, and I still hated how seriously everyone took themselves around here. But I understood it now. You've got to believe in *something*.

I still felt sort of trapped, but it didn't feel quite as much like forever. That's because I finally had something to look forward to: Devektra's concert at the Chimæra. I was going to ditch my butt-ugly tunic, sneak off campus and sneak *into* the club.

Yes, I knew that if I got caught, none of my technical

skills and no amount of groveling would save me from a fate worse than the Kabarak. I also knew that Devektra hadn't really even invited me in the first place.

Neither of those things mattered. First off, I wasn't going to get caught. Second, it didn't matter whether Devektra had been totally sincere. She had invited me knowing there would be no way for me to actually go. I figured if I pulled off the impossible, she'd have to be impressed.

It was a big task, but I was up to it. Planning it had been my main source of entertainment ever since I'd come back from the trip with Daxin. It had even gotten my mind off the nagging worry that I was missing something around here—that something wasn't quite right.

The first thing I'd done was to to scope out the nighttime security situation at the academy. That wasn't so hard, because it turned out there basically wasn't any. Students weren't allowed to leave the grounds after dark, but all the other students here were so boring and committed that no one bothered actually enforcing it.

There were no security guards, no cameras, no sensors, no nothing. They didn't exactly advertise it, but it was honor system all the way.

The more complicated part of my plan would be Daxin. I'd done a little spying on him, and had discovered that he had a single-occupancy bedroom down the hall from me, and a habit of going to bed early. I'd briefly worried that Daxin, as an active Mentor Cêpan, might have the privilege of a lock on his dorm room. But on the last night before Quartermoon, I snuck out of my room at midnight, crept down the hall, and quietly tried turning the knob. It opened without any resistance at all.

After listening carefully for the sound of his snoring, I crept into the room and approached Daxin's bed. There it was: his ID band was lying right there next to his pillow, and he was curled up next to it, sawing logs, oblivious to my presence. This was going to be too easy. The following night, I would sneak in, snatch the ID band, commandeer the Egg from the transport hangar— I had already covertly preset the time and coordinates for my departure—and make my way to the Chimæra for Devektra's performance. Then I'd sneak back, return the Egg to transport, return Daxin's ID band to his pillow, and no one would be any the wiser for my absence. Sneaking around, conniving, scheming: it would be just like the good old days.

The Saturday of Quartermoon was my best day yet, a half day of classes followed by a quick workout in the gym and an early dinner in the commissary. A professor had authorized a screening during mealtime of an intercepted satellite transmission of a visual entertainment from the planet Earth.

It might have been an overall pretty crappy place to live, but they sure knew how to do their visual entertainment right. Although the transmission was video only, I had seen my share of Earth intercepts and had no problem following the story.

It wasn't really that complicated. At all. A well-dressed man traveled the world, hung out with beautiful women, snuck around to retrieve valuable objects, chased and got chased by bad guys.

While watching the movie I thought, *I want to be like him one day.*

But then, taking another bite of my dessert and smiling up at the screen, I realized that I already was.

The Egg handled like a dream.

Despite its silly name, it was a sleek and sexy machine, especially from behind the steering wheel—not that different from the transports in the Earth movie I'd watched earlier that day. I had preprogrammed the journey so it would start at my command, but once I'd snuck into transport and slipped inside the vehicle, it occurred to me that would create a potentially incriminating log of my route, so once I'd started the engine, I deleted the preprogrammed route and began my trip to the capital manually. Whizzing out of the hangar and through the Alwon Kabarak, I felt grateful for that decision: driving the Egg was a lot more fun than sitting back and letting the car do all the work.

While the LDA campus was quiet and sleepy at that hour—just like at any other hour, really—the Kabarak was in full swing for the Quartermoon festivities as I passed over it. The Chimæra had been let out of their pens and were frolicking freely while the Kabaraki-ans ringed around campfires in the dark, laughing and dancing and shooting off fireworks and waving spar-klers. I knew that behind me, from Alwon to Tarakas, from Deloon to the Outer Territories, people would be celebrating until dawn.

But the sights and sounds of revelry diminished as I crossed the border into the city, where the Quarter-moon holiday was observed with less enthusiasm.

One hand on the wheel, I removed my tunic and threw it on the passenger seat revealing the contra-band Kalvaka T-shirt I was wearing underneath. I was still wearing what Devektra had called my pajama pants, but they really weren't so bad without the tunic. Around my wrist, the bulk of Daxin's ID band made a striking counterpoint to the rest of my ensemble.

All in all, I looked pretty good. Not that it even mat-tered that much how I looked. What mattered was that I'd gotten out.

My escape had gone so smoothly that I almost felt guilty. I'd made such quick fools of everyone at the LDA, none of whom had any reason to suspect that my changed attitude was due in large part to the planning and execution of this grand deception. But before I could succumb to guilt or regret, I was distracted by the Spires of Elkin on the horizon, which were lit up in pink by the mysterious column of light behind them. This time, I didn't pay them any attention. I was almost there.

At the Chimæra, the ID band worked like a charm. No one even looked at me sideways as I glided in. I was almost offended. Had they forgotten me so quickly?

Maybe they just didn't recognize me anymore. I felt more confident than ever, like a totally different person from the one who, at the first sign of trouble, had gone pushing through the crowd like a frightened little kid just a few weeks ago. It had hardly been any time at all, but I felt like I'd grown up so much since then.

The club was packed tonight, almost twice as busy as the last time I'd been here, which was saying something. Devektra's appearance weeks ago had been a surprise, but this Quartermoon performance was well publicized, and it had attracted an even wider audience. I spotted homemade Devektra T-shirts on every fifth patron. The Chimæra was the largest club on Lorien by far, and she had filled it to capacity. I felt a surge of pride. I'd known that Devektra was a big deal and all, but I hadn't known *how* big of a deal she was until now. And I knew her. You could almost even say we were friends.

"Well, well, well." I turned to see Paxton and Teev, holding up half-finished ampules and staring at me with amused grins on their faces.

"Look who doesn't give up," Teev said, draping her arm around me in greeting. "After we saw you get busted last time, we figured we'd seen the last of you."

I just shrugged and smiled my cagiest smile, and they looked at me, for the first time, as if they were actually sort of impressed.

I was just about to pat myself on the back for it when I heard a voice I recognized.

"Someone told me you might have found your way in here somehow."

I turned around to see Mirkl, Devektra's perpetually annoyed right-hand man, standing behind me with an ampule in each hand. He looked me up and down with predictably annoyed eyes.

"Hey, Mirkl," I said, in the most casual tone I could muster. My heart was thumping in my chest, knowing that if Mirkl was talking to me I was one step closer to seeing Devektra again, but I played it cool for the benefit of Teev and Paxton. I wanted them to think it was no biggie for me to be on a first-name basis with a member of the headlining performer's entourage. I snuck a glance in their direction, and saw that they were looking at me with stunned eyes. Mission accomplished.

"Devektra wants to see you," he said.

As well as things had been going tonight, I still hadn't expected it to be *this* easy. How had Devektra even known I was here?

Mirkl must have seen the surprise on my face. "Telepathy, remember? Neat little trick to have. I think you know where the dressing room is. Here—bring her these." He pushed the ampules into my hands and began to walk away.

"You're not coming in?" I asked after him, suddenly nervous about waltzing into Devektra's dressing room unaccompanied. It seemed too good to be true. With Devektra you never knew what you were getting into.

He turned, looked over his shoulder and waved me off. "I'm on a break. Those ampules were my last errand for her until showtime." He smiled wryly. "She's all yours." Then he disappeared into the crowd.

Devektra faced her reflection in the vanity mirror, her back to the door. She was wearing slim-fitting red metallic pants and a shimmering top made out of a liquid-like material that I'd never seen before. Her shirt flowed around the curves of her body in undulating cascades as she stood tall, stared straight ahead and gently massaged her temples with her fingers. She didn't acknowledge me.

But she knew I was here—last time I'd been in this room, I'd had to bust through the entrance with all the strength I could muster. This time I hadn't even had to knock. The door had just swung open for me as I'd approached it, clutching the ampules Mirkl had given me to deliver. It suddenly occurred to me that maybe Devektra had used her telekinesis to "help" me get through the locked door last time too.

It was ironic that I'd been more comfortable making my entrance breaking down a door and crashing through an entire rack of clothes than I was just walking right in. I just stood there, feeling a few steps beyond awkward as Devektra gazed at herself in the mirror and rubbed her forehead.

"Did you bring them?" she asked without turning.

"Yeah," I said. I walked over and handed her an ampule. She took it, downed it in one gulp, then reached out for the second and downed that too. She still hadn't bothered to look at me.

When she tossed the second spent vial aside and onto the floor, I understood what her deal was. I had to hold back a laugh. For once, I was the one who knew what she was thinking instead of the other way around. Or, at least, I knew what she was feeling. You didn't need to be a telepath to figure it out.

"Wow. You're actually nervous," I said.

"So?" She finally turned her attention from the mirror and locked her gaze on mine. Her eyes were hard, but underneath the steel, I saw a hint of fear. Of vulnerability. "Who wouldn't be?"

"You weren't nervous last time," I pointed out. "I didn't know you *got* nervous. I kind of thought that was, like, your whole thing."

"Last time was different."

"Why?"

"It just was," she said. "It was a smaller crowd. It wasn't Quartermoon. It was just different. Plus, there's just something about tonight. I don't know. I sort of have a bad feeling I guess."

"It's just nerves," I said.

"I know. I'll be fine."

Then it was like I wasn't there anymore. Devektra's attention was back on herself as she ran her fingers through her hair and gingerly began to pile it, one tendril at a time, on top of her head. Each carefully arranged lock somehow managed to stay perfectly in place. She looked more frightened than ever.

I didn't know what to say, so I decided to try something else. I decided not to talk. Out loud, at least.

How does it work? I thought. *Can you hear everything I think? What about the people outside? Can you hear them? What about the whole world? Can you hear them all?*

Devektra's lips didn't move, but she answered me anyway, in a voice I heard inside my head that was both hers and not hers.

"It's like standing waist-deep in a rushing river and trying to catch a million tiny floating leaves as they race past you. Some of them you catch. Most of them you don't."

You invited me here tonight, and summoned me back here. But why me? I wanted to know. *Who am I to you? You're Devektra. I'm a nobody in a green tunic.*

"No. You're like me. You're different. Neither of us fit in on this world. I knew it as soon as I met you. Before I met you, I knew.

"I sensed you out there in the crowd that first night. All those people and their thoughts all zooming past me. Except yours. Yours just bubbled up, and I could reach down and pull up each one, like every fear and hope you had was meant for me. It sounded like you were singing."

But what about tonight? I had to know. *Why am I here now?*

"I knew you would make me feel less alone. Especially tonight. I can feel that something terrible is about to happen."

I looked over. Devektra was staring at my reflection in the mirror. She had the strangest look on her face, both peaceful and surprised. Something told me that she'd never done this before, had never used her Legacy to speak to someone wordlessly like this.

I knew then, without understanding why, that this might be the only chance I ever got. So I leaned over, closed my eyes and kissed her. Her lips were soft and she smelled like something I recognized but couldn't describe, even to myself. Her lips tasted like something I'd tasted in a dream, one of those dreams you forget as soon as you wake up. When I opened my eyes she was gone.

CHAPTER
NINE

"DELOON THIS TIME OF YEAR IS *MISERABLE*,"
said the guy. "You couldn't pay me all the money in the
world."

"No argument there, bro," I said, even though I'd
never been to Deloon. I truly didn't want to argue.

I was on the balcony above the stage waiting with
Mirkl and the rest of the entourage for Devektra's performance to start. She was behind schedule, but most
of the people on the balcony were pretty buzzed and no
one seemed impatient, least of all me.

Instead, I just felt strange. I was lightheaded and
euphoric. I didn't know where Devektra had gone after
she'd left me, but, even after her warning—*something
terrible is about to happen*—I wasn't worried about her.
My brain was still buzzing, turning loops and cart-
wheels on itself.

Our kiss had been incredible. But it was the

telepathic rapport that we'd shared that I was still reeling from. Speaking only with our minds, we'd managed to communicate on a level more pure—more real—than anything I'd ever experienced. No kiss could ever compare to that.

The lights finally came down on the club, and as they did, a spotlight, positioned stage center, took shape, a blindingly white oval. Every single person in the place gazed into the brightness, our breaths all held together, in anticipation of what was coming next.

Then came a sound, a thin, heartbreakingly fragile warble. It seemed to be coming from inside that small pool of light. As the warble grew in volume and intensity—never losing any of its beautiful fragility—the disc of the spotlight began to bend and twist, as if willing itself to break.

Where was Devektra? It sounded like she was somewhere inside that orb of light.

The light kept rising off the stage floor, and the voice contained inside it rose in pitch. It stopped, hovering in the exact center of the club, only yards away from where I stood at the edge of the mezzanine. It was so bright it hurt to look at, but I couldn't pull away.

The volume and pitch rose and rose. Some members of the crowd plugged their ears from Devektra's sonic drill. But still no one dared to look away from the ball of light.

Then it exploded.

Suddenly light was everywhere. There wasn't a single shadow left anywhere in the usually shadowy club. People spun around, dazed, staring at their fellow concertgoers with new eyes. Every pore on every face was exposed, illuminated. The sound of Devektra's voice had shattered too, into tiny cascading tinkles, equal in volume at any point with the club's space.

"There she is," said a voice in the crowd.

Devektra stood above the crowd. Her crowd. Not on the stage but on top of the bar near the entrance. The tinkling sounds evaporated from the air like smoke.

She had been throwing her voice—and shaping it into that orb of light—the entire time. All the while, no one had noticed she'd been somewhere else.

It was amazing. And she was only getting started.

Devektra stepped forward off the bar and walked through the crowd towards the stage. Under normal circumstances, people would have been clamoring and elbowing each other, rushing forward to get closer to the performer. But they stepped back to let her through, still in awe of what they'd just seen.

She began to sing. No microphone, no amplification, no Legacy-assisted manipulation. She just sang. No one in the audience made a sound. Her voice came through as clear as a bell.

This wasn't one of her usual dance numbers. It was

a simple song, and a sad one. I barely understood the
words, but I knew that it was a song of love and loss.
She stepped onto the stage without missing a beat, and
then turned back to her audience, her eyes sparkling
with tears.

I was rapt. I wondered what she was singing about.
I couldn't help wondering if she was singing about me.

I didn't have to wonder, really. I knew. It was about
me but it wasn't. She was singing *for* me. The sadness
at the heart of this song was bigger than any one or any
two Loric: it was as big as the planet itself. It was a song
for Lorien.

As entranced as I was, I jumped when I felt something vibrating at my wrist. I looked down in surprise,
forgetting that I still wore Daxin's ID band. It was rattling, buzzing urgently. I silenced it and turned back to
the stage.

Devektra was still singing, her eyes closed.

The band vibrated again.

I pulled the ID band off to inspect it, to figure out why
it was rattling so insistently. As I held it in both hands,
the vibrating band tickling the bones of my fingers, I
inspected the digital interface. The small rectangular
screen was blinking, as was the single word, "Alert."

Panic began to rise in my chest. Maybe Daxin had
woken up, seen his missing ID band and triggered some
kind of alarm. Maybe I'd been caught.

No. I knew somehow that the alert signaled something far worse than that. I thought of the control panel outside the club just weeks before, about the sorry state of the grid. I thought of Daxin in the Egg, behaving as if something was seriously wrong. I thought of the unexplained column of light. And I thought of the Elder Prophecy I'd been ignoring my whole life.

One day, a great threat will come . . .

And I thought of Devektra: "Something terrible is about to happen." My knees went weak. I looked up to hear her finishing her beautiful song.

Devektra closed her mouth. The song ended. The crowd held its applause, fearful of breaking the spell.

And then the roof came down.

CHAPTER
TEN

RETURNING TO CONSCIOUSNESS, I TOOK INVEN-
tory.

Blackness.

Silence.

And—there it was—pain.

I forced myself up through the blackness, clutching blindly forward with my hands. I felt smashed stone, the wetness of my own blood in my palms, the acrid tang of smoke against my still sightless eyes.

Sound returned faster than vision. It was a ringing in my ears, the exact opposite of the hypnotic, unfettered emotion of Devektra's music. This was concussive, ear-splitting.

In agony, I clutched my head to force it out but the pain kept rising.

The club had been bombed.

Then more sound emerged through the tinnitus-like buzz.

Moaning. Screaming. Crying.

I turned my head left and right, trying to find a source of light, anything to help me figure out what had just happened.

That's when I saw the fire, rising up the entrance wall, small but getting bigger.

It wasn't until I tried to stand that I realized I was on the ground floor of the club, not on the mezzanine. I turned around and saw that the entire balcony had been knocked from its struts, smashed like a dropped dinner plate on the floor of the club.

No, I thought. *No.*

Not just on the floor of the club. On top of a mass of crushed concertgoers. They were already dead.

The stage was intact, as was the other half of the dance floor that hadn't gotten buried by the collapsing mezzanine. But the people there hadn't been spared. The sheer force of the blast, in combination with the shrapnel from the shattered roof, had killed most of the audience members who hadn't been crushed. Bodies littered the floor, while bloody and dazed survivors struggled to their feet from out of the sea of corpses.

My leg was stuck, wedged between two crushed stones. I feared it was broken, or worse. But I needed to get up.

Devektra, I thought. I needed to know she was okay.

I strained against the rubble, but it wouldn't give. I looked around for something I could use to pull myself out.

That's when I saw the guy I'd been talking to only minutes ago, the one who didn't like Deloon this time of year. He was flat on the ground, the balcony a broken jigsaw beneath him. His eyes were wide open, his body eerily intact except for his jaw, which had been sheered clean off by shrapnel.

I turned away from the grisly sight, and felt a hand on my shoulder. Mirkl stood above me, a shocked look on his face and caked in dust but apparently unharmed by the explosion.

"Help?" he said.

In my confusion I froze, unable to decide if he was asking for help or offering it.

Mirkl didn't wait for me to figure it out. He crouched down by my side and looked around, determining which rock to lift in order to free me. His slender arms looked weak, but when they found the chunk of rubble that trapped my leg, he pulled it away like it was nothing at all.

I stared down at my knee. It was bloody and bruised, but not broken. I was going to be okay.

Without knowing where I found the strength to do it, I stood up, first on my strong leg and then on my tingly weak one, wobbling on the uneven rubble beneath me. I turned to thank Mirkl. He had already disappeared into the mass of wailing, screaming and silent shell-shocked survivors.

I looked towards the entrance. There *was* no entrance anymore. The doors and entire front wall of the club were now nothing more than an orange, raging inferno. My forehead prickled with sweat.

The fire exit. It was the only way out. Or, it would have been. The fire exit had only been accessible from the balcony.

I felt all hope slip out of me like a vapor.

Then I saw a few survivors crowding at the base of the wall below the escape. Despite the balcony's collapse, the struts, a few chunks of concrete and some girders remained at the base of the exit. It was enough. Barely. The survivors were hurriedly scrambling against the wall, grabbing on to whatever handholds they could manage and hoisting themselves out of the burning club.

I was torn. I knew I had to run, to save myself, and still I couldn't. I wanted to find Devektra.

I was still trying to make a choice when I saw her shiny red pants sliding up the wall and out of the exit. After all that, she hadn't thought twice about taking her first chance to safety. Had it even occurred to her to look for me?

There was nothing keeping me here now. I ran to the crowd at the base of the wall. I tried to resist casting one glance back at the smoky, bloody, ruined club. *Don't look back.*

But I looked back and my eyes went straight to him.

It was Paxton. He was alive but he was just crouched on the ground in despair, rocking back and forth.

I knew I was being an idiot, but I didn't care: without thinking twice, I gave up my place at the back of the line and rushed over to help him. As I got closer, I understood why he had given up. At his feet, crushed by concrete, was Teev.

I grabbed his hand and tried urging him on towards the exit, but he wouldn't budge.

His eyes met mine. "She's stuck," he said. "Teev. We have to get her out."

I didn't need to look down to know that Teev was dead. Paxton didn't get it, though.

"I'm sorry," I said. "But there's no time. We have to go now."

Slowly, he began to move away from the corpse of the girl I'd once had a crush on, the girl he had loved. I pushed him forward over the balcony's rubble, trying not to imagine all the Loric bodies mangled and bloody beneath the stone.

We were the last two up the wall. As I pushed Paxton up and out of the exit, I spotted Daxin's band poking out of the rubble a few yards away. I must've dropped it when the roof caved in and the balcony collapsed. The smoke was overwhelming, and the flames had nearly reached the exit but I took one last risk anyway.

I lunged for it.

I put the band back on my wrist, leapt up the wall, and crawled out into the night.

On the street, a bloody woman in tattered clothes milled among the survivors. "Devektra tried to kill us!" she screamed. "Devektra did it!"

She was clearly hysterical, and most of the people gathered around her were far too shocked by the explosion to pay her much heed. But a few people seemed to be nodding in agreement.

The shock was only just now hitting me. There was something about the stillness—the *ordinariness*—of the street outside the club that truly made me understand the horror of what I'd just escaped.

The band was vibrating on my wrist again. alert alert alert.

Devektra was nowhere to be seen among the survivors. She hadn't hesitated for a second, or stopped to help anyone. She'd gotten her sparkly red ass out of there.

Still, despite the screaming woman and the hushed murmurs of the crowd, I knew Devektra hadn't been the cause of the explosion. She had even tried to warn me about it, sort of. In her own way, she had tried to warn us all. With that song. She just hadn't known she was doing it, I don't think.

It hadn't been her. *They were right all along,* I thought.

Everything I had learned at the LDA. The grid. The Prophecy. Our sacred duty to safeguard our perfect planet. It had all turned out to be true. There was some force willing and able to bring our entire planet down after all. This was the first strike.

A Munis vehicle had double-parked outside the club and its driver was rushing to attend the victims. I climbed up the side of the truck to get a better view of the city.

It was as I'd feared.

Everywhere I looked on the horizon I could make out the sight of yet another destroyed landmark. The North Arena. My former school. They were all burning.

I turned around. There was no smoke, but the Spires of Elkin, the largest structures on Lorien and home to almost a third of the city's population, were gone too, leaving a soul-shattering void in the skyline. With no obstruction, I stared up at the column of violet light pulsing malevolently on the horizon.

That was no "Herald."

In a burst of understanding, I saw it all clearly. If only I hadn't been so convinced that everyone at the

LDA was a self-important fool, I would've seen it so much sooner. It was obvious now: the column of light was responsible for the grid's burnout. Whoever had just attacked us must have known about the weaknesses in the grid, and sent that light down to screw with our only mechanical form of defense. It had been draining our defenses this whole time.

I clutched my head, my heart thumping in my chest. The attackers had sent missiles through the holes in the grid, targeting high-density structures like the Chimæra and the spires. I had just replaced the wiring in this sector days ago, but the security patches were interdependent and I knew there were outages all over the city. We'd been unprotected.

It was as clear a night as I'd seen in a while. There were no clouds at all. Just smoke, flame, and the brilliant blue light of the Quartermoon.

I couldn't take any more. I jumped down from the Munis vehicle and raced to the Egg, which I found still parked exactly where I'd left it. Amazingly, it was all in one piece.

I had to get back to the academy—or whatever was left of it. I had to explain my theory to whoever would listen. Surely the council and the academy faculty had been apprised of the attacks on the city, and Daxin would be awake, wondering where his ID band was.

As I opened the door to the Egg, I heard a voice.

"Sandor."

I turned around. Devektra and Mirkl stood in the shadows. I had never seen Devektra look so lost before, not even during her little panic attack before the show. All the anger and betrayal I'd felt toward her just minutes ago disappeared as soon as we collapsed into each other's arms.

After just a moment she pushed me away and shook her head sadly.

"I just came to say good-bye. I know we won't see each other again. Whatever this thing is, Sandor, it's bad. It's the thing they warned us about. I'm going to find some of my Garde friends and we're going to do whatever we can to stop it."

Mirkl had been standing there the whole time but he was staring straight ahead with a dead look in his eyes. Whatever fight he'd had in him looked like it was long gone now.

"Let me come with you," I said. "I can help."

Devektra shook her head. "No. We have to do it on our own." She looked at the band on my wrist. "There are people who need you more than I do right now."

She was right, but I wasn't ready. Not yet. Tears were streaming down my face. I tried to fight them back. There was no time for crying.

"Why did you leave me in there?" I knew the answer. It didn't matter. I had to ask anyway.

Devektra put a finger to my lips, as if to say *listen carefully*.

"I left because I was scared, Sandor," she said. At least, I think she said it. "We were never perfect. There's no such thing as perfect. But it's not too late for us. We can still be good."

CHAPTER ELEVEN

I PROGRAMMED THE EGG TO RETURN ME TO THE LDA on autopilot. In the driver's seat, I folded my arms across my chest and stared straight ahead. I didn't want to see the devastation as I passed my charred school, or any of the other now ruined landmarks of my home city.

But even with this cultivated tunnel vision, I couldn't help noticing the smoke coming from the Elder Gardens.

Hundreds must be dead, I thought.

I closed my eyes. I didn't want to think about it. I just wanted to get back to the LDA, to do something.

I opened my eyes as the Egg passed through Alwon. Chimæra still frolicked by the light of the campfire, and the Kabarakians clustered together in merriment. They were unaware of the destruction to their west. It wouldn't be long before they found out.

The first thing I had to do was make sure academy officials and councilmembers were even aware of the attack on the city. I was pretty sure they were, but even so, it was still possible I had firsthand information that would be important somehow. I would confess to having snuck out and brief them on my experience of the attack. I'd share my theory that the column was some kind of attack intended to disarm the grid in advance of the wave of missile attacks that had decimated our city.

Once that was accomplished, I would locate Daxin, apologize for taking his ID band, and return it to him.

Then there was Rapp. I had to make sure he was okay.

I smelled it before I saw it. A coppery, dusty tang in the air, somehow strong enough to reach me even through the Egg's high-grade air filters.

The first thing I actually saw was an absence: the LDA building, the hangar, and the council chamber behind it were all usually bathed in security lights. But as the Egg approached the academy's coordinates, I saw nothing but blackness.

The academy had been hit.

The Egg whirred to a halt in the darkness. journey complete, read the dashboard monitor. Dazed, I stepped out into the eerie blackness of the night.

As my eyes adjusted, I began to make out tiny shards of light on the ground.

It was all gone. Razed. The entire structure had been pummeled into the ground by a weapon the likes of which I had never even imagined. The entire campus had been crushed and melted simultaneously. The green-tinged shards of light I was looking at were the smoldering edges of this black, toxic pancake on Lorien's surface.

Hundreds more, I thought, stumbling back and forth over the black crust, looking for some unruined piece of the campus and finding none. My professors. The tech students. The Mentor Cêpan trainees and the resident Mentor Cêpans. All those Garde children.

Orkun. Daxin.

Rapp.

I fell to my knees on the crust. It was warm, ash black, but surprisingly soft. This time, I allowed myself to cry.

How could I let this happen? I thought.

The fumes rising from the crust—probably chemicals from the bomb mixed with whatever debris the academy's destruction had unleashed—burned my throat and my eyes. I didn't budge.

Let them kill me, I thought.

I had no plan, no home to return to.

I could go to my parents. Deloon, a minor city on the other end of the planet, was probably safe. But for how long? And even if it remained untouched, the thought of programming the Egg to take me there, of spending the rest of my life with my parents in their two-bedroom chalet in bourgeois seclusion made me ill. The only things I had ever cared about were gone. The worst part was that I'd never even really known I'd cared.

With my head pressed against my knees, still fuzzy and throbbing from the rising vapors, my ears suddenly pricked. I heard something approaching. A vehicle.

The attackers, I thought. *The ground invasion has begun.*

I had no weapons, no means of defense. The attackers, whoever they were, were probably coming to make sure they'd left no survivors at their target. When they found me, they would kill me.

This had been my home—not just the school, but the whole planet. I had been too busy wanting it to be something it wasn't that I had never realized all the ways in which it was mine.

Maybe there was nothing I could do. I was just one Cêpan with a busted leg, with no Legacies and not even a weapon. I stood up anyway, turned around to face whoever it was head-on and prepared to fight.

The footsteps approaching me were heavy and purposeful, and as they got louder, the melody from Devektra's final song came back to me. I began to hum. But before I could see my enemy, I had collapsed.

CHAPTER
TWELVE

I FELT MYSELF LIFTED FROM THE GROUND, AND carried to a vehicle. I was thrown inside and landed with a thump on my back. I heard the sound of the door buzzing shut, and felt the transport lurch as it speedily resumed its course on autopilot, throwing me hard against the back.

The lights came on and the world around me began to blur back into focus. I tried to make out the shape of my captor.

Brandon stared back at me.

"You?" I said, shocked not to see some hideous alien face. Stunned to see Brandon *alive*.

Brandon fell to his knees.

"No," he said. "It's not possible." He looked as bereft and lost as I felt. Then he lunged at me, yanking my wrist forward. He inspected the ID band in disbelief, then grabbed my shoulders and started shaking me so hard I thought I might throw up.

"How did you get this?! How did you get this?!"

I tried to answer but he wouldn't let me. He just kept shaking me. When I couldn't take it anymore, I finally tipped over and retched all over the corrugated steel of the vehicle's floor.

Brandon crawled back, away from my heaving. But by the time it had stopped, he was looking at me apologetically. "Sorry."

"It's not your fault," I said. "I don't think it was you anyway. The fumes from the explosion made me sick. Made me pass out, I guess."

I moved to the other side of the still-moving vehicle, sat down, and explained how I'd come to be here. I told him how I'd stolen Daxin's ID band to get into the Chimæra, and how I'd raced back to campus only to find the place a tarry smear on the ground.

Finished, I looked up at Brandon sheepishly. He was quiet for a minute, his expression impossible to read.

Finally, he spoke. "I never would have come back to the LDA if I'd known it was just you. It was a pointless risk."

Ouch.

"I came for Daxin. I just wasted hours, exposed in the city, trying to locate Daxin, and all I find is *you*?"

I felt my insides twist with shame.

"He might've gotten out. If he'd had his ID band, he

might've lived," said Brandon, his anger rising. "When the first Mogadorian missile hit the grid, a warning was sent to us, the academy's nine Mentor Cêpans. We were to immediately evacuate whatever structure we were in, to make our way to our assigned Garde using their locator bands, retrieve them and bring them back to the secret base. Eight of us succeeded, but Daxin must've slept right through the attack."

The evacuation plan Daxin had cryptically alluded to. I'd assumed it was just Lorien defense paranoia, but he'd known this was coming.

"I'm sorry," I croaked. The words sounded so pitiful, so puny, in light of the havoc and death I had created. All so I could go to a concert and mess around with Devektra. Now my city lay in ruins, and Daxin was dead. He would never complete the mission he'd spent his whole life preparing for.

"The Elder Pittacus designed the evacuation protocol many years ago, but we Mentor Cêpans were given very little information beyond the mere fact of our enrollment. Weeks ago the Elders went off on a secret diplomatic mission from which they've yet to return. They'd set the protocol to be activated preemptively if the council lost touch with them during the course of their absence." Brandon clutched his head. "They were worried. From what little I've learned, a race of aliens called Mogadorians is coming. Has already come.

The Elder Prophecy has come to pass. We knew of the Mogadorians' existence—had even had some dealings with them long ago—but we never anticipated that they might prove hostile to us."

I nodded along with him as he spoke, trying to absorb as much of what he was saying as I possibly could.

"Lorien as we knew it has already ceased to exist," he said. "And," he added, punctuating himself with a bitter laugh, "we've already botched the evacuation. Nine Mentor Cêpans, nine young Garde. Just as there are now nine Elders. The number must matter, it must've been for a reason. With Daxin dead . . ."

His voice trailed off. He turned towards the console at the front of the transport, and sighed. "We're almost at the airstrip," he said. "We'll just have to make do with eight."

The vehicle came to a stop and Brandon stepped out.

I followed him outside. We were parked fifty yards from a small airstrip, deep in the Outer Territories. A medium-sized aircraft was parked in the distance. I could make out people congregating near the craft. Without a word to me, Brandon was charging away from the vehicle towards them.

"Wait," I called.

He turned around, an impatient look on his face.

"The kid," I said. "What about the kid?"

I already bore some, possibly all, of the responsibility

for Daxin's death. But the boy had been earmarked for survival and he was still out there. As far as I knew, the Malkan Kabaraks hadn't been hit yet.

"His Mentor Cêpan is already dead," said Brandon. "And even if he weren't, the trip there and back would take two hours. We need to be off this planet as soon as possible. It's too big a risk, and it's a risk that none of us, with Garde of our own to protect, can afford to take."

So the kid was doomed?

"I can't live with that," I said.

"You won't have to," said Brandon. "Not for long, anyway."

Fear gripped my heart and I suddenly realized— there was no place for me on the evacuation ship. I would perish along with the rest of the planet during the next wave of the attack.

"So me, the kid, and everybody else on this planet . . . we're just fucked, huh?" I knew I sounded pathetic, but I couldn't help myself. "Left to die as the invasion begins?"

Brandon didn't skip a beat. "Yes," he said. "This is no longer about saving individual lives, Sandor. This is about saving an *entire race*."

So that was that.

"I'm sorry, Sandor," said Brandon, softening a little. "I have no reason to believe the Mogadorians will leave a single Lorien soul alive when they come, but for your sake I hope—"

Brandon drifted off, unable to finish his sentence.

He didn't need to. I understood perfectly. Death would be better than the alternative.

There was nothing left to say.

"Okay then," I said, pitifully sarcastic. I gave Brandon a little wave good-bye. "Guess I'll be seeing you!"

I was alone again.

I'd fallen to my knees in the dirt by Brandon's vehicle.

The only illumination came from its interior lights. Brandon hadn't bothered to close the door when he'd left it behind. I guessed there was no point when the entire planet was set for destruction.

I twisted Daxin's ID band around the flesh of my wrist. It was amazing how much trouble this little device had caused, what a trivial and tragic mess I had made with it.

Disgusted with myself and my own predicament, I pulled the band off and raised it over my head, ready to toss it into the darkness.

I hesitated, thinking of Devektra. I wondered where she was, if she had found any other Garde to help her. I wondered if she was still alive, knowing that even if she was, her chances of survival, even with her

Legacies, would be slim to none.

Really, death was probably the best thing that could happen to her. She wouldn't give a shit about that. We were too alike that way. She didn't believe in perfect. That would be her strength. I decided it would be mine too. If I was going down, I was going to make it as messy as I could.

"Nine young Garde," Brandon had said. "That must've been for a reason."

Yes, I thought, looking down at the ID band I was still clutching in my white-knuckled fist. Something had been set in motion a long time ago that had brought me to this point, on my knees in the Outer Territories, this ID band and locator in my hands.

It's all for a reason. There had to be nine. Nine Cêpan, nine Garde. I had fucked up so badly. It wasn't too late, though. I could still be good.

CHAPTER THIRTEEN

THE VEHICLE RUMBLED AND BUCKLED OVER THE unpaved earth, its course set for the Malkan Kabarak. With the thing on autopilot, I was free to dig around in the back, trying to find a weapon. I had no idea if the Mogadorians' second wave would be another round of missile hits or a ground invasion, but I figured it wouldn't hurt to arm myself. Unfortunately, all I managed to find was a long, sharp knife. Not especially powerful, but it was something. I also grabbed a spare info-mod, hoping that it might somehow come through with news of another attack.

I booted it up not expecting much, but it was still picking up scattered, patchy transmissions. The ones that *were* coming through were mostly dedicated to Munis communications about rescue efforts in the city.

They'd caught us off guard, just like the Elders had predicted. Even now, people didn't seem to get it. Not a single one of the transmissions I was able to hear made any reference to the fact that we'd been attacked—or the fact that it wasn't over yet.

Maybe the rest of Lorien was still mostly oblivious. *I* knew the truth, though. I knew what I had to do.

I was going to save the boy, or die trying.

The vehicle pulled up to the edge of Malka and I made my way up the dirt path in the dark. I couldn't see much, but I let my memory guide me towards the hut the boy had shared with his grandfather. The closer I got, the more the locator band vibrated, signaling that I was heading in the right direction.

In the distance, I could hear the hubbub of the Malkans' Quartermoon revels. They still didn't know. For a brief moment, I considered running onto the Kabarak and warning them about the upcoming invasion, telling them to arm themselves. But I didn't have time for that, and it wouldn't make any difference anyway. I had to keep my focus. This was about the survival of our whole race. Brandon had said there had to be nine.

When I reached the hut, the boy, his grandfather and the frolicking chimæra were nowhere to be seen. But the band continued to vibrate in my hand. By moving forward in a couple different directions, testing the vibration's frequency, I was able to get a bead on him. He was farther up the path.

I rounded a crest that gave out to a narrow field among other hills. A large campfire blazed nearby, and as I moved closer, I saw the boy's grandfather crouched next to it. He looked up at me.

The boy and his chimæra were nowhere to be seen.

The man gestured at the seat beside him. Nervously, I stepped forward and took my place at the campfire. Whatever he was cooking, it smelled delicious. It was nearly dawn, and I hadn't eaten since dessert the night before. Teased by the smell, my mouth began to water.

The man gestured at the pot. "Eat," he said.

I did as I was told, using the stone ladle jutting out of the pot to fill a small earthenware bowl with the rich stew.

"It's delicious," I said, nodding with gratitude.

"You've come for my boy," said the grandfather.

"Yes," I said, realizing that he had known why I was there all along.

"He is all I have," he said. "Anyone can see that there is something special about him. My gift allows me rare glimpses at the threads of destiny, and I have always known this day would come. The day I met you, I could see that it wouldn't be long."

Daxin's ID band hadn't stopped vibrating crazily since I'd sat down, and now my tab was going off like crazy. Here by the campfire, with this strong, simple man staring me down, I felt like a tech-addled slob.

"One second," I said, feeling like a total idiot. "Excuse me."

I stood, pulled the mod out of my pocket and looked down, reading the newest update. approach of second wave confirmed. missile attack followed by ground forces. Some surviving LDF warrior, or perhaps a Munis employee, had managed to make it onto the com-network and had finally managed to sound out the real alarm.

I was still wondering what it all meant when I felt my legs give out from under me. The mod went flying out of my hands and landed with a thud on the ground.

But it was only the boy, who'd lunged at my legs and knocked me onto the ground. He was stronger than he looked and he knew it. He threw himself onto his back in the grass and giggled with wild pride, the metal band on his wrist glinting under the firelight.

"Gotcha!" the boy exclaimed. I wondered if he would remember this night, and if he did, whether he would remember with sadness what he was about to lose or with happiness for what, for a few more moments at least, he still had.

I mustered up a smile in response. "Not yet, pal." I retrieved my mod from where it had landed in the grass and picked myself up, kneeling in the dirt with the fire at my back. I opened my arms and the boy ran into them unquestioningly. I scooped him up and stood, and as I did, I looked over at his grandfather, just for a moment. He stared back at me with a great sadness.

I knew I had to leave. But I had to ask him one more thing. "You said your Legacy allows you to see people's destinies," I said. "Can you see anything now?"

"He will be important," the man said sadly. "That's all I know."

"What about me?" I asked.

The man smiled sadly. "You will be important also," he said. "But you will die."

I knew he was right. It was okay, though. We were all going to die. At least I would do it making a difference.

As I walked away, back down the path to the van, the boy's arms wrapped around my neck, I looked over my shoulder and took one last look at the man who had raised him. It was streaming with tears that ran in deep furrows through the caked dust on his cheeks and into his beard.

And then the second wave of missiles came down, booming in the distance.

CHAPTER FOURTEEN

THE GROUND ON THE TRAIL WAS UNEVEN UNDER my feet as I raced down the path, the branches and brambles scratching my face in the dark. I cursed under my breath and stumbled at every third step. The kid in my arms had started to cry as soon as his grandfather had disappeared from view, but he was doing it quietly.

"It's okay," I said, rubbing his back. "It's okay, little guy."

It wasn't okay. But maybe things would be better someday—for the kid in my arms, if not for me. First, though, I had to get him to the evacuation site without getting us both killed on the way.

That was going to be easier said than done: I gasped when I emerged from the trees into the clearing near the hut and saw the sky.

It was as bright as day, bright blue punctuated with quick-fire bursts of pastel pinks and purples all up and down the horizon. It was like the entire world was on fire. Maybe it was. The explosions were coming faster than I could count.

I couldn't stop to think about it. Panic wasn't going to do me any good, and there would be plenty of time for mourning later. Brandon and the evacuation ship would be leaving soon if it hadn't already left. There had to be nine Garde. Brandon had said it and somehow I knew it in my gut. I had to get him to the ship before takeoff.

The vehicle was just up ahead. One step at a time.

When I strapped the kid in next to me and fired up the autopilot system, the screen on the console lit up in a sea of red. The system was still linked in to an LDF satellite that was reading conditions all over the planet, and the devastation already wrought across the surface of Lorien—rendered in blinking red patches on the screen—had most routes back to the evacuation airstrip looking risky at best. The route I'd taken to get here was completely obstructed.

With that no longer an option, it seemed like my best bet was to pass through Malka, and then rejoin the original route at its midpoint. I fired up the autopilot, cranked it up to the highest speed it could achieve, and took a deep breath. It would either work or it wouldn't. The engine began to whir. The vehicle lurched forward and we went hurtling out into the burning night.

Then I turned to the still crying kid. I had no experience with children. I wasn't even a Mentor Cêpan *trainee*. Once I dropped him off at the airstrip, he would go on to whatever his great destiny was and would cease to be my problem.

But I hated hearing him cry. I looked him in the eye and he gasped for breath a little bit as his wails became weaker. It was like he didn't want me to see him like this. It was like he was trying to be brave.

"Listen, kid," I said. When I spoke, his sobs got even quieter. "Things are going to be a little dicey for a little bit. You need to be brave. You're a Garde, you know? Someday you're going to have a lot of power. You'll be able to be whoever you want to be. But first, you need to keep your chin up. After all, you're the future of the whole damn Lorien race, right?"

The boy was looking at me intently now, no longer crying at all. He was hanging on my every word, his eyes wide and his small mouth formed into a tiny O. "You got it, buddy?" I asked. "We need you."

He gave me a stern look and waved his fist in my face. "Kow kow," he said.

"Yup," I said, smiling. "Kow kow is right."

SKWONNNNKKK. SKWONNNNNK.

Instinctively, my hands flew to cover my ears. The boy yelped. It was the sound of some kind of horn, deep and booming. It rumbled up through the wheels of the van, right up into my bones.

I had a feeling I knew what it was—the sound of a Mogadorian ship. There was nothing else it could be. This was not good. I checked the console. We were getting there, but we still had a ways to go.

The road ahead of us was littered with rubble, fallen trees and dead bodies every here and there. I tried not to look at them. To the right was a void in the sky where the Elkin Spires had once been. In the distance, the smoking ruins of Capital City were getting closer.

We had just reached Eilon Park, on the outskirts of the city, when we were hit.

I'm not sure what got us. It wasn't a missile, or else we would be dead. It might have been flying debris from a bomb. It might have been something else. It really doesn't matter. Whatever it was, a massive blast knocked against the van and sent us flying. Everything went dark.

I came to on my back. My head was bleeding and my vision was blurred. There was some horrible grinding squeak above my head. The boy was kneeling over me, looking down into my eyes with a concerned expression. "Kow kow?" he asked.

I looked up past him to see the bottom of the van—the seats, the center console—above me. I was lying with my back against the interior roof. We were upside down.

In pain, I moved my head and could see, through a freshly smashed window, the grass of the park.

I didn't know what we were going to do. There was no way we were going to be able to get the van right side up again, much less running. I climbed through the shattered window, ignoring the glass that scratched my arms. When I was through, I turned around, reached out, and yanked the boy through with me. We rolled back into the grass together, out of breath.

SKKKWONNNK. SKKKWONKK. That noise again. Suddenly, next to me, the kid's eyes widened. His jaw dropped. I flipped around and saw the monster standing right above us, so close I could smell the stink of his breath.

It was the ugliest thing I'd ever seen, probably a full two heads taller than me, with pale white skin and a mouth jammed full of tiny, crooked teeth that were pointier and sharper than knives. I know what his teeth looked like because he was smiling. At his side, a giant curved sword dangled.

This, I knew, was a Mogadorian.

He growled at us with narrowed eyes. The noise was low and menacing, throaty and guttural.

The beast raised its sword over its head.

I had tried. I had. We had almost made it. Now it was over.

There was no use pretending my body would make any real shield for the kid. We would both die from the same blow.

Then I heard the strangest thing. It was something like music. I recognized it. Before I could react, there was a giant flash of light, and the music got louder, so loud that it sounded like it was coming from inside my skull.

It was Devektra's song. It was beautiful.

The Mogadorian reeled backward and dropped his sword. His face twisted into a horrified mask of pain. He let out another growl—really more of a roar—and fell to his knees.

I didn't even think about it. I knew what I had to do. I sprang to my knees, grabbed the sword and, with dazzling white lights flashing all around me, swung it with every bit of strength that I had. A geyser of blood erupted into the air as his head went flying.

I never saw her. I don't know how she found us, or why she didn't reveal herself. There probably just wasn't time. But it was her. Devektra had saved me. More important, she had saved the boy.

He stood up, looked up at me quizzically, seemingly unfazed by what had just happened, and pointed to something that was lying in the grass a few yards away.

"Motorcycle?" he asked.

CHAPTER FIFTEEN

WE ARRIVED AT THE AIRSTRIP IN TIME.

I parked the cycle and raced to the ship with the kid in my arms, searching for Brandon, pushing past a group of Kabarakians and LDF Garde who were chaotically arranging a perimeter around the airstrip.

The Mogadorians would be here soon. These Loric would be the only thing protecting the ship as it took off. Like me, they would remain behind. We were going to die. There was no way around it. But with a little luck, the nine children and their Mentors would live, and with them, the Lorien people would survive.

The eight Mentor Cêpans stood outside the ship, waiting to go, while eight young children—ranging in age from infancy to six years old—were arrayed in a circle on the ground. Another man was leaning over each of the children, touching their heads.

It was the Elder Loridas. It looked like he was

blessing them or something. Well, if I was going to die, at least I could say I finally saw one of the Elders.

When Brandon saw me approach, a look of disgust began to creep into his face. Until he saw the boy.

"This is the ninth," I said. I knew they'd be leaving any minute and, anxious to make my case, the words tumbled out in a rush. "It's not too late. You have to . . ."

"Quiet," said Brandon, taking the child. He rushed over to Loridas, who had just finished whatever he was doing with the children. I nervously watched them confer, wondering how Loridas had made it to the planet.

"He's the last." I turned to see a woman with long dark hair in her early thirties. She had read my look of confusion. "The other Elders are gone. They sacrificed themselves for us."

"Pittacus too?" I asked, stunned. I had never really thought much about Pittacus Lore, never reacted to his name with the unreserved awe that so many other Loric had for him, but it was still a shock. Even with everything that had happened tonight, it had never occurred to me that he could be *gone*. It was almost unimaginable.

An uncertain frown crept across the woman's face. "Pittacus is . . . missing," she said. "He may still be alive. We don't know."

I didn't respond. What was there to say?

"You look awfully young to be a Mentor Cêpan," she said.

"I'm just a trainee," I said, my eyes locked on Brandon, Loridas, and the boy. "Engineering. Not a Mentor."

"Could've fooled me," she said, glancing over at the boy. Loridas took him by the hand and laid him down in the sole remaining part of the circle. The other children all looked on as Loridas began to perform some kind of ritual.

"Why are they all so young?" I asked the woman. "They're too young to have been trainees at the Academy."

"These children were identified by the Elders as the most powerful of their generation," she told me. She sounded wistful as she said it. "They have a long road ahead of them. They will have to learn to adapt to a new home, and a new way of life that's unlike anything we know here. It will be better if they have as little memory of Lorien as possible. It will be easier for them."

I nodded sadly and turned back to watch the ritual. I was eager to take the whole sight in, but Brandon pulled me out to the edge of the airstrip.

"He has been admitted. The Eight is now Nine," he said. "Funny thing is, Elder Loridas wasn't fazed at all. When I said the ninth had arrived, he turned to me and looked at me as if he'd known he was coming all along."

I turned back to the collected Mentor Cêpans, to the

Garde arrayed on the ground, to the ship that would take them off this planet. I feared what my own fate would be, but was determined not to let Brandon see my fear. I wanted to make a gracious and noble exit.

"Go," I said. "I'll join the perimeter guard."

The suns were just starting to come up, the dusk colored by the flame and smoke of the planet's destruction.

"Good luck up there," I said.

"Stop," said Brandon. I turned back. "You're coming with us."

"Me? There's not room." I felt my heart rise in my chest. But I couldn't go along. "What about the rest of the people here? The ones who have been fighting all along? The ones who actually believed?"

"The boy needs a Mentor. You brought him here. He trusts you. And the bond has taken place—I can sense it. It has to be you."

"But I haven't been trained."

"The only thing any of us really need to know is to always put our Garde's survival ahead of our own." Brandon cast a glance back at the boy. "And it looks like you've got that part down."

Another explosion rumbled about a mile off, bringing our gaze across the sky to the approach of a massive Mogadorian ship. What looked like little wisps were parachuting out of the ship and landing gently, soundlessly on the ground.

But of course, that was a trick of distance and perspective. They weren't wisps. They were Mogadorian ground troops. And there was nothing gentle about them.

My fate had been decided. We rushed to the rest of the group to board the ship and leave our beloved Lorien before it was too late.

CHAPTER
SIXTEEN

"OOF." BARELY AWAKE, I WAS ALREADY IN AGONY.

The boy had just stepped hard on my legs, and was now jumping up the rest of my body, crushing my stomach, then my ribs.

"Wake up," he said, still jumping painfully all over me. It was a hell of a way to wake up in the morning, but I was starting to get used to it.

"Wake up," repeated the boy, who we had all started to call "Nine." He was bright-eyed, playful, and so full of energy that five minutes in his company was enough to make me pray for his bedtime.

Nine and the other young Garde had made a quick recovery from the horrors of that awful night, barely a month ago, when Lorien had fallen to the Mogadorians. The other Mentor Cêpans couldn't believe the childrens' resilience. We envied it. None of us would ever get over what we'd seen.

"I'm getting up," I said, swinging my legs over the bed and swiping my Kalvaka T-shirt off the hook on the wall. All of the other Mentor Cêpans were stuck with their LDA tunics, but I had only my street clothes from my last night out in Lorien.

"You're too slow," said Nine, yanking my arm as I tried to finish dressing.

"Sorry, buddy," I said. "Had a late one last night."

"What else is new?"

I looked up to see Brandon, smiling at the edge of the partition separating my sleeping quarters from the rest of the ship. Brandon was always getting on my case for being a late riser, for always being the last Cêpan socializing into the wee hours in the ship's canteen. If Brandon had gone to bed there was always Kentra, or one of the others.

"Today's the first day of pre-combat training," he said. "I'll take Nine, it's not a problem."

"Pre-combat? Already?" I had a hard time under-standing that they were already going to start conditioning some of the Garde as warriors. Brandon and Kentra had explained it was just simple calisthen-ics and drills at this point, but still. The kids were so young.

I saw Four, Brandon's Garde, poking his head out from behind Brandon's back. He shyly put his hand out for Nine to take, inviting him to walk to pre-combat together.

Seeing this, I hoped Nine would take Four's hand. It was a sweet gesture.

"Prucawbat! Rawr!" squealed Nine, and jumped back onto the bed, either unaware of Four's overture or too keyed up to notice.

I smiled, simultaneously exhausted by and proud of my Garde's hyperactivity. I scooped Nine off the bed and put him on the floor.

"You go off with Brandon and Four, okay? I'll see you at One-on-Ones after." One-on-Ones were training and development sessions between Mentor Cêpans and their Garde. It had been decided that my One-on-Ones with Nine would be overseen by another Mentor Cêpan, owing to my inexperience and lack of training. But even with Brandon or Kater breathing down my neck, One-on-Ones were my favorite time of the day: just me and the kid.

The large ship had an open plan with no walls, but in the interest of our privacy and sanity, programmable holographic partitions separated areas of the cabin into "rooms."

The canteen was one such space, located close to the ship's cockpit. It was nearly empty when I finally got there, and the food options were slim: a packet of freeze-dried karo fruit; a plate of mushy, lukewarm flurrah grain.

Ah, I thought. The perils of oversleeping.

I settled for the Karo and took a seat next to Hessu, the only Cêpan there. Hessu was the oldest of the Cêpans, and shy to boot. I never knew what to say to her so I just nodded at her and ate my breakfast in silence.

As tended to happen when I had a moment to myself, my thoughts drifted to the events back on Lorien, both the things I had witnessed—the destruction of the capital; those heartbreakingly muddy tears on Nine's grandfather's cheeks—and those I had only imagined: my parents' chalet in Deloon blasted by Mog missiles; Devektra, finally succumbing to the Mogadorian ground troops while valiantly defending her beloved city.

I also thought back to the ship's takeoff, watching out the window as we pulled up and over the airstrip. The Elder Loridas, who had insisted not to be taken on board, faded to a dot on the ground as we breached the planet's atmosphere, with the fighting Lorien Defense Forces and Kabarakians still down there, holding off the advancing Mog horde.

The first few days in space had been the worst. We Mentor Cêpans had all huddled in the canteen together, our impatient, traumatized charges in our laps, waiting for word from the ship's pilot about the fate of Lorien.

Brandon had explained that the vast majority of the council, the academy and the LDF had been killed in the first wave, but there were bound to be survivors, heroes like Devektra who would fight off the invading forces no matter how bad the odds. It had been decided by a vote that once we had reached a distance of relative safety, the ship would hang back, watch, and wait. If there were any sign that the defeat of Lorien was incomplete, that whatever resistance movement had formed stood even a meager chance of survival, we would turn back and aid however we could.

But after many sleepless days and nights, the pilot emerged into the canteen from the front of the ship and shook his head. "From the ship's scans . . ." he said, fighting back tears. "There's nothing. Nothing's left."

For every horror I had endured, that was the worst, the most devastating.

Slowly but surely, things improved. And as dark as my thoughts got, it was hard to stay down when we had nine rambunctious, energetic kids all around us, every second of the day.

"She's sick," announced Hessu. I almost did a double take: Hessu never spoke without first being spoken to.

It took me a second to realize she must be talking about her Garde, the girl we called "One."

"I woke up in the middle of the night with a bad feeling, so I went to the children's quarters to check, and sure enough when I touched her forehead it was hot. A bad fever." Hessu's aversion to eye contact was just part of her personality, but the intense way she avoided my look made me fear the worst.

"Where is she?" I asked. "Is she okay?"

"She's in the Autodoc." Because no one on board had any medical knowledge, the ship had been outfitted with a small climate-controlled area called an Autodoc. It monitored a patient's vital signs and administered medicine as needed through the air vents. "Machine says she'll be fine."

"Well then," I said, relieved. "That's good."

Hessu merely shrugged. Her mouth was pursed, bitter-looking, like she'd been sucking on something sour.

"She's going to die," she said.

I froze in my seat, speechless. It felt like Hessu's words had sucked all of the oxygen out of the room.

"She will die. I'm certain of it."

"Hessu, I'm sure she'll be fine—"

She turned at me, a look of rage and contempt burning on her face. "I don't mean *now*, you idiot!" She began to laugh bitterly. "Don't you realize, we're *all* going to die?"

My blood turned to ice. What was this woman getting at?

"Right. Right," she said. "You haven't been fully briefed yet, how would you know? This is a suicide mission. We are going to some distant planet to hide from the Mogadorians, to run from them, to make whatever pathetic efforts to survive we can make before they hunt us down and kill us. It's useless. I don't know why we're even bothering."

Her words seeped into my brain like a poison, but I tried to focus on the matter at hand: her hysteria. "You need to calm down," I said.

"Easy for you to say. You're last. You and your boy get blessed last out of sheer luck, because you were running late!" The bitter laughter came back. "While me and my girl . . . we're first. First blessed, first to die."

The laughter gave way to tears, and Hessu threw her face into her hands. I fought through my own horror and embraced her.

We stayed like that for a while. I rocked her in my arms while the terrifying truth of our situation bled into my heart.

Later, I made my way down the virtual corridor, towards the empty barrack in which my One-on-Ones with Nine were held. I felt like a fool. For allowing myself to be optimistic about the Elders' plan for us all, for believing that the road ahead would be any brighter than the one behind us. To hear it from Hessu, it was only going to get grimmer once we reached our destination.

And I felt like a fool for not inquiring deeper into

the nature of the ritual Loridas had performed on Nine. I had foolishly assumed it was just some meaningless pagan blessing. But according to Hessu it was much more than that. It was a protective spell that granted total immunity to the children. All except One.

Her blessing was just a link to the others. She was not invulnerable. Once she died, Two would be vulnerable. Once Two died, Three would be vulnerable. On and on up the chain of their precious young Garde.

Put in those terms, it no longer felt like any kind of blessing at all. It felt like a curse. And it made me sick just thinking about it.

I paused outside the barrack's door and looked out the window of the ship. All I could see were stars. We still had many galaxies to travel before we reached our destination. We were heading to Earth. A planet that was far from perfect. It was nothing like Lorien had been.

But even with all the terrible stories I'd heard about Earth's misery, about the war, the famine, the pollution, I was looking forward to it, at least a little bit. I still remembered that transmission I'd watched on the night of Quartermoon, before I'd made the fateful decision to take Daxin's band and leave the academy, and I knew that Earth couldn't possibly be *all* bad.

I entered the barrack to find Nine waiting on the floor, his back to the virtual door. Adel, Seven's Mentor

Cêpan, sat in a chair in the corner, having been assigned supervisor duty for the day.

"Hey, Adel," I said, giving her a smile and a little wave. Adel waved back.

At the sound of my voice, Nine jumped up, whirled around and raced right at me, grabbing me by the knees.

Nine looked up at me, his eyes gleaming. "Sandor?" he asked, drawing my name out and wagging his head back and forth. "Are we going to play today?"

I looked down at him and smiled.

"Yeah, buddy," I said. "We're going to play."

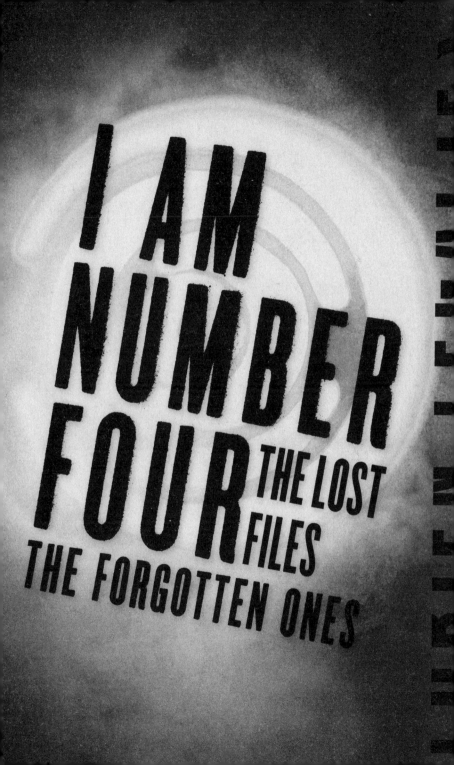

CHAPTER ONE

MY EYES FLY OPEN, BUT I DON'T SEE ANYTHING. Just darkness. My lungs feel weak and heavy, like they're coated in a thick layer of grime, and when I cough, a cloud of dust swirls around me, making me cough more until I'm about to hack up a lung. My head is throbbing, foggy and immobile. My arms are pinned to my sides.

Where am I?

As the dust settles, my coughing finally subsides and I begin to remember.

New Mexico. Dulce. Wait—did all that really happen?

I want to believe it was all just a dream. But by now I know enough to realize that there's no such thing as *just a dream* anyway. And this was no dream. I was the one who brought this place down. Without even knowing how I did it, I took the power that One had given me and brought a whole government base crashing down to its foundations.

Next time I pull a stunt like that, I'll wait till I'm not *in* the place before I tear it apart. It made sense at the time. I guess I have some things to learn about having a Legacy.

Now everything around me is silent. I'll take that as a good sign. It means that nobody's trying to kill me anymore. Which means that they're either just as buried as I am, or they're dead. For now, I'm alone. One is dead. Malcolm and Sam are gone—they probably think I'm dead too. As for my family, they'd prefer it if I *was* dead.

No one would even know if I gave up here, right now, and there's part of me that wants to. I've fought so hard. Isn't it enough that I came this far?

It would be so easy just to stop struggling here, to stay buried. To stay forgotten.

If One were still here, she would toss her hair impatiently and tell me to snap out of it, to get over myself. She'd tell me that I'm not even halfway finished with the job she left me with and that there are bigger things to worry about than myself. She'd remind me that it's not just my life that hangs in the balance.

But One isn't here anymore, and so it's up to me to tell myself those things.

I'm alive. That in itself is amazing. I'd triggered the explosives in the armory with the full knowledge that it might be the last thing I did. I'd done it so Malcolm

Goode, the man who'd started to feel like some kind of dad to me, could escape with his real son, Sam. I figured that if they got away, at least I would have died doing one good thing.

But I didn't die. For now, at least. And I figure that if I'm still alive despite everything, there has to be a reason for it. There's still something I need to do.

So I try to slow my racing heart, breathe steadily, and assess the situation. I'm buried, yes. But there's air here, and I can move my head, my shoulders, even my arms a little. Good. My breathing stirs up more dust and that shows me which way is up, and also that there's a little light seeping in from somewhere. And if there's any light at all, it means I can't be too far from the surface.

There's no room for me to move my arms, but I struggle anyway, trying to push against the shattered stone and concrete I'm trapped under. It doesn't do any good, of course. I'm not a vatborn with genetically enhanced strength or even a natural powerhouse like my adoptive brother, Ivan. I'm tall but slight and built like a regular human, with only moderately more physical ability. I'm not even sure if the most highly trained of the vatborn would be able to dig his way out of here; there's no way *I* have any shot at all.

But then One's face enters my mind again—her wry, affectionate eye roll, the way she would look at me like,

Really? That's all you've got? And something occurs to me. It's *not* all I've got. Not anymore. I may not have strength, but I *do* have power.

I focus on the rocks around me, knowing that, with my Legacy—the Legacy that One gave me—I can shake all this debris clear. I close my eyes and focus on it, picturing the rubble shaking and splitting, moving away from me until I'm free.

Nothing happens. It doesn't budge. *Move, dammit,* I think, and then I realize that I've actually said the words aloud without meaning to. Either way, the rocks don't pay any attention.

Suddenly I'm angry. First I'm angry at myself: for being so stupid, for being so weak, for not having mastered the gift that One gave me. For getting myself to this place at all.

But it isn't my fault. I was only trying to do what was right. It's not myself I should be angry at—it's my people, the Mogadorians who got me here. The Mogadorians, who worship brute force and believe that war is a way of life.

Soon I can feel my rage coursing through my body. Nothing in my life has ever been fair. I never had a shot at all. I think about Ivan, who was a best friend to me. We grew up together, and then he betrayed me. He tried to kill me—more than once.

I think about my father, who didn't think twice

about letting the Mogadorian scientists experiment on me with machines that had been completely untested and came close to frying my brain. It was nothing to him to risk sacrificing me for *the cause*.

And what cause was that? The cause of creating more destruction, of killing more people and gaining more power for himself. But power over what? When we'd conquered Lorien, we'd left it a lifeless, destroyed husk of a planet. There was nothing left on Lorien to rule. Was that what we were going to do to Earth too?

For people like my father, that's not the point. The point is war. The point is winning. To him, I was just another potential weapon to be used and discarded. That's all anyone's ever been worth to him.

The more I think about it, the more I feel my mind racing with rage. I hate him. I hate Ivan. I hate Setrákus Ra and the Good Book for teaching them all that this is the right way to live. I hate them all.

My fingers and toes start to tingle. I feel the rocks around me start to tremble. I'm doing it. My Legacy is working. You can let your anger destroy you, or you can use it for something. I close my eyes again, clench my fists and scream as loud as I can, letting all my fury out in one big burst. And with a massive whoosh, the dirt and stone and rubble begin to crumble. My body is shaking all over, and the ground is shaking too. Before long, it's all slid away, and I'm free again. It's as if a giant shovel has scooped me out.

But someone else isn't as lucky. Not ten feet away from me, a Mogadorian soldier is wedged beneath what looks like part of a shattered steel doorframe.

He groans and stirs now that the weight's been lifted.

He's as alive as I am. Awesome.

CHAPTER TWO

I PULL MYSELF TO MY FEET, STAGGERING A bit. My whole body aches like I've just been squeezed in a giant vise, but I don't think anything's broken. I'm covered in dirt and dust and sweat and, yes, some blood, but not a lot of that either. Somehow, I've managed to avoid any serious injury. I don't know how, and I don't really care.

The other Mogadorian isn't so lucky. As I stand, he lets out a low groan, but he doesn't look up at me or move. He's so beaten up that he barely seems to realize he's not buried anymore. I don't even think he realizes I'm here.

He must have gotten hit pretty hard, because this guy doesn't look like the type who would be easy to take out. He's as big as Ivan and built like a pro line-backer, with a thick neck and bulging muscles, but I can tell even from here that he's not vatborn—his facial features are too clean lined and too even to be one of the genetically altered warriors who make up the majority of the Mogadorians' army.

This one is a trueborn, like me. Like my father. From the tattoo on his skull I can tell that he's an officer, not a grunt. It figures. The vatborn are bred to be cannon fodder, while the trueborn give the orders. Maybe that's why I don't remember seeing him while I was holding back the troops. Unlike Ivan, who charged after me and got himself killed as a result, this guy must've been leading from the rear.

I actually feel a stab of disgust at the thought. A good commander leads by example, not by cowering behind his men. Not that it did him much good. Anyway, none of it matters much. I need to figure out what I'm going to do with him.

First things first: I check him over for any weapons. He grunts a little as I pat him down, and his eyes flutter for a moment, but he doesn't resist my search. Not that I find anything useful on him—if he had a blaster it's long gone, and he doesn't seem to have a knife on him either. I don't find so much as a breath mint in his pockets. Which, from the foul stench of the air emitting from his mouth in wheezing bursts, would probably do him more good than a weapon right about now.

The one thing that I can't help but notice is the blood. This guy's practically covered in it. It's seeping out from under the dust and dirt that coat his pale skin, and staining through the torn-up clothes he still has on. I don't see any one big injury, but he's a mess for sure.

When I'm satisfied that he's not going to jump to his feet and take me down the moment I turn my back on him, I look around the area I'm standing in and try to get my bearings. The bulk of Dulce Base was built underground to keep it away from prying eyes, but I guess my little stunt changed all that. I'm standing in a giant crater at least a hundred feet across at the top, and there's a clear blue sky above. The only problem is, I'm at least twenty feet down from where rock ends and sky begins.

The wreckage is everywhere—rocks and cement and toppled columns, busted computers and equipment with their exposed electrical wires sparking dangerously. When I smell the familiar stench of gasoline, I realize that I'm basically standing in the middle of a huge powder keg. This place could go up in flames at any second. It's sort of a miracle there haven't been any more explosions yet.

I have to get out of here quick. Luckily, despite the fact that we're so far down, there's so much debris piled high in every direction that I figure it won't be too hard to climb my way to the surface.

I figure out which direction will be the easiest to negotiate, and start to head that way—and then stop. I look behind me, at the guy lying there on the ground—the Mogadorian who still hasn't stirred beyond a groan.

I could leave him here to die alone. I have myself to worry about, and besides, one more dead Mogadorian is a good thing. But something stops me.

It's not that I'm just being nice. It's way too late to start having moral qualms now. After all, I've killed more than my share of Mogs since all this started.

For a moment I wonder if my dad ever would have guessed that I had it in me. I wonder if it would give him even a tiny bit of pride if he knew.

Of course, my dad's pride is the last thing I'm looking for now. That's not why I decide to turn back, though. Instead, it's because I know that a single, unarmed Mogadorian officer can do me more good alive than he can dead. For one thing, if he was stationed here he'll know his way around the surrounding area and any nearby towns. Deep in the middle of the desert, without even a compass to guide me, that stuff matters if I want to get out alive.

So I head back to the guy, grab him under the arms and start hauling him along.

This guy's really heavy, and it's all I can do to drag him over the craggy piles of junk and rocks as we make our way across the vast expanse of the base's ruins towards the edge of the crater. The sun is higher in the sky now and we're completely exposed to it. I feel a bead of sweat forming at my brow and making its way down my face and then, before I know it, I'm completely drenched. I try to clear a path as I move, kicking aside dusty monitors and crushed aluminum piping and whatever else is blocking the way.

Not that it does much good. Within minutes, my arms feel like noodles, my legs hurt and my back is killing me. We're not even halfway to where we need to be. This isn't going to work. Finally, when I drop the Mogadorian to the ground to catch my breath, he stirs.

"Hey," I say. "Can you hear me?"

"Uhhhrm," he replies. Well, it's not that helpful, but it's better than nothing, I figure.

"Hey, listen," I try again. "We've got to get out of here. Can you walk?"

He peers up at me, his heavy brow furrowed, and I can guess why. He's trying to figure out who I am and what I'm doing here. I'm covered in grime, so he probably can't tell that I don't have the skull tattoo that denotes Mogadorian rank, and he looks up at me in confusion.

I don't have time for him to be confused, or time for him to come to his senses—assuming he ever will. We have to get out of here *now*. I have no idea whether there are any others still alive elsewhere on the base, or if reinforcements are on the way. Plus, I'm half expecting

THE FORGOTTEN ONES

the whole place to go up flames at any second. That's *if* I don't die of thirst before it happened.

I try a different tack. I speak to him in our native Mogadorian tongue, the language that's mostly only ever used now for ceremonial purposes. I quote the Good Book. "*Strength is sacred,*" I say. It's one of the most important tenets in Mogadorian society. His eyes come into focus.

"On your feet, soldier!" I snap. I'm only half surprised when it does the trick and he slowly levers himself up onto one knee and raises himself to his feet. Typical Mogadorian—there's nothing my people respond to more enthusiastically than empty authority. He's swaying a bit as he comes to a standing position. His left arm is hanging funny, and he's pale, sweat popping out across his forehead and along his upper lip, but he's up. For now.

"Let's go," I tell him, pointing towards the opening high above. "March." Without a word, he lumbers past me.

I follow him, realizing that I'm not in much better shape than he is. As we scramble over the heaps of rubble, I find myself thinking of Sam and Malcolm. I hope they made it out of here okay. My cell phone got crushed when I brought down the base, so I can't call Malcolm to find out what happened, arrange somewhere to meet up or even ask for help. All I can do is have some hope.

It feels like hours before we finally come to the edge of the blown-out base, though the sun is still high in the sky so it can't have been that long. So far none of my fears has come to pass: there have been no explosions or fires and no sign of Mogadorians coming back to dig through the wreckage.

The pit is deeper than it appeared earlier, and I look up and see exactly how far we have to climb to get out of here. Luckily there's enough junk piled up around the edge that we'll be able to find a path to the top, but it won't be easy.

Is anything ever easy?

I'm soaked in sweat, though, and practically panting for air as we pull ourselves up the side of the cliff, using toppled girders and jutting pieces of cement and whatever we can find to use as handholds. My new best friend is pushing through the pain, his black eyes glassy and unfocused, but he's doing it. I'm embarrassed to see that even in this state he's still at least as strong as I am.

I'm guessing he took a blow to the head from the explosion. The good news is, it's made him nice and docile—when I tell him to do something, he does it. The bad news is, he has no idea what he's doing. I need him alive, so I've got to keep a close eye on him every second in case he does something stupid.

"What's your name?" I ask him once I've got my

breath back. Might as well know who I'm dealing with.

"Rexicus Saturnus," he answers after a minute. The name sounds vaguely familiar. He doesn't look that much older than me, and I wonder if I'd ever seen him when I lived at home with my parents and sister. Ashwood *is* the largest Mogadorian community on Earth, after all, so there's a good chance he grew up there too. Even if he was a bit older than me, I'd have seen him around occasionally, or heard his name. I study his face, though, and find that I don't recognize him it all. "They call me Rex."

I just nod. There's nothing to say right now. We just have to keep climbing. So we climb.

And then, after who knows how much time, we emerge from the pit and stumble over the edge into a vast desert. I didn't think it would be possible, but the sun on my brow feels even hotter than before.

I only take a few seconds to rest and catch my breath before I dust myself off and scan the horizon, looking for something—anything—other than dirt and rocks, and after a minute, my eyes settle on what looks like a small building. I don't know what we'll find—there could still be Mogadorians inside, for all I know—but I decide I don't have much choice, especially if it means finding water and some respite from the heat.

"All right then, Rex," I say, pointing to the building in the distance. "Let's get moving. That way."

He just nods and starts walking. I follow him, wondering again if I'm doing the right thing. It would be so easy to kill him. For now he's weak, his reflexes dulled, his mind fuzzy. It would take nothing for me to sneak up behind him and get rid of him once and for all. This could be my only chance. Once he's recovered, he'd be able to overpower me easily. Then he might not think twice before killing *me*.

But he's a Mogadorian officer. I have no idea what information he has or how valuable he is to my people. All I know is that if he knows anything that can help Malcolm and the Loric people, it's worth it to keep him alive even if it means risking my own neck. It's what One would want.

CHAPTER THREE

MY FEET FEEL LIKE THEY'RE MADE OF LEAD; it's a supreme effort to lift each one and set it back down. My head is throbbing, my tongue feels swollen and my nose is so dry it hurts to breathe in through it, but my throat is coated with sand and swallowing makes me want to retch. My skin is tight and crinkly, and I itch everywhere—when I glance at my arm I realize it's bright red, the harsh sunlight already burning me. Every movement sends little jolts of pain washing across my every joint, over every inch of exposed flesh. I can't see straight—the desert stretches out ahead of me, and the building we're heading towards doesn't seem to be getting closer. In fact, part of me is starting to wonder if it's even real. When I stare at it for too long it begins to waver, like it's just a mirage that will always remain a few thousand paces in the distance.

I'm not sure, though. I'm not sure of anything

anymore. I've never felt more alone in my life. In the past, even when things were at their worst, I always had One urging me along, reminding me of what was right. Then One was gone, but at least I had Malcolm. Now he's gone, too, and I only have myself. I just wish *myself* was someone I had more faith in.

Of course, I'm not actually alone. Rex is here too. But Rex is not my friend. If he knew who—or *what*— I was, he'd probably kill me on the spot. Killing the traitor Mogadorian who turned on his father and brought down the Dulce Base would earn him at least one promotion in rank.

At the moment, though, Rex is useless. His stride's become more erratic, his head is down like he can just bull through the entire New Mexico desert and he keeps muttering to himself. I don't know what he's say- ing, but I get the impression he's talking to somebody else. Somebody who obviously isn't here right now.

So it's just me, the desert and a hallucinating Mog soldier.

And then the building we're heading towards begins to transform from just a thick smudge in the distance where sand meets sky into a real shape that I can recog- nize. It's getting bigger, closer. We're almost there. And it dawns on me exactly what it is—with everything that's happened I'd practically forgotten.

Miles out from the main base, along the perimeter,

there was a watchtower. *Was.* When Malcolm and I first got here, it had been the first thing we spotted, along with a generator right behind it that was powering the base's electric fence. I decided to bring it toppling down, sending it crashing into the generator, in order to sneak in and rescue Sam.

I thought I'd destroyed the tower completely, but now as we approach it, I begin to see that the actual guard station at the top survived, a metal-and-concrete room that's now lying on its side a hundred feet from the ruined generator. It's not much, barely bigger than a bathroom, really, but we can hole up there for a while. We're almost there when I hear the most wonderful sound in the world. I try not to run—at this point if I fall down I doubt I'd be able to get back up again—but I hurry towards the noise. And there, jutting up within the tower's twisted, bare foundation, is a jagged, broken pipe.

Bubbling up from it is water.

I drop to my knees right next to the fallen tower where the spouting water has formed a little pool around the pipe. I would jump in if I could; I'd let it soak in through every pore.

Since I can't do that, I scoop up as much water as I can into my cupped palms and splash it on my face. Then I take another scoop, raise it to my lips, and drink. The water is warm and metallic but tastes like life itself.

I feel immediately better. I'm filled with a burst of

energy spreading through my body, from my chest all the way to my toes and fingertips. I take another greedy sip. I can think clearly again.

Then I remember Rex. He's on his knees beside me, staring at the pool with bloodshot eyes, but he's not drinking. It's like he doesn't remember how. I reach down and splash some water on his face. His eyes widen. He licks his lips, and then he's hunched over the pool, scooping handful after handful up to his mouth, lapping at it furiously.

I pull away and just sit back on my haunches, taking it all in. We've got water now, and shelter. Maybe there are even some rations in there, if we're lucky. We might just survive this yet.

Or will we? As I've started to feel like things are going to be okay, I hear a low, threatening rumble. A growl.

I turn my head, startled by the noise, and come face-to-face with a huge, powerfully built beast. It's a wolf—the largest I've ever seen. His golden eyes are narrowed menacingly; his tail is twitching and his ears are pricked for a fight. He bares his fangs.

CHAPTER
FOUR

"EASY THERE, BIG GUY," I SAY CAREFULLY, clambering up as gracefully as I can manage, hoping not to spook the animal any more than I already have. "We're not here to hurt you."

He digs his paws into the ground and hunches forward. If he decides to pounce, we're done for, but if I can call up One's Legacy again, I might be able to shake things up enough to knock the wolf off his feet, giving me time to run for the protection of the guard station. It's not the best plan ever, but it's the only one I've got.

The water's refreshed me a bit, but my head's still throbbing. I'm swaying on my feet and my skin's burning. Not the ideal circumstances to try to use the Legacy I don't have a complete handle on yet.

But I concentrate as hard as I can and clench my hand into a fist. I raise it slowly and point it at the ground. There's a soft rumble, and the earth below us stirs like a table that's been bumped by accident. It's something, but it's not going to help much.

I'm surprised at how the wolf reacts: he gives a small yelp and backs away a step, eyeing me now with curiosity rather than anger. He tilts his head to one side like he's trying to figure me out, and then slowly begins padding toward me. This time, he doesn't growl. He almost looks friendly. Whatever I was expecting when I tried to nail him with my Legacy, this wasn't it.

"Uh, hey there," I say, trying to modulate my voice so that it's soft and nonthreatening, holding out my upturned palms. No sudden movements.

He's right in front of me now, studying me, sniffing me. A low whine is coming from his throat. I didn't have a dog or any pets growing up—my father, the great general, didn't see any value in pets that couldn't do something useful—so I have no idea how to read this animal and no idea whether or not I should be running right now.

When he licks the palm of my left hand, though, I'm pretty sure it's not the prelude to an attack.

"Good boy." I reach out and, ever so slowly, pet him on the head. His fur is thick and soft, and he gazes at me steadily. I have no idea why, but he suddenly seems to trust me.

I turn to see what Rex thinks of all this, and discover that he hasn't been watching any of it: he's passed out. For a second I worry that he's dead, but then I see that he's breathing, but barely. His injuries—in addition to the exertion and dehydration—must have caught up with him.

I need to get him out of the open desert. The sun's starting to sink toward the horizon. I've heard it gets cold in the desert at night. The temperature's already starting to drop. If nothing else, it would be nice to have four walls protecting us from the elements.

"You gonna stick around?" I ask the wolf as I lift Rex up by his armpits and begin to drag him toward the guard station. I feel stupid talking to an animal, but it's not like I have any better options for conversation. He looks me up and down and then begins to follow me, silently loping along.

Luckily it only takes us a few minutes to reach the structure. All the windows have shattered from when it collapsed, but there are wooden shutters that look intact. After a couple of hard shoves, the door swings open.

The place is on its side, but it looks mostly intact. The inside's got a few desks, some chairs, clothes lockers, filing cabinets, a smashed computer, and a busted-up minifridge. Yeah, this should do nicely.

I step inside, dragging Rex with me, and the wolf

follows behind us. I'm not sure why, but I feel strangely reassured to have him with us.

Unfortunately the place is pretty tiny. After I drop Rex's body to the ground, there's barely space to turn around without tripping over the wolf. I'm thinking maybe there isn't room for all of us in here.

He studies me for a second, as if he knows exactly what I'm thinking. He lets out a bark.

And then he starts to change. First the edges of his body lose focus, and then his fur begins to glow, somehow smoothing itself out into a glossy shell around his body almost like armor. He turns from white to green.

I take a shaky step back. I wonder if this is what happens when you spend a whole day wandering around a desert dragging a guy almost twice your size. I open my mouth to speak and then realize I have no idea what to say.

He's not done yet either: now his skin is rough and scaly, and then his whole body begins to ripple like water in a pond just after you've tossed a rock into it. He's shrinking.

It's all happening so fast that I barely have time to wonder what's going on. But then it's over. Sitting at my feet, blinking up with huge, glittering eyes, is a lizard.

"Holy shit," I mutter. They're suddenly the only words I can remember.

It's not like my life has been boring. I was raised in a secret community of alien conquerors, had my mind grafted onto the mind of a dead girl, recently developed superpowers.

But none of those things has been weirder than watching a wolf transform into a lizard right before my eyes.

CHAPTER
FIVE

"I KNOW WHO YOU ARE."

It's the first time Rex has spoken to me directly. We've been here a few days now. I decided to stick it out to let both of us recover, although I'm barely sleeping because I worry that every little noise I hear could be the Mogs—or the U.S. military—coming to see if anyone survived the explosion. Oddly enough, I haven't seen a hint of anyone—Mog or human. They must assume that everyone is dead and there's no urgent need to sift through the debris.

We've got shelter and water, and although we went through the meager rations in the guard tower pretty quickly, I've managed to find small stores of food scattered around the ruins of the Dulce Base: military rations and crackers and chips and dried fruit. We're not exactly living large, but it could be worse.

I was able to patch myself up pretty quickly using

the first aid kit mounted to the wall of our hideout, and with rest and hydration, Rex is getting better too. His color's improved each day, along with his breathing, although his arm still looks like it might be broken.

For the past few days, he's been drifting in and out of consciousness, sometimes sleeping fitfully, other times passed out cold. Yesterday he spent most of the day awake, but he just sat in the corner, staring at the ceiling, totally silent. It was hard to tell if he *couldn't* speak or if he just didn't want to.

But now he's decided to talk, and the thing he says is the one thing I've been dreading. He recognizes me.

I just shrug, trying to act like I don't know what he's talking about. "Yeah?" I ask, noncommittal.

"You're Adamus Sutekh," he continues. "Son of General Andrakkus Sutekh." Now there's no mistaking the contempt in his voice, or the way his lip curls in disgust. "You're a traitor."

I freeze. He knows everything. I stare at him, trying to figure out what he's going to do next. I can still take him out if I have to—I won't have that chance once he's back to full health.

I shake the idea off one more time. I might be making a huge mistake, but I still think he's too valuable to kill. It's a risk I'm willing to take.

"I saved your life," I say evenly. Rex snorts.

"You betrayed our people. You blew up the research

lab at Ashwood." That's not strictly true—I shattered the lab, yes, with the Legacy that One gave me—but I let it pass as he raises his voice. "And I'm willing to bet that you're responsible for all this too. Aren't you?"

I turn away. I can't even look at him. Even though I know I was doing the right thing—the thing I *had* to do—there's still a part of me that feels ashamed.

Now he's almost yelling, although he's still too weak and hoarse to summon the strength to really scream. "You're pathetic. I don't know how a weakling like you managed to do it alone, but you're the one who blew up the base. You killed everyone. Your own people."

What I don't tell him is that I wasn't on my own. From the pieces of the puzzle that I've managed to put together—the chaos and noise during the attack, the extent of the wreckage afterwards—I'm pretty sure I wasn't the only one attacking the base when it collapsed. If he wants to think I did all of this myself, that's fine, but I know that the Garde must have been there too.

I just shrug. "I was looking for somebody," I tell him. "You guys were holding him here. I took him back."

Rex is still glaring at me. "You killed all those soldiers to save one person?" he asks. "That human we were holding, the boy? Why?"

My new friend saves me the trouble of answering. He's been out and about all day, scouting as usual, and now he swoops in through the open doorway of our shelter and settles on my shoulder. He's taken on the shape of a hawk today and his talons grip tight through the T-shirt I scavenged from a locker.

Rex recoils when he sees the bird. "What the hell is that?"

"It's Dust," I say, happy for the change in conversation. Rex just narrows his eyes at me. I can see the wheels turning in his head. I can't figure out what he's thinking, but whatever it is, it's nothing good.

I reach up and stroke Dust's head, and he ruffles his feathers contentedly. He and I have already become buddies. The name "Dust" seemed appropriate out here in the middle of the desert, and he seems perfectly happy to be called anything at all. I don't know *what* he is or why he's out here, but I'm starting to have a feeling we've both been lonely for a pretty long time.

Rex, on the other hand, doesn't seem at all pleased to have company. He eyes me and Dust for a moment longer and then, out of nowhere, springs to his feet. Before I know what's happening, he's got me pinned up against the wall, his fingers wrapped around my neck. Dust flutters from my shoulder and alights on the table across the room. He lets out an earsplitting squawk, but Rex ignores it.

"I don't know what you're up to, traitor," he snarls at me. "And I don't know what that *thing* is. But your days are numbered. Look at how weak you are. Even injured, I could kill you right now."

"Then do it," I say. I'm bluffing, of course. "Kill me," I tell him.

Then there's a roar from behind him and Rex spins around to come face-to-face with Dust. Only now he's not a hawk. Or a lizard. Or a wolf. He's shifted into a huge lion, so big the shack can hardly contain him. Having successfully gotten Rex's attention with the growl, he now opens his huge jaws and licks his chops as if to say, *Go ahead, try me.*

Rex jumps back, startled, but he isn't as surprised as I thought he would be. He pivots his head towards me with a nasty frown. "I knew it," he said. "Only a turn-coat like you would keep a Chimæra for a pet."

I look at him blankly. "Chimæra." It rings a bell, but I have no idea what it means.

Rex snorts. "You don't even know what he is, do you? That's what it is. It's a Loric beast, a shape-changer. High Command thought they were just legends, but when we invaded Lorien it turned out they were real. Nasty things, and vicious."

Of course. "Chimæra." Now I remember the word. They're mentioned in the Good Book—something about evil little pests, I think—but the days I used to spend poring over Setrákus Ra's sacred book of directives feels so long ago that I can barely remember any of it.

Then I remember something else. I've seen these creatures before—in One's memories of escaping Lorien. But I thought they were all dead now, that they'd been exterminated by my people along with the rest of her planet.

The thought that I'm wrong makes me smile. The Garde still have a few tricks up their sleeves.

And Rex isn't as tough as he wants me to think. I'd been shocked he'd had the strength to attack me at all, but it must have taken all he had out of him, because now he sinks back to the floor. Dust is still watching him warily, ready to pounce if necessary, but I wave him off and just like that, he's back to his bird form.

I should be getting used to it, but I'm not. It amazes me every time he transforms, and now that I know what he really is, it gives me a glimmer of hope too.

"What's he doing *here*, though?" I ask, more to myself than to Rex.

A smirk flashes across his face. He knows something.

Then I get it. "You were holding him prisoner, weren't you? Like Sam. Like Malcolm."

Rex looks up at me with fire in his eyes. "You just don't get it, do you?" he says. "We're at war. It's not a contest to see who can be the nicest. Prisoners get taken. People die. My *friends* have died. They should have been your friends too. If you hadn't decided to betray them."

I almost let his words sting me, but then I push them aside. "You're wrong," I say. "I do get it. Prisoners get taken. Come to think of it, it looks like I've taken a prisoner myself: you."

CHAPTER SIX

I'M MORE WORRIED THAN I LET ON.

A few days after my confrontation with Rex, he's healthier than ever. I've got Dust for protection—I know by now he won't let anything happen to me—but if it weren't for him, Rex would be able to overpower me easily. I'm starting to realize how lucky I've been so far, and what a mistake it could have been for me to keep Rex alive.

It's not just that. I'm getting antsier than ever about the Mogadorians showing up again and finding us. I've frisked Rex at least ten times by now, looking for communications devices and weapons, but I'm still worried he could have some way of getting in touch with them, of bringing them back for us.

We need to get out of here. We need a plan. Every day I go out scavenging the base for food, and every day I'm coming back with less and less of it. It's time to move on. But to where? I have no clue.

I wish I had a way of getting in touch with Malcolm. Assuming he made it out of here alive, he'd know what to do. But all the equipment in the base is damaged beyond repair, and I haven't been able to dig up so much as a cell phone. Until I'm back in civilization, I'm on my own.

I try to think about what One would say if she were here. I'm so used to having her kicking around in my head that if I try hard, I can summon her image as if we still shared a mind. When I close my eyes and picture her face, I see us back in California, standing on the beach. She's barefoot in the surf, her arms crossed against her chest, her hair pinkish in the sunset and curling in the breeze.

Rex is better. His bruises have faded and the cuts and abrasions crisscrossing his body seem to be knitting back together. The big gash on his side that was squirting all that blood when I first found him will take time to heal properly, but it's really only a surface wound. As for his arm, it wasn't broken after all, just a dislocated shoulder that he managed to pop back into place with a casual grimace when he put his mind to it.

His mood, though, is as bad as mine. Maybe worse. He spends most of his time sitting in the corner with a dark look on his face, sometimes muttering under his breath to himself and other times scowling silently for hours on end.

If I didn't know better, I'd say he was depressed. But that's impossible—real Mogadorians don't get depressed. They get even.

Strangely, the only thing that seems to snap Rex out of it is Dust. They've reached a tentative truce with each other, and despite his attempts to appear unimpressed, Rex seems just as fascinated by the Chimæra's transformations as I am. One day when Dust is in a playful mood and flitting from one shape to another—from rabbit to parrot to chimpanzee to Labrador—I even see Rex watching him with something approaching a smile.

It gives me an idea. "How much do you know about him?" I ask, nodding toward the Chimæra. I'm not really expecting anything, so I'm taken aback when Rex actually answers me.

"Not a lot," he says. "I don't know where they found him, or how long he was at Dulce. I just know that we've been running experiments on them."

Experiments. I give an involuntary shudder at the word, imagining Dust in some underground lab while a Mogadorian scientist tortures him in the name of Setrákus Ra. I know all too well what that's like. I was one of those lab rats myself once.

I don't want to think about it, but I can't *help* thinking

about it. And something clicks in my mind. Something about what Rex said that strikes me as odd. I just can't quite place what it is.

"'Them'?" I ask.

"Huh?" Rex says quizzically. He tries to play off the mistake, but the guilty flicker in his eyes lets me know I'm on to something.

"You said they've been doing experiments on *them*. As in, more than one. Are there more Chimæra out there? Somewhere on Earth?"

His eyes shift to the ceiling. He shrugs.

"I thought all the Chimæra were killed on Lorien," I muse, circling the question carefully, trying not to remind him that he's supposed to be giving me the silent treatment.

He remembers. He doesn't take my bait.

The next day, though, when I find him in his usual spot in the corner again, his chin resting on his fist, I give it one more try.

"There's more of them out there, aren't there?" I ask. "Dust isn't the last Chimæra."

Rex glares at me. His eyes are dead and distant, black holes. Dust is a cat now, snoozing under the table.

"Listen," I say. He doesn't even look at me. "Dust would kill you if I wanted him to. You know that, right? You're still weak, and even if you weren't, he's more powerful than both of us put together."

"So have him kill me," Rex says dully, still not meeting my gaze. It almost sounds like he means it.

I can't hide my surprise. "I can't believe a true-born would say that," I say. The shock in my voice is genuine.

Rex's head snaps up and he looks me right in the eye, his brow furrowed in some combination of anger and shame. It was the right thing for me to say.

I push it further. "To stop fighting—that would make you even more of a weakling than I am."

"I'll never stop fighting," he snaps. "I'll see the Loric dead if it's the last thing I do. But killing you, Adamus Sutekh—that's going to be the *first* thing I take care of."

"Fine," I say. "Kill me."

He knows he can't. Not yet, at least. Because I have Dust.

"I know my days are numbered anyway," I tell Rex. "You'll kill me eventually, or my father will, or some vatborn who doesn't even know my name. But right now, I'm the one with the power. You try to leave and that cute little guy napping under the table will turn into a ten-ton gorilla and peel you like a banana."

Rex rolls his eyes, angrily hocks a giant wad of saliva onto the cement floor and goes back to staring at the ceiling. He knows I'm right.

I push on, knowing that I'm making progress. "I need you too, Rex. There's a reason you're alive. It's because

I can use you. You have information. And information is what I want."

"I don't know anything," he spits out.

"Tell me what I want to know," I say, "and we'll get out of here. There will be plenty of time for you to kill me once we've made it out of this wasteland. I won't even stop you."

I can see him considering it. I hold my breath. If this doesn't work, I really *will* kill him, I decide. When I can see he's at his most vulnerable, I lean on him with one last question. "'They.' You said 'they.' Where are the rest of the Chimæra?"

"I haven't seen them," he mutters. "But there are a bunch of them. At least ten. Maybe more. They came on a separate ship from the Garde—at least, that's what I overheard some of the other officers saying."

Suddenly it all feels incredibly important. "You said they were experimenting on them," I say, trying to keep the sense of urgency from creeping into my voice. "What kind of experiments?"

I guess Rex doesn't see the point in clamming up now that he's said this much already, because this time he answers my question without hesitation. He sounds almost proud as he explains it. "They're trying to figure out how Chimæras' transformations work. Setrákus Ra thinks that if we can isolate the gene that gives them their abilities, we can duplicate the process with the vatborn."

The way he says "we" chills me. I'd forgotten what it was like to live among them, to believe that your own self-worth is bound up in the messed-up glory of a war-lord who chased nine teenagers across a solar system just to make sure they were all good and dead.

"Where are they?" I ask. "Tell me where they are, and we'll go there together."

He looks shocked at my intensity, but he takes a deep breath. "They're not here. Dust got separated from the rest of them somehow and they were keeping him here until someone could take him back to the main facility."

"Tell me where, Rex."

Only now does it seem to dawn on him exactly how much he's said and what the consequences of that could be. Revealing the secret goes against all of his training, against everything in the Good Book. His voice wavers a little, but he tells me anyway. "New York," he says. "A place called Plum Island."

CHAPTER
SEVEN

"NICE CITY," REX REMARKS, HIS TONE HEAVY with sarcasm as we set eyes on the town. "This was all totally worth it."

It's been a long day for all of us. After trying and failing to find a working vehicle anywhere on the grounds of the base, we'd had no other choice but to cajole Dust into carrying us. On his back. As a donkey.

He'd brayed and stomped his feet as first Rex and then I had climbed on top of him, but he'd done it, and after hours of trudging we were finally here. As civilization goes, the town we finally stumbled upon is a step up from the ruins of Dulce Base, but only barely. It's dusty and run-down, and half the storefronts on Main Street are boarded up. The other half are just weird, junk shops and drugstores that look like they haven't changed their window displays in about thirty years.

Still, there are paved roads, cars and working street-lights.

Not to mention hot food. When we make it to the center of town I can't help stopping outside Celia's Café and peering in the window to stare at people sitting in booths, looking happy as they chow down on hamburgers and pancakes and eggs and bacon. I can practically feel my mouth watering. After living on whatever canned and boxed and wrapped food we could scrounge up from the guard station's lockers and the base's remains, the thought of a real, proper meal is enough to make me drool.

Rex reaches for the door of the restaurant but I grab him by the shoulder. "Later."

He makes a sour face, but drops the door handle. He knows as well as I do that we don't have any money to pay for a meal. Food can wait. The first thing we need is cash. I'm still standing on the sidewalk, wondering how feasible it would be to rob a bank, when a stout, middle-aged couple exits the diner and brushes past me. They continue on down the street, and I watch as a skinny young guy carrying a tattered gray backpack bumps into the husband—and swipes his wallet.

It happens so fast that I almost can't believe what I saw. For a second I consider running after the pick-pocket, taking the wallet away from him and returning it to the couple.

But Rex has a different idea.

"We need money, right?" he asks, his eyes following the pickpocket, who's now strolling down the street, the very picture of nonchalance. "Follow him, but not too close. We don't want him seeing us."

I don't know what he's thinking, but I nod, and together we start after the pickpocket. Whatever he has in mind, I hope it works.

The criminal works hard, I'll give him that. From what I can see he swipes three more wallets and two purses over the course of the next hour, stuffing everything into his bag without pausing for a second. Somehow he never doubles back, never walks the same street twice.

At one point I spot a cop car, but the thief spots it too, and lays low until he's well out of sight. This guy's obviously a pro.

After the cops are gone and the guy's just swiped his second purse, Rex nudges me. "Get ready." He crosses the street, picks up the pace to get a block ahead of our prey and then cuts back over and starts heading towards me.

There's an alley up ahead, and Rex times it perfectly—he's just passing the pickpocket on the outside when they both reach the alley, and with a quick shove he sends the smaller guy tumbling sideways—right into the alley and temporarily out of sight. Or at least as close as we can manage. I hurry to catch up.

The thief doesn't waste any time complaining, or asking what we want, or anything like that. Instead he bolts for the alley's far side as I follow them both into the narrow brick corridor that dead-ends against a brick wall with one lonely dumpster. I can already see his plan—he's going to spring up its side, launching himself partway up the wall, and then grab the top and lever himself over. Leaving us in the dust. Frustrated, I pick up my pace, as does Rex, but it's obvious we're not going to catch up to the pickpocket before he hits that dumpster.

I stop short—we don't have much time and I can think of only one other way to stop this guy in his tracks. I channel my angry emotions, raise my hand and focus on the ground below that dumpster.

"Come on!" I mutter, gritting my teeth. And just as the thief makes that first jump, I feel a small tremor in the ground. The dumpster comes flying towards us. It slams into the pickpocket, hurling him against the alley's side wall. He hits it hard enough that we hear the air escape his lungs as he collapses in a heap on the ground.

"What was that?" Rex says as he runs back.

"Looked to me like he was planning to go up and over," I reply as I crouch down next to him. He's still breathing, which is good—there's a big difference between killing Mogs who are attacking you and killing some idiot who steals people's wallets for a living. The impact just knocked him out. I glance over at the dumpster. "Guess he didn't realize the dumpster was on wheels." I rifle through his backpack, finding all of his stolen goods and passing them back to Rex one by one. "Grab the cash, leave the rest." A minute later we've dropped the empty bags back in the guy's lap and are on our way. We've now got about thirteen hundred dollars between us. Not too shabby.

"First things first," I tell Rex as we exit the alley. "Supplies, a decent meal and then we'll figure out how to get to Plum Island from here."

Rex nods. "Supplies, food, transportation, check."

It's a little weird to find ourselves suddenly working together so easily—I could almost forget that we're supposed to be enemies. And while I'm glad that Rex isn't attacking me or trying to get in touch with Mog base command, I remind myself not to get too comfortable. It's nice to finally have someone to talk to, but I can't let myself think he's my friend.

Still, it won't hurt to get some food together, right?

We turn back towards the center of town, but as we're looping around I'm distracted for a second by what looks like the shadow of a figure running past us. I jump a little, and Rex gives me a funny look.

I must just be tired and hungry. When I scan up and

down the sidewalk, there's no one at all in sight.

All the way back to the restaurant, though, I can't quite shake the fear that we're being followed. And I don't mean by Dust, who's currently circling overhead as a hawk.

In a booth at the diner, even the taste of French fries and a milk shake doesn't help me shake the feeling that I'm being watched. And that can only mean one thing. Mogadorians.

CHAPTER
EIGHT

TWO HOURS LATER, WE'RE SITTING ON HAY BALES in the back of a pickup truck, the wind whistling through our hair. We both ate well—and I got a doggie bag for Dust—and even picked up some new clothes, then rented a room at a motel to shower and change. I managed to snag a burner cell phone too when Rex wasn't looking, but Malcolm didn't answer his phone and I didn't want to leave a message—just in case someone else gets their hands on his phone. I hope he and Sam are okay, but it's impossible to know. Just another thing to worry about.

Get yourself together, I tell myself. *You've come this far. Just put one foot in front of the other. This is important.*

And what I'm doing *is* important. I'm sure it is. I've already seen how powerful Dust is just on his own. Finding the rest of the Chimæra and reuniting them with the Garde might turn the tide in their favor. It could easily mean the difference between victory and defeat, not just for the Loric but for all of Earth.

However, if my people crack the genetic code allowing them to breed an endless supply of new vatborn soldiers with the Chimæra's shape-shifting abilities, the fight is as good as over.

One's death will have been for nothing. My betrayal will have been for nothing too.

So even though I'm tired, lonely and feel like I'm starting to go a little bit crazy, I know that I have to get to Plum Island. I have to free the Chimæra. If I can do it without getting myself killed in the process, that will be a bonus.

Before I can do any of that, though, I have to get out of New Mexico.

It turns out that's easier said than done. There's a train. Unfortunately it only makes three stops—one here, one in Colorado and a final stop in Wyoming. None of that was going to bring us anywhere near New York.

The bus isn't an option either. The nearest Greyhound station turns out to be in Colorado as well, a town named Alamosa, about forty or fifty miles from here. That's one hell of a walk.

Rex suggested stealing a car, but besides the fact that it's something I have no idea how to do, it feels too risky. You can't save the world if you're in jail for carjacking. I briefly consider trying to rent a car, but without any credit cards or ID, I doubt we'd get very far with that plan.

That leaves hitchhiking. Rex and I have the pallid, whiter-than-white skin of Mogadorians, and Rex has his military tattoo on his skull, none of which makes us particularly appealing passengers. But we both pull the hoods of our new sweatshirts up and hope to hide our more recognizable alien features.

I'm not sure how well it works, but we also have a secret weapon: Dust has had the good sense to turn himself into the world's most appealing golden retriever. The kind of dog people slow down just to look at.

Before long, it works. The third vehicle to pass us is a slightly battered pickup truck. It pulls right up ahead of us on the shoulder of the road. The middle-aged driver who rolls down the window has "rancher" written all over him, from the weathered skin to the callused hands to the worn flannel shirt and blue jeans. "Give you fellas a lift?" he asks.

"That'd be great, thanks," I answer, stepping up to the passenger side. "We're trying to get to Alamosa."

"Easy enough," he assures me. "Don't think I can fit all three of you up here with me, but you're welcome to hop in back."

I glance down at the passenger seat, which is covered with a bunch of packed grocery bags. "Back sounds good, thanks," I assure him. I gesture for Rex to climb in, and Dust hops over the side after him. I jump in last, and then we're off.

We're in Alamosa an hour later. "Where're you going in town?" he calls back through his open window as we pull up to a stoplight. "Anywhere in particular?"

"The bus station," I shout back, and he nods. Ten minutes later he brakes in front of a small redbrick building with a big Greyhound sign out front.

"Thanks again," I tell him as we all clamber out. "Can I give you some money for gas?"

He waves that off. "I was heading this way anyway," he assures me. "You boys get home safe now!" I wave back as he drives off.

He didn't have to take us here or turn down our money. He could have taken one look at us and figured us for hoodlums. But this isn't Mogador. Here, it's not considered weak to help someone else.

This driver is exactly the kind of person One and the other Garde are fighting to protect. The kind of person my race wants to enslave or slaughter.

I can't—I won't—let that happen. So I buy two tickets to Kansas City.

Dust is safely tucked away in my pocket, in lizard form, and we all settle in for the trip.

As our bus speeds off down the highway, Rex closes his eyes. I look over at him and wonder what he's thinking. Part of me wants to believe that spending time with me and Dust has changed him. That maybe he's struggling with himself the way I once did, questioning the tenets of the Good Book that have been drilled into his head since he learned to walk.

I wonder too if he wants to know why no one's out looking for him. If he's angry to learn exactly how disposable he is to the Mogadorians. I know how it feels.

Eventually I drift off to sleep. As I do, One appears to me again. I know it's not really her. Sometimes a dream is just a dream. But she speaks to me in her own voice for the first time in ages. "You're different from him," she reminds me. "You can't trust him. Hate is in his blood. It always will be."

"It's in my blood too," I say.

"*Was* in your blood. Until you met me."

When I wake up, I wonder if she's right. I honestly don't know the answer. Maybe I never will.

Almost exactly a day later, we pull into Kansas City. Union Station is a big, imposing stone building, easily a city block in every direction, and I gaze up at it as we step out of our bus.

"You think we can catch a train straight to New York from here?" Rex asks as we walk across the polished marble floor. I feel strange to be back in a crowd after the loneliness of the last few weeks. The place is packed, with lots of people coming and going, including plenty of college kids. The hectic nature of it all makes me a little antsy, but I know it's a good thing. We can blend right in.

"I don't know," I admit. There's a row of ticketing machines off to one side of the actual service counters, and I step up to one of those. When I punch in New York as our destination, I get an unpleasant surprise.

"No, there's nothing that goes straight there," I reply finally, staring at the screen as if that'll make it change its mind. "We can get from here to Chicago, though, and then from Chicago to New York." I study the information a bit more. "It'll take thirty-three hours in all," I report, "and cost us about three hundred per ticket." That's more money than I'd like to spend—it will leave barely any cash in our pockets—and I don't want to spare the time either, but I don't see much we can do about it.

The way Rex sighs, I'm pretty sure he agrees. "Fine," he says finally. "Just do it."

As I'm about to hit PURCHASE TICKETS I see a strange reflection in the screen. Someone is walking by and glancing my way—I know because there's a faint flicker of pale skin with a dark band across it—sunglasses. The rest of the reflection is dark too—dark coat, dark hat. Almost exactly like Mog scouts wear. Panic flashes through me and I whip around, but I can't find the figure or anyone like him in the crowd.

I get an idea. I change our destination to St. Louis—that's only thirty bucks apiece instead of three hundred—and buy the tickets. I take the tickets but leave the receipt behind, and turn away fast. "Come on."

Rex sticks with me without a word as we hurry down the hall to our platform. I keep moving to the end, then quickly push through the door marked EXIT—AUTHORIZED PERSONNEL ONLY.

"What're we doing?" he asks as we step outside. Just as I'd hoped, we're in the rail yard itself. There're trains everywhere, and a few people loading luggage or refueling or just walking around checking on things. None of them pays us any attention, and I don't look their way more than a second either. The best plan, I figure, is to move fast and look like I know what I'm doing.

Maybe I'll even convince myself.

There's still Rex to deal with though. "We're not getting on our train, are we?" he asks, putting a hand on my arm and pulling me to a stop. "What's up?"

Well, the moment of truth. I square my shoulders. "I think I saw a scout," I tell him, watching him closely. And then I wait. And tense, gathering my strength. If he tries to grab me, I think I can use my Legacy to knock him down long enough for me to lose him in the yard, but I'd rather not do that unless I really have to. And I still have Dust in my pocket.

After a few seconds that feel like forever, he nods. "So what now?"

"Now we hitch a ride instead." I gesture toward the freight trains on the other side of the yard.

Surprisingly, Rex grins. "All right, then!" And he breaks into a jog. I guess it makes sense he'd get into the idea of something as physical—and as dangerous—as train hopping. Ivan probably would have loved it too.

"How're we gonna know which train to hop?" Rex asks over his shoulder as he slows by the first group of cars. "Are they labeled or something?"

I glance at the cars, hoping they have address labels or big destination signs like buses, but each one just has a number, plus stuff like the manufacturer and model. "I don't know," I admit. "I'm making this up as I go along." Rex snorts. But then I spot a guy walking around in a rail-yard uniform, carrying a clipboard. "I bet he'd know."

"Yeah?" Rex scoffs as we both slide between two cars so the guy won't see us. "What, you gonna go ask him?"

The man's past us now—and as I watch he heads to a little shack in the center of the yard and enters it. But not before hanging the clipboard on a hook outside. "Not me, maybe," I answer, grinning. "Dust?"

I pull him out of my pocket and hold him in my palm. He twitches his tail as if to tell me he's ready for action. We've developed such a rapport that it some-times feels like he knows what I want before I know it myself.

"We need that clipboard." In a flash, he's a hawk again, arrowing across the yard. He swoops down, snags the clipboard between his talons and then soars up into the sky. The few people who see him gasp and stare, but lose him in the sun—which is why nobody notices when he drops down to my shoulder a minute later. He changes back into a lizard as he lands, and the clipboard falls free, right onto the ground for me to scoop it up. "Nice one," I say.

I scan the list. "Here," I say after a second, stabbing a finger at one line. "There's a train heading to Philly in a few minutes. Track twelve." All the tracks are num-bered, and twelve is only a few rows away. "Let's go."

Rex nods and we take off, but then he pauses, stoops down—and comes back up with a thick, blackened metal spike. "To jam the door open," he explains. "Slid-ing doors, probably won't open from the inside." That makes sense. Of course, it also means that now he has a blunt object that he can use as a weapon.

He doesn't try anything, though. We get to track twelve just as the train starts to rumble into motion. I quickly spot a boxcar and start moving toward it, but Rex is on board before I'm even to the train: he jogs over, hauls himself onto the ladder affixed to the side and yanks the door right open. Then he swings in and, kneeling down, slams the spike under the door's bottom edge to keep it from closing.

It bothers me a little to see exactly what a miraculous recovery he's made. When we left the base, he could barely move his arm and now he's swinging around like a champion athlete. As if it's nothing. Instinctively I pat my pocket, reassured by Dust's very presence.

"Come on!" Rex calls. "Let's go!"

I pick up the pace. Unfortunately, so does the train. I manage to get a hand on the ladder, but I can't jump up without stopping first.

My feet are scraping the ground now, the train accelerating beyond what I can manage, and I'm forced to pull my legs up and grip the ladder for dear life. If I fall now I'll probably get pulled under the wheels. My hands are starting to lose their grip, my feet are drifting down again and the ground is now whistling past below me. If I don't do something, and fast, I'm not going to go any farther because I'll be nothing but a smear across a few miles of Missouri track.

Rex solves that problem. He reaches down and grabs me around the chest just below my arm, then he just lets himself fall back, pulling me with him into the boxcar. We both land on the worn wooden floor with a thud and lay there a second, winded.

Then he starts to laugh.

"Woo!" he shouts, still laying there, the biggest grin I've seen yet plastered all over his face. "We just jumped onto a moving train!"

I smile too. Rex just saved my life. Now we're even. Maybe there's hope for him after all.

We have to hide once, in Columbus, Ohio, when the train stops and rail-yard cops check all the cars for stowaways like us, but it's easy to hear them coming. We just duck out of the boxcar as soon as the train lurches to a halt, taking the spike with us, and then circle around, hopping back on once they've gone.

It would almost be fun if I wasn't so preoccupied with what's going to happen once we get to New York. I still have no idea how we're going to make it to Plum Island at all, much less how I'm going to get inside, get past whatever security measures the Mogs have and free the Chimæra.

It's overwhelming, but I'm starting to doubt myself less now. When I look back and think of how much I've managed to accomplish since I left Ashwood, I'm amazed. I could actually pull this off.

However, I still haven't managed to get in touch with Malcolm, and *that* is worrying me. Why wouldn't he be answering his phone? Unless he never got to the Garde at all.

I can't let myself think about what that would mean.

Rex and I are silent for most of the trip, but somewhere halfway through the journey, as I'm watching the countryside fly by, I surprise myself with the sound of my own voice.

"Why destroy it all? What's the point?"

Rex doesn't hesitate before he rattles off one of the most important tenets from the Good Book. "*Conquer, consume, cauterize.*" He shrugs. "It's what we do."

It's a phrase I've heard so many times that I'll be able to repeat it by heart for the rest of my life. It's the perfect summation of the Mog objective—travel to a new world, conquer it completely, drain all of its resources, then leave it a burnt-out husk and move on to the next one. It used to make sense to me.

"But why?" I ask. "Don't you ever question it?"

"Because it's the way of the universe. It's the way progress happens. The Piken eats the Kraul. He doesn't feel guilty about it. He just does it."

"Because he has to," I argue. "Survival is one thing. This is different."

Rex's face hardens into a stubborn frown. "Look at what happened on Lorien. They had so much power. Their Legacies alone should have allowed them to fight us off easily. But they'd gotten soft. Even with all that power, they were weak. Their world was stagnating. It was disgusting."

"They were happy. What's disgusting about that?"

He fixes me with a glare so hard that I can practically feel it. "I almost forgot who you are," he says coldly. It's the voice of the old Rex. "I forgot *what* you are. And what you've done. I won't forget again."

Then I know that, whatever came over Rex on the course of this trip, it was only temporary. He's not going to change. It's in his blood. And when we get to Plum Island, he won't need me anymore. He'll be back with his true people; he'll have no reason not to turn on me.

I look away. I'm alone again. I don't even know where Dust is—he turned himself into a mouse a few hours ago and has been exploring the train on his own ever since.

Ten hours after Rex pulled me on board, we arrive in Philly in silence. We haven't said a word since our argument.

Dust appears from behind a crate and slides into my pocket as Rex is jumping out into the rail yard. I'm about to follow behind him when I see that he's left the railroad spike behind. I guess he thinks I'm so weak that he doesn't need it. I shove it in my pocket and leap out into the chilly Philadelphia night.

We've still barely spoken more than a few words to each other as we're boarding the bus to Manhattan. Then, in theory, it's just a quick hop over to Plum Island.

After that . . . I don't know. I've been weighing my choices. I wonder if Rex has too. As we were buying our bus tickets, I thought about ditching him altogether. Losing him in the crowd and trying to make it to Plum Island on my own. I came pretty close to doing it, and I would have if I thought it would help. It would be pointless, though. He knows where I'm going and what I want. On top of that, I have a feeling I'll need his help getting inside.

Then again, it's entirely possible he's already alerted the Mogadorians that he's on his way with his trophy—me—in tow.

"Last stop before we hit the Lincoln Tunnel," the bus driver announces, pulling into a rest area. "Twenty-minute break. I suggest you stretch your legs and use the facilities, people. Traffic in the tunnel can get pretty crazy."

I signal that I'm going to pee, and together Rex and I climb out of our seats and follow most of the other passengers off the bus. The ride's been uneventful so far, which suits me just fine. We should be in Manhattan in about an hour, maybe less.

"I'm gonna grab some more snacks," Rex tells me sullenly as we're walking across the parking lot. I just nod. He nods back and heads off towards the cluster of vending machines.

In the bathroom, I lock the stall door behind me and try Malcolm one more time, praying that this time he'll answer.

Still nothing.

As soon as I allow myself to consider the worst, my mind feels like a big ball of yarn that's coming quickly unraveled. I can't stop the what-ifs: What if they got caught fleeing Dulce? Or worse, what if the explosion took them out along with all the Mogs there? What if I killed my only friend, and his son we went there to save?

What if he never found the Garde? He's the only one who can lead me to them. If he's not with the Garde, that means I have no hope of finding them myself. Ever.

No, I tell myself. Malcolm's smart, and he's cautious. He's probably being careful about how he communicates. If he *is* with the Garde, he won't want to risk having his cell phone traced and their location discovered. Anyway, it's not like he's not expecting to hear from me. As far as he's concerned, I'm dead.

It all makes perfect sense. It just doesn't make me feel any better.

I'm stepping back out of the bathroom a few minutes later when it happens: I find my way blocked by two men. They're dressed identically in black trench coats, black hats and black sunglasses. They're both pale beneath those outfits—a little too pale. As soon as I lay eyes on them, they both smile at me, their wide mouths spreading open to reveal toothy, shark-like grins.

I turn around instantly and try to shove my way back into the bathroom. Maybe there's a window I can escape through or something.

I never get that far. They have me by the arms. Rex is nowhere to be seen.

The Mogadorians have found me.

CHAPTER
NINE

"TOOK A WHILE TO CATCH UP WITH YOU, ADA-mus," the one on the right says. "You almost managed to slip past us."

"Almost," the one on the left echoes. He pulls his hands out of his pockets. No surprise, he's holding a dagger in one and a blaster in the other. Standard Mog scout weaponry.

Lucky for me, what I'm carrying is nonstandard. And after my initial shock, I'm more resigned than frightened. I've been looking over my shoulder for Mogs this whole time, and in a way it's almost a relief that they're finally here. Still, there's something I need to know. "How'd you find me?"

They just laugh at that. Unlike me and Rex and the rest of the trueborn, most scouts are vatborn and have the triangular, fang-like teeth to prove it. Their smiles really do look like a shark's.

They don't need to tell me the answer. I already know: it was Rex. It had to have been. While I was in the bathroom trying to call Malcolm, he was calling in the big guns. He was betraying me. And I hate him for that.

I'm not scared. I'm not sad. I'm certainly not relieved anymore. I'm just angry.

The vatborn's laughter stops when the ground beneath them ripples upwards like it's water, tossing them off their feet.

The one on the left loses his grip on his blaster, and I dive for it, scoop it up and shoot him point-blank. Poof. I'm already sighting on the second one by the time he crumbles to ash. If Rex thinks I'm not a worthy opponent just because I'm not as big as him, or because I don't believe that Setrákus Ra's stupid fortune-cookie rules are words to live by, he needs to think again.

I have to get out of here. There are too many people in too small a space, and if there's going to be a big battle here there's no telling how many innocent people could be hurt.

Before anyone can stop me I make a beeline for the rear exit and slam right through it without stopping. A hundred heads turn to stare at me, but I don't care.

Outside, I find myself in a wide-open parking lot, empty except for a few untended sixteen-wheelers. I'm looking frantically for cover when I hear the distinctive, high-pitched whine of a Mog hand cannon powering up to fire from somewhere behind me. I hurl myself to the side, hitting the ground hard just as the energy blast sizzles past me. The pavement is smoking, a circular hole in the exact spot where I was just standing.

Glancing up from the ground, I see a quartet of Mog soldiers tromping toward me, rifles and hand cannons aimed in my direction.

Too bad for them. Now they've pissed me off.

I feel my face clenching up in fury, and my body trembles as I send a quake through the ground. The two Mogs nearest to me go toppling like bowling pins. In the confusion, I dive behind one of the trucks, buying myself some time while my remaining pursuers split up to look for me.

When I don't hear anything for a minute or so, I peek out quickly from behind the cab and see another soldier coming toward me. He's alone—too easy. He's a goner before he even knows I've zapped him with my stolen blaster.

Five down, one left—not counting Rex.

Of course, that's assuming that there aren't more I don't know about yet.

I should be so lucky. I hear more footsteps approaching—and getting louder. They're coming fast.

I suppose it was too much to hope the High Command had only sent two scouts and four soldiers after me. But when I poke my head over the cab again and see dozens of Mogs pouring through the parking lot from every possible direction, blasters and cannons at the ready, I have to say it seems like overkill. I guess I should be flattered, not just that they think I'm worth the trouble, but that whoever sent them here considers me such a formidable adversary.

Ducking down, I peer below the truck and spot a Mog marching toward me, shooting at my shelter to keep me pinned down while he advances. Too bad he wasn't watching the tires. I shoot him in the leg and, when he drops, put another blast in his head, finishing him off. Then I pull myself to my feet and scan the area. "Dust!" I scream. Where the hell is he?

For that matter, where's Rex? Not that I really want to know.

More soldiers round the corner of the building, and my stomach clenches. They're spreading out in front of me, so I won't be able to take them all down at once. I crouch behind the truck again, but I know I won't be able to hold out like this much longer.

How is this at all worth it?

I've never hated my own race more than I do right now. Mostly, though, I hate Rex. Not because he betrayed me. No. I hate him because, before he could betray me, he made me trust him.

At least my anger's good for something. I focus in on it and stomp a foot on the ground. This tremor is the strongest one yet. I can feel it flowing out through my body like a giant ocean wave originating in my rib cage.

Some of the soldiers topple. Others wobble but stay standing. One or two drop their weapons.

I grit my teeth. Using my Legacy is exhausting me and I don't know how much longer I'll be able to keep it up. But I have to. I stomp again.

A few more go down, but now the rest are shooting at me.

I'm trying to figure out what to do next when I hear a ferocious roar. Glancing over my vehicular shield I see a large, tawny shape leap from the trees and grab one soldier by the shoulder, yanking him to the ground. Dust roars and lunges again, his massive jaw snapping shut like a trap around his quarry's neck. The soldier's scream dies mid-shriek, his body convulsing as it turns to ash.

But the lion has already moved on. He's ripping through the soldiers easily, their fire barely slowing him down. Dust claws and bites, not stopping to consider any individual enemy for more than a split second before moving on.

The Mogs still left standing are confused—they didn't plan for this, and now they're not sure whether they're supposed to be shooting me or Dust, or whether it's time to retreat altogether.

I take advantage of the confusion. Two soldiers are backed up almost to me, and I shoot them both before they remember that I'm still a threat too. Dust's finished off another soldier, and several more have taken shelter around the side of the main structure—collapsing something is one trick I got pretty good at with Malcolm, and though it causes spikes of pain to shoot through my forehead I shake the roof loose and drop it on those soldiers, easily crushing them. That leaves only two, and they move away from Dust and me both, shooting at him to keep him back and edging away toward the trees where they must have a ship waiting.

If they reach it I'm toast.

I'm using my Legacy far beyond anything I've ever tried in the past, and every time I cause a new quake I'm more and more exhausted. My vision's starting to go dark around the edges, but I know I don't have any choice except to fight through it. I concentrate and send a tremor under a nice thick tree, the same way I did to the guard station back at Dulce Base. It topples with a loud groan and crushes one of the soldiers beneath its trunk. The last Mog simply turns and runs, but Dust is on him in an instant in a blur of teeth and claws. A few seconds later he's trotting back toward me, his mouth coated in ash. He doesn't seem fazed by this. That makes one of us.

"Thanks," I manage to mumble weakly when he reaches me. Then everything goes black.

When I wake up, I'm in the passenger seat of a car flying along the highway. My head's still pounding and my vision's still blurry. The New York City skyline is barely recognizable over the dashboard as an abstract haze of lights. I have no idea how I got here or where I'm headed. The events of the past few hours bounce around in my skull like a million Ping-Pong balls. Everything's jumbled and hard to make sense of.

Groaning, I look over to the driver's seat. Behind the wheel is Rex. Even in my messed-up state, I fumble with the door handle. *I'll jump out right here,* I think. *I'd rather be instant roadkill than spend another second letting him think I trust him.*

"Hey!" he says when he sees me fumbling to escape. Before I can get the door open, he reaches to the console on the dashboard and locks all the doors. I'm trapped.

"Calm down," he says. "I don't know what you did in that parking lot, but whatever it was it took a lot out of you."

I don't want to hear it. "Where the hell were you?" I demand. "What the hell happened back there?"

Rex barely glances up from the road. "Same thing that happened to you," he says calmly, as if I'd just asked him to remind me of tomorrow's weather forecast. "The Mogs got to me too. They must think I'm on your side now. I fought them off, but by the time I got rid of them and made it to you, this guy was already on it." He points to a lump on the dashboard, which I only then realize is Dust, in his lizard form. "When I found you, you were passed out on the pavement, and Dust's just sitting there, practically on top of you, watching over you like he's your mom or something. He barely even let *me* come near you. Anyway, what's done is done. We got away. What do you think of the car? I stole it."

If he expects me to believe any of that story, he's an idiot. I want to tell him so, but with my head still swimming I only manage to spit out one short sentence. "Screw you, Rex," I say just as everything fades to black again.

CHAPTER
TEN

I COME TO IN ANOTHER PARKING LOT, FINALLY
feeling myself again. Sort of, at least.

Based on the light streaming into the car, it must be
morning. Rex has the windows rolled down and the air
smells vaguely of the ocean.

"Finally," he says when he sees me stirring. "I was
beginning to think you were gone for good."

I sit up. I look at him. I can't believe how stupid I feel.
I knew exactly what he was up to all along and I let him
get away with it anyway.

"You betrayed me," I say.

He just laughs. "I knew you were going to say that.
Kind of funny, right? You're a traitor to your entire race,
and you're mad at *me*?"

I get ready to hit him with every bit of tectonic force
I have left at my disposal, but as soon as I so much as
think about it I start to feel faint again.

"You seriously expect me to believe you weren't the one who called in the Mogadorian mafia? You go mysteriously missing just as they show up and then you somehow don't reappear until I've fought them all off?"

"I told you," he said. "They attacked me too."

"Sure. Right." I know he's full of shit, but I honestly don't know what to do about it. What I don't understand is why he's toying with me like this. If he wanted to kill me, he could have killed me by now. He could have called in more Mogs.

Instead, I'm still alive, still uncaptured, sitting unscathed in the passenger seat of a carjacked sedan with Dust on my lap, whining at me.

I look out the window and I see where we are. Sort of, at least. We're somewhere on the water. A foghorn blares and I squint out the window to see a ferry crawling across the water and into view.

"You wanted to go to Plum Island, right?" Rex says, seeing the confused look on my face. "How else are we going to get there except by boat?"

I still don't believe he didn't give the Mogs our location. But then that doesn't explain why he came to get me, why he helped me escape. He could have just left me at the rest stop, left me to get caught by the Mogs, by the cops, whoever. I need some air. I need to get out of this car. Rex doesn't try to stop me when I open the car door. Dust jumps out onto the pavement and I'm right behind him.

Rex finds me on a bench half an hour later. I don't know what else to do, so I'm just sitting. I've tried calling Malcolm. No answer. I tried picturing One in my head. It would have helped just to imagine her face. But it wouldn't come to me. Even golden retriever Dust has given up trying to make me feel better. He's just lying at my feet.

"I didn't tell them," Rex says. He's standing a few paces away but doesn't try to come any closer. "The scouts have been following you all along. They missed you a few times and then I think you gave them the drop when you decided to hop the train. But they were going to catch up eventually."

"Where were you, then?" I ask. "Don't try to tell me they attacked you too."

"The truth?"

"Yeah," I say. "For once. The truth."

Rex pauses. "I was hiding," he finally says. "They might have already seen me with you, but I didn't want them to see me fighting to save you—to think that I'm a traitor. So I hid."

I examine his face for signs that he's lying. I honestly have no idea. I don't know why it matters. But it does.

"So you were just going to let them kill me?"

He looks at the sky. "Yeah," he says. "I guess I was. If it came to that."

"But now you're helping me?"

"Yup."

"I don't get it. Why?"

Rex shuffles his feet nervously. "I don't know," he says. "I still believe in the Mogadorian cause. I still believe in Setrákus Ra's principles. When it comes time to fight, I'll be there with the rest of my brothers—if I'm still allowed to be. War is in my blood. But I'm helping you anyway. You don't have to believe me if you don't want to. I can't explain it even to myself. But it's the truth."

I don't answer him. I don't know how.

"So do you want to go to Plum Island and rescue the Chimæra or not?" he finally asks.

The ferry doesn't go to Plum Island. There's no reason it should—normal Americans need the highest level of clearance even to set foot on the island. That rules out getting there openly.

But in a seaside community like this, most people own a boat, at least a little one. Rex and I spend the afternoon peering into unattended garages until we find ourselves hauling a small rowboat towards the harbor. We stash it behind some trees in the neighboring park until the sun's going down and we see the last ferry pull in. Then we wait another half hour just to be sure no one will spot us and drag it to the end of the dock. From there it's easy enough to flip it over and lay it into the water, climb in and start rowing.

While I'd spent my morning passed out, Rex had been coming up with a plan to get us inside the facility. Sitting across from me in our rowboat, he explains it to me. It's so simple that it sounds absurd.

"I'll tell them you're my prisoner," he says. "That I tracked you from New Mexico until I captured you and brought you here. They're looking for you, right? They send that many scouts to get you, they think you're important. It might even go all the way up the chain to Setrákus Ra. If I bring you in, there's no chance they'll turn you away."

"They could just shoot me on sight," I say.

Rex scrunches his face and shakes his head. In the distance, I see lights. We're getting closer. "Nah," he says. "First, they'll want to know how you took down Dulce. Hell, I want to know that myself." A quick grin surfaces. "Then they'll shoot you."

"Gee, thanks." I glance over to where Dust is gliding along beside us in hawk form, tilting to one side from time to time so a wingtip knifes through the water. "We don't know anything about who they've got there, how they're set up, what they've heard, what—"

Rex stops me. "Will you relax? Trust me, I know how our military works. I've got this covered."

If I had to make a list of all the people I trusted, it would be a really short list, and Rex wouldn't be on it. Even if I did trust him, I still wouldn't like the plan. What if they know Rex has been working with me all this time? What if they kill us before we even get the chance to explain ourselves? It all relies too much on faith—and after yesterday, faith is something I'm pretty much all out of.

But before I can argue, Dust lands on the edge of the boat. He's flapping his wings furiously, and then he shifts into cat form. Just as quickly, he changes again, this time into a wolf. He's too big for the boat and nearly tips over, but now he's shifting so quickly that I start to lose track of what he's even supposed to *be*. And he's making a noise that's so loud I have to put my fingers in my ears, halfway between a howl and a trumpet blast, deep and quivery. I've never heard anything like it.

"Dust," I say. "What's wrong?"

I put my hand out to rub him in the hope that it will calm him down. His body feels like liquid, but it does the trick— he's starting to get control of himself again. As he settles into lizard form, he finally quiets down. He's still agitated though. He's darting around the floor of the boat, cocking his head frantically in every direction, sniffing the air. It looks like he's hearing something that Rex and I can't—almost like there's something calling to him.

It's very weird, but I don't know what to do about it. The island's close enough now that I think I can just see where that harbor opens up. Rex pulls the oars in. "You ready to do this?" he asks. I'm not ready at all, but I nod. At least Dust has settled down enough to climb into the pocket of my hoodie. I can still feel him twitching nervously in there, but it seems like he's getting back to normal.

Rex doesn't pay any attention to how uneasy this is making me. He just digs through his pockets until he pulls out the plastic ties that he bought from a local hardware store while we'd been waiting for the ferries to clear out for the day.

"Give me your wrists," he says. Every bit of my common sense is telling me not to do it. Letting myself be tied up and marched into a Mogadorian stronghold by a Mog I barely trust—doesn't sound like the most brilliant scheme, does it?

Certain I'm walking into some kind of incredibly elaborate trap, I offer up my hands anyway. I've come this far. What else can I do but take the risk?

Within seconds Rex has me expertly bound. It's almost like we're back to the way we started at Dulce: one guard and one prisoner, this time with our roles reversed.

Hopefully it's just for show.

We're a few meters from the shore when a blinding

searchlight engulfs us in its dazzling beam and a booming voice calls out. "Stop! Identify yourself!"

Rex straightens. "Rexicus Saturnus, from Dulce," he shouts back. "And a prisoner!" He grabs my hands and raises them so those watching can see the restraints.

The pause has me sweating despite the chill coming off the waves, but finally the voice replies, "Come ahead." They don't offer to pick us up, but instead stay back and let Rex row us the rest of the way in. Typical Mogs.

"Shouldn't there be regular soldiers here?" I whisper. "Instead of Mogadorians?"

"Used to be that way," Rex says. "But we're getting more and more power in the American government lately. Pretty soon the White House'll be run by Mogadorians too."

It's a scary thought—and one that would have made me incredibly excited just a few short years ago.

At the sound of the Mogadorians shouting at us, Dust has crawled from my pocket. And before I have time to even say good-bye, he's turned into a hummingbird and is gone into the night sky.

I know it's for the best. If I'm going to be thrown into a cell, I don't want him trapped in there with me. Nonetheless, I feel incredibly vulnerable without him.

The feeling only intensifies when I see the squad of soldiers waiting for us on the dock, weapons drawn.

They wait until our little rowboat bumps up against the logs and then reach down and haul us up.

"Who's this?" the Mog officer in charge demands, staring into my eyes and grabbing me roughly by the arm.

"A low-life traitor," Rex replies. "Adamus Sutekh, son of General Andrakkus Sutekh." He punches me in the stomach, hard enough to double me over and leave me gasping for breath.

The captain's frowning at us. He's trueborn, of course, but the underlings flanking him are all vat-born, big and pale and typically creepy. "Why bring him here?" the captain asks after a second. "And what exactly happened at Dulce? We lost all communication with it—sent some scouts in but they reported the whole place destroyed."

"*He* happened," Rex replies, gesturing towards me. The captain's frown deepens, and Rex hurries to explain. "I was stationed at Dulce Base. This traitor showed up with a human ally and attacked. They blew up the base. I was only stunned—I woke up in time to see him slip away, so I followed him all the way from Dulce to here. Once I was sure this was his next target, I captured him and brought him in for questioning."

The captain nods. I can't believe he's buying this load of horseshit, but he is. "Good job," he says. "We'll notify the general and find out if he wants to question his son personally. In the meantime, Rexicus, you'll need to be debriefed."

He gestures at two of the soldiers. "Throw the traitor in a cell for now, but don't get too carried away—the general will want to handle his punishment personally."

Then he leads Rex away while the guards grab me and march me toward a long, low building a few hundred feet from the harbor. Damn. It's not even in the main building. This is going to make things very difficult. When they throw me into my cell, I'm still trying to decide whether Rex sold me out or if everything's going exactly according to plan.

CHAPTER ELEVEN

I DON'T KNOW HOW LONG IT'S BEEN. HOURS? Days? But no one has come by since those guards threw me in here. I guess they're taking their commander's orders to leave me alone until my father comes to retrieve me to heart. I'm cursing myself for thinking Rex was actually on my side, for letting him get the better of me. I thought I could trust him.

Then I hear the click of the lock on my cell door. It's too dark to make out who's standing there, but I easily recognize Rex's voice. "Sorry I took so long," he says.

Then something hits me in the face and chest—something lightweight, flexible, a little scratchy. "Put those on!"

It's pants and a jacket, all standard military issue, and I hurriedly do as I'm told. "Where have you been?" I demand as I change.

"I had to be sure they didn't suspect anything," Rex

replies, holding the cell door wide-open and beckoning me to follow. "And I had to find out where they were holding the Chimæra. Here." He hands me a military cap, and I pull that on as well. Smart thinking—I'm clearly a Mog but my long hair definitely isn't a soldier's cut. Plus the cap helps hide my face, in case anyone might recognize me.

"So? Where are they?" I ask as he leads me out of the building. I'm surprised there aren't any guards at all, until I see a small pile of ash in one corner and another behind a desk near the entryway.

I'm a little surprised Rex was willing to kill to get me out of here. Surprised, but grateful.

"They're keeping them in the Disease Center," he replies, easing open the brig's front door and glancing out before nodding and motioning me through. "But not the main annex—that's mostly marines and human scientists. There's a second building off to the side, staffed entirely by our people. They're in there."

That makes sense. Even though the High Command clearly has some kind of deal with the U.S. government, they wouldn't want to let any of the humans close to anything that could be used against us. And the Chimæra would definitely qualify. "How do we get there?"

He grins as we step around the side of the jail and stop at a military jeep that's sitting there, already idling. Rex doesn't hit the lights until we're clear of the last building and our view of the harbor is swallowed up among the trees.

It only takes a couple minutes to curve up and around to the Disease Center—the advantages of an island that's only a few miles in any direction. The main building is enormous and looks like a research lab crossed with a school, but sure enough there's a smaller, warehouse-like building off to one side. We head over that way. There are Mog soldiers standing guard outside, but they salute Rex and step aside to let us pass. Interesting.

"This is our main base on the island," he explains once we're through the doors and walking along a wide, rough, cement-floored hall. "Where they're keeping the Chimæra will require security clearance, but out here we're good." Which is obviously true, but I can't help wondering how we're going to get back out past those same guards without setting off alarms. Especially with however many Chimæra there are in tow.

"We lucked out too," Rex is saying. We head up one flight of stairs, then another. "They were being held in the basement, but two days ago I hear they all went nuts. They trashed the place completely. So they were moved up here until stronger cells could be built."

Two days ago? I bet that's about the same time that Dust started freaking out on the boat. It's all got to be connected.

Speaking of which . . . "Have you seen Dust? Do you know where he is?"

"He's out there," Rex answers without glancing back. "He found me when I was grabbing the jeep. He knows what he's doing. He'll find you when the time's right."

I nod slowly. I wish Dust was with me right now, but I know Rex is right. Dust hasn't let me down yet.

We stop on the fourth floor and exit the stairwell. The ceilings up here are twelve feet tall at least, and enormous windows cover most of the walls, though they're barred. Despite the concrete floors and thick stone outer walls and corrugated metal inner walls, the space still has a light, airy feel.

And doors. Lots and lots of doors.

"They're up here somewhere," Rex assures me, opening the first door at hand and peering in. He shakes his head and slides it shut again. I open another door, but it leads to a small office. Empty, fortunately. "Nope." The next one is a supply closet, also not much help. The door after that, however, opens onto a large room that looks like an operating theater—there are instruments arrayed on trays positioned around a large exam table. It's also empty, which I consider a very good thing. I really wouldn't want to walk in on a surgery, especially not one performed by my people. They're a lot more interested in carving up than in putting back together.

"Over here!" Rex calls, and I see he's one door down from me but on the other side of the hall. I cross quickly and peer inside with him. It's like a big kennel, with wire cages lined up against the far wall. Could this be it?

"Shut the door," I whisper, stepping through to study the cages and their inhabitants. The first cage looks empty, save for some sort of goo smeared across the floor. But when I step a little closer, the goo suddenly rears up, flowing into a shape like a raccoon or maybe a weasel, narrow and wiry with dark, matted fur, a sharply pointed face and beady little eyes.

And then it screams.

I've never heard anything like it. And I hope I never will again. It's high and shrill and makes my entire body feel like a glass that's about to shatter. I stumble back a pace, off balance, then another, until the screeching stops. The goo settles, dropping back to the cage floor. Rex and I stare at each other. What the hell was that?

Whatever it was, there's nothing I can do to help it, not if it's going to scream bloody murder and completely paralyze me every time I get close.

The next cage is empty, though judging from the soiled newspapers on the bottom, it hasn't been that way for long.

The third cage contains a bird. About the size of a

parrot, it has blue feathers ranging from a deep purple so dark they look almost black to a pale blue-white like winter itself. The bird has no wings, though—where those appendages should be are two stumps, stitched and bandaged. It caws at me, a single long, chirp-like wail, and the sound brings tears to my eyes. I look over at Rex but he looks just as horrified. Either he's a better actor than I realized or he had no idea what we'd find.

"Are these . . . Chimæra?" he asks, his voice hushed and rough.

"I don't know. They might be." I shake my head. "I don't think either of those two are going anywhere, though—even if we opened their cages, how would we get them to follow us? Especially without risking whatever others we find?" I hate to abandon any of them, but I think we have to leave this pair here. I glance in the other cages quickly but they're all empty. I see a second door against the sidewall, and I hurry over to that, pull it open, and rush through, almost slamming into a pair of Mogs that are standing in front of another row of cages. One of them is short and wiry and wearing a lab coat—definitely a scientist. The other one's big and burly, though, and in military gear. They both look up as I barrel in, and the soldier's hand automatically goes for the blaster at his side. Great.

"What—who—?" the scientist starts, but I shut him

up by slamming into him as hard as I can. He flies backwards into the soldier who stumbles a step, his hands going up automatically to catch his companion. They both turn to ash a second later, and I glance back to see Rex in the doorway, blaster in hand.

He did that. Just like he killed the Mogs who were guarding my cell.

"Why . . . ," I start.

"I promised you I'd help you and I'm helping you," he says. "Let's just leave it at that." Then he looks past me. "Jackpot," he whispers.

I follow his gaze to see what he's talking about. At least four of the cages here are occupied—no, five. And all of them . . . well, the first one has a small dog, the second a little pig, the third a cat, the fourth a raccoon, and the fifth a brightly colored bird. Then I blink, and now they're an owl, a goat, a rat, a beaver, and a monkey. Then they shift again, and again, a lot like Dust did the other night, only this is constant, cycling from shape to shape to shape fast enough to make them dizzying to watch.

"Is that normal?" Rex asks. He sounds just as surprised as I am. The continual shape-shifting is unsettling, to say the least.

"I don't know," I admit. Then I notice a clipboard on the ground by my feet. The scientist must have dropped it. Picking it up, I see a list of subjects, with notes next to each one. Notes like "100cc injected, change rate increased tenfold" and "lobotomy performed, cohesion shattered." Bile rises in my throat, and I have to gulp a few times before I can answer. "No. They've been experimenting on them already."

At this point, I have no idea how useful these surviving creatures will be. I'd hoped to find a bunch more like Dust, and instead I have five out-of-control shape-changing animals. Still, there's no question they're Chimæra, and I don't waste any more time wondering. Instead I step over to their cages and yank them open one by one.

"It's okay," I assure them, loud enough for all of them to hear me at once but low enough that I hope my voice won't carry beyond these walls. "We're here to help." I have no idea if they understand me, but I figure it can't hurt.

For a minute none of them move, and I can't blame them. I don't know how long they've been here, or what's been done to them, but they don't have any reason to trust a Mog—or, for all I know, humans. The one that's now—for the moment—back to being a monkey is the first one to edge over to its open door, poke its head through and then chitter at the others, shifting back and forth between forms as they pour out of their prison. A second later they're all loose, crawling and swinging and pacing and fluttering every which way.

"Right," I tell Rex. "Time to go."

Almost on cue, a siren starts blaring. Flashing lights accompany it out in the hall. Then a voice erupts from speakers in the ceiling.

"Attention, a prisoner has escaped the brig. Adamus Sutekh was last seen wearing blue jeans and a black shirt. He is five-ten, slight of build, with long hair. He is unarmed but a known traitor. If found, detain if possible—shoot if necessary. The same for any accomplices."

"Yeah," Rex agrees, shaking his head. "Definitely time to go."

CHAPTER
TWELVE

WE RACE OUT OF THE ROOM, INTO THE HALL AND down the stairwell with the Chimæra following behind us. Rex clamps a hand on my arm and hauls me back just before I start bounding down the stairs. "Not that way!" he calls after me. "They'll start checking the building at the bottom and work their way up. But there's an elevator in the back that you can only access from up here. If you can fight your way to it, you can get out that way."

I nod and let him wheel me around and half drag me up the stairs to the fifth floor. Judging by the door we've come to, which is painted bright red and is made from some kind of heavy, extra-reinforced steel, we've reached the part of the building that they really *really* want to keep people out of. With a grunt, Rex yanks it open and we step inside.

The ceilings are just as high up here, but there aren't any inner walls. Instead it's just one big room, crowded with computer stations around the edges and a massive topographical map of the East Coast in the center of the room. This is obviously the command center.

"Quick, hide!" I whisper, and duck behind a computer station. Rex does the same. I worry what the Chimæra will do, but they all stick with me, and even though they're still changing shape constantly they all shift to smaller creatures—mice and lizards and dragonflies.

Peeking out I see a few Mogs here, typing in front of monitors or marking things on transparent touch screens suspended in midair. Others are gathered in small clusters, discussing something in low tones. Nobody's noticed us yet, and they aren't mobilizing to hunt for an escaped prisoner either. I guess their work is more important. Our luck can't last though.

And—next problem. Other than the stairs we just ran up, I don't see any other way out. This may not have been Rex's best plan.

A siren begins to blare again, and I cringe, figuring this is it. They've spotted me, and they're calling guards to surround and overpower us. Even if I bring the whole building down the way I did Dulce Base, I might still be trapped. And we're currently five floors up—if the building goes, that's a long way down.

But this siren is different, more of a whoop than a shriek. And when someone starts speaking over it, what he says is not what I expected.

"Attention, all units," the announcer states, his words slightly rushed but clear. "Assemble at once. Garde located. Full-scale assault about to begin. Repeat, all units assemble at once. Full-scale assault about to begin."

They've found the Garde? Full-scale assault? I look at Rex, whose own eyes are darting everywhere. He looks worried—but excited too, with that same gleam he had when we jumped onto the train. He zeroes in on something, and I follow his gaze to a Mog officer leaning over a console. His screen is showing something—I realize all of them have the same image up now—and I rise to a crouch and edge closer to get a better look. It's a street map, but it doesn't look familiar—there's a lake instead of an ocean. It's not New York. The others in the room are rushing about, either speaking quickly into walkie-talkies or racing towards the stairs, but this guy's still at his desk. What if he turns and sees me? I've apparently just moved down on the priority list, but I'm sure if he realizes who I am he'll still grab me. I have to chance it, though. If that's where the Garde have been hiding, Malcolm may be there as well.

I take a few more steps, and now I can make out more details, including place names. Shedd Aquarium, Water Tower Place, North Lake Shore Drive, Lake Michigan—it's Chicago. They're in Chicago. And the building that's dead center on the screen is the John Hancock Center. That must be where the Garde are.

Just as I realize that, the Mog sitting there turns. And sees me.

"Hey—" he starts, half rising from his chair. He looks confused, like he knows I'm not supposed to be there but hasn't totally figured out that I'm the escaped prisoner. Then he notices something at my shoulder, and his eyes go wide. Out of the corner of my eye I see a butterfly there—and a second later it's a hummingbird, then a bumblebee. Crap. He's just realized who I am.

I'm only a few steps away from him at this point. I close the distance fast, and slam my fist into his jaw as hard as I can. His eyes glaze over and he slumps back into his chair. A quick scan of the room tells me no one else noticed.

I guess all those years of sparring with Ivan were worth something after all.

"You've got to get out of here," Rex warns, moving up beside me and grabbing my arm again. "Now, while everyone's rushing to deploy."

I nod, then stop. "*I've* got to get out of here?"

He looks down, then away. "Look," he starts. "You saved my life. I owe you. And I didn't betray you—I haven't and I won't. But—" He shrugs. "I'm not like you. I already told you that. I was just keeping my promise. I get that you probably have reasons for what you did, and maybe they make sense to you. But not to me. This is where I belong. It's who I am."

It's obvious that there's no changing his mind. And he's *not* like me. As far as I know, no other Mog is. He believes everything we were taught about being the superior race and having the right to rule, to control, to destroy. Maybe he's come to appreciate things a little more from our time together, but at his core he's still a loyal soldier. And sooner or later I believe he'd betray me—our beliefs are just too different.

So I just nod, and hold out my hand. He clasps it, claps me on the back and gives me a quick grin. "Tell Dust I said good-bye," he says, already turning towards the stairs. Then he's gone. If he's lucky, no one will realize he helped me. I actually hope that's the case.

I'm left alone in the command center, me and a handful of messed-up Chimæra—and a bunch of Mog officers who are just starting to notice the fugitive and his strange menagerie in their midst.

"It's the traitor!" one of them shouts, breaking that frozen moment of recognition. "Get him!"

He rushes towards me, along with a few of the others. That's when a huge white owl comes crashing through the window.

It's Dust. Shattered glass is flying everywhere, and before it can even hit the ground he's already shifting.

By the time he lands, he's blocking the way between me and the Mogadorians. He's a wolf again, just like the first time I saw him.

This time, though, he lets out a guttural, almost primordial howl. The first of the guards doesn't even have time to disintegrate before he's been torn to shreds. At that, the rest of them do something I've never seen a Mogadorian do before. They run.

CHAPTER
THIRTEEN

SEVERAL HOURS LATER, I'M SPEEDING ALONG the highway in a stolen car packed with Chimæra, heading toward Chicago. The creatures have finally stabilized their shapes and have mostly managed to settle down.

It's still the weirdest road trip I've ever taken. Not to mention the smelliest.

But I'm making good time. I'm almost to the Illinois border when, after the fifth try, Malcolm's phone finally picks up.

"Malcolm!" I shout immediately, juggling the phone to my other hand as the light changes and I ease through the intersection. "Where have you been?!"

But the voice that answers isn't his. "This is Sam." There's a pause. "Adam, is that you?"

"Sam?" It takes me a second—we didn't exactly get introduced, and I'm a little stressed right now.

Then I remember. "Sam! Where's your father?"

"He's—"

"Never mind! It doesn't matter!" I switch the phone to my other hand so I can drive properly. "Listen to me, Sam. You're in Chicago, right? The John Hancock Center?"

I can hear him suck in his breath. "How—how did you know that?"

"They know, Sam!" I don't mean to shout, but I know I am. "They know and they're coming for you!"

An oncoming car honks at me as I swerve into its lane, and I'm forced to drop the phone onto the seat beside me and concentrate on driving. I warned them. That's all I can do right now. I can only hope they listen, and that they're prepared. They've just got to hold out for a little while. I glance behind me to the backseat. Dust has taken the form of a cat again, and is curled up around his recovered kin. He looks up and meets my gaze, his golden eyes to my black ones, and growls slightly, but I know that warning isn't meant for me. It's for the ones who did this to the other Chimæra.

Just hang on, Malcolm, I pray as I press down on the gas and the car leaps forwards, racing into the night. I'm coming. And I've got the cavalry with me.

I hope One, wherever she is now, knows what I've done. What I'm doing. I'd like to think she does, that there's still a part of her out there somewhere.

No. One's gone. I finally accept the truth: if she lives on in any way at all it's not because she's a ghost or a lingering psychic imprint. All that's left of her is what I've held on to in my memories. The things she told me; the way she taught me to live.

She's not coming back. I don't need her to. I know she's proud of me because I'm proud of myself.

Because I remember her.

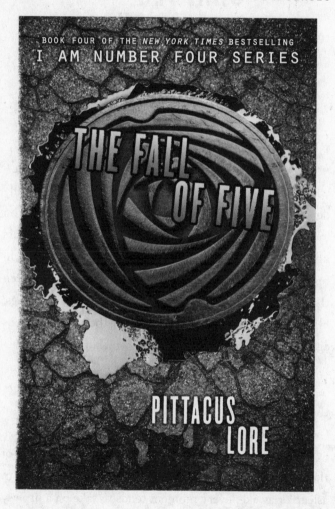

BOOK FOUR OF THE *NEW YORK TIMES* BESTSELLING
I AM NUMBER FOUR SERIES

THE FALL OF FIVE

PITTACUS LORE

CHAPTER
ONE

MOGADORIANS STANDS BETWEEN HER AND MY CELL—which isn't technically realistic. The Mogs don't usually devote any manpower whatsoever to keeping watch on me, but this is a dream, so whatever. The Mog warriors unsheathe their daggers and charge forward, howling. In response, Six tosses her hair and turns invisible. I watch through the bars of my cell as she slices through the Mogs, blinking in and out of visibility, turning their own weapons against them. She twists her way through an ever-increasing cloud of ash, the Mogs soon completely decimated.

"That was pretty awesome," I tell her, when she reaches the door of my cell. She smiles nonchalantly.

"Ready to go?" she asks.

And that's when I wake up. Or when I snap out of the daydream. Sometimes it's tough to tell whether I'm asleep or awake; every moment tends to take on a drowsy sameness when you've been kept in isolation for weeks. At least, I think it's been weeks. Hard to keep track of time since there are no windows in my cell. The only thing I'm really certain of is that my imaginings of escape aren't real. Sometimes it's like tonight and Six has come to rescue me, other times it's John, and other times I've developed Legacies of my own and I fly out of my cell, pummeling Mogadorians as I go.

It's all fantasy. Just a way for my anxious mind to pass the time.

The sweat-smelling mattress with broken springs that dig into my back? That's real. The cramps in my legs and my backache? Those are real, too.

I reach for the bucket of water on the floor next to me. A guard brings the bucket once a day along with a cheese sandwich. It's not exactly room service, even though, as far as I can tell, I'm the only prisoner being held in this cell block—it's just rows and rows of empty cells connected by steel gangways, and me alone.

The guard always sets the bucket down right next to my cell's stainless-steel toilet, and I always drag the bucket over next to my bed, the closest thing I get to exercise. I eat the sandwich right away, of course. I don't remember what it feels like not to be starving.

Processed cheese on stale bread, a toilet without a seat, and total isolation. That's been my life.

When I first got here, I tried to keep track of how often the guard came so that I could keep count of the days, but sometimes I think they forget about me. Or ignore me on purpose. My greatest fear is that they'll just leave me in here to waste away, that I'll just pass out from dehydration, not even realizing that I'm living my last moment. I'd much rather die free, fighting the Mogadorians.

Or, better yet, not die at all.

I take a deep swig of the warm, rust-flavored water. It's disgusting, but I'm able to work some moisture back into my mouth. I stretch my arms above my head, my joints popping in protest. A jolt of pain comes from my wrists, my stretch pulling at the still-fresh scar tissue there. And that's when my mind starts wandering again—this time not into fantasy, but memory.

I think about West Virginia every day. I relive it.

I remember darting through those tunnels, clutching that red stone Nine had loaned me, shining its alien light on dozens of cell doors. In each one I hoped to find my father, and each time I was disappointed.

Then the Mogs came, cutting me off from John and Nine. I remember the fear that came from being separated from the others—maybe they could fight off that many Mogs and Piken with their Legacies. Unfortunately, all I had was a stolen Mog blaster.

I did the best I could, shooting any Mog that got too close, all the while trying to find a way back to John and Nine.

I could hear John shouting my name above all the fighting. He was close, if only we weren't separated by a horde of alien beasts.

A monster's tail lashed across my legs. My feet went out from under me. I lost my grip on Nine's stone and went tumbling to the ground. I hit face first, opening up a gash above my eyebrow. Blood immediately started trickling into my eyes. Half blinded, I crawled for cover.

Of course, considering the lucky streak I'd been on since arriving in West Virginia, it wasn't that surprising that I ended up right at the feet of a Mogadorian warrior. He aimed his blaster at me, could've killed me right then, but reconsidered before pulling the trigger. Instead of gunning me down, he clipped me in the temple with the butt of the gun.

Everything went black.

I woke up suspended from the ceiling by thick chains. Still in the cave, yet somehow I could tell they'd taken me deeper, to a more secure area. My stomach sank when I realized the cave was still standing at all, that I was being held prisoner—what did that mean about John and Nine? Had they gotten out?

I didn't have much strength in my limbs, but I tried pulling against the chains anyway. There was no give. I felt desperate and claustrophobic, was about to cry out, when a huge Mogadorian strode into the room. The biggest one I'd ever seen, with an ugly purple scar on his neck and a strange-looking golden cane clutched in one of his massive hands. He was absolutely hideous, like a nightmare, but I couldn't look away. Somehow, his empty black eyes held my gaze.

"Hello, Samuel," he said as he stalked towards me. "Do you know who I am?"

I shook my head, my mouth suddenly beyond dry.

"I am Setrákus Ra. Supreme commander of the Mogadorian Empire, engineer of the Great Expansion, beloved leader." He bared his teeth in what I realized was supposed to be a smile. "Et cetera."

The ringmaster of a planetary genocide and the mastermind behind an upcoming invasion of Earth had just addressed me by name. I tried to think of what John would do in a situation like this—he'd never flinch in the face of his greatest enemy. I, on the other hand, started to shake, the chains that bound my wrists clanking together.

I could tell Setrákus appreciated my fear. "This can be painless, Samuel. You've chosen the wrong side, but I am nothing if not forgiving. Tell me what I want to know and I'll set you free."

"Never," I stammered, shaking even harder as I anticipated what would come next.

I heard a hissing noise from above and looked up to see viscous black goo dribbling down the chain. It was acrid and chemical, like burning plastic. I could swear the sludge was leaving rust marks on the chain as it dribbled down towards me, and soon it was coating my wrists and I was screaming. The pain was excruciating and the goo had a stickiness to it that made it even worse, as if my wrists were covered in scalding tree sap.

I was about to pass out from the pain when Setrákus touched his staff to my neck, lifting my chin with it. An icy numbness flowed through my body and the pain on my wrists was momentarily eased. It was a twisted kind of relief; a deathly numbness radiated from Setrákus's staff, like my limbs had been drained of blood.

"Just answer my questions," snarled Setrákus, "and this can be over."

His first questions were about John and Nine—where would they go, what they would do next. I felt relieved knowing that they'd escaped, and even more relieved that I hadn't a clue where they'd be hiding. I had been the one holding on to Six's instructions, which had meant John and Nine would need to figure out a new plan, one that I couldn't possibly give away while being tortured. The paper was now missing, so it seemed like a safe bet that the Mogs had searched me while I was unconscious and confiscated the address. Hopefully Six would approach with caution.

"Wherever they end up, it won't be long until they're back here kicking your ass," I told Setrákus. And that was my one badass, heroic moment, because the Mogadorian leader snorted and immediately pulled his staff away from me. The pain in my wrists returned—it was as if the Mogadorian goop was eating right down to my bones.

I was panting and crying the next time Setrákus touched his staff to me, giving me a reprieve. The fight, what little there'd been to begin with, had completely gone out of me.

"What about Spain?" he asked. "What can you tell me about that?"

"Six . . . ," I mumbled, and regretted it. I needed to keep my mouth shut.

The questions kept coming. After Spain it was India, and then questions about the locations of Loralite stones, which I'd never even heard of. Eventually, he asked me about "the tenth," something that Setrákus seemed particularly invested in. I remembered Henri writing about a tenth in his letter to John and how that last Garde didn't make it off Lorien. When I told Setrákus that—information I hoped wouldn't somehow hurt the remaining Garde—he was infuriated.

"You're lying to me, Samuel. I know she's here. Tell me where."

"I don't know," I kept repeating, my voice shaking more and more. With every answer, or lack thereof, Setrákus pulled back his staff and let me feel the searing pain again.

Eventually, Setrákus gave up and just stared at me, disgusted. I was delirious at this point. As if with a mind of its own, the dark ooze slowly crawled back up the chain, disappearing back into the dark recess it'd come from.

"You're useless, Samuel," he'd said, dismissively. "It appears the Loric only value you as a sacrificial lamb, a diversion to be left behind when they're in need of a hasty escape."

Setrákus swept out of the room and later, after I'd hung there for a while slipping in and out of consciousness, some of his soldiers came to retrieve me. They dumped me in a dark cell where I was sure they'd leave me to die.

Days later the Mogadorians dragged me out of my cell and handed me over to a pair of guys with buzz cuts and dark suits, and guns holstered beneath their coats. Humans. They looked like FBI or CIA or something. I don't know why any human would want to work with the Mogs. It makes my blood boil just to think about it, these agents selling out humanity. Even so, the agents were gentler than the Mogadorians, one of them even mumbling an apology as he clasped a pair of manacles over my burned wrists. Then, they pulled a hood over my head, and that was the last I saw of them.

I was driven nonstop for at least two days, chained in the back of a van. After that, I was shoved into another cell—this cell, my new home—an entire block in some big base where I was the only prisoner.

I shudder when I think about Setrákus Ra, something I can't help but do every time I catch a glimpse of the lingering blisters and scars on my wrists. I've tried to put that horrifying encounter out of my head, telling myself that what he'd said wasn't true. I know John didn't use me to cover his escape, and I know that I'm not useless. I can help John and the other Garde, just like my father was doing before he disappeared. I know I have some part to play,

THE FALL OF FIVE

even if it isn't clear exactly what that's going to be.

When I get out of here—if I ever get out of here—my new goal in life is to prove Setrákus Ra wrong.

I'm so frustrated that I pound the mattress in front of me. As soon as I do, a layer of dust shakes looses from the ceiling, and a faint rumbling passes through the floor. It's almost as if my punch sent a shockwave through the entire cell.

I look down at my hand in awe. Maybe those daydreams about developing my own Legacies weren't so farfetched. I try to remember back to John's backyard in Paradise, when Henri would lecture him about focusing his power. I squint hard and ball my fist up tight.

Even though it feels nuts and a little embarrassing, I punch the mattress again, just to see what happens.

Nothing. Just a soreness in my arms from not using those muscles in days. I'm not developing Legacies. That's impossible for a human being and I know that. I'm just getting desperate. And maybe a little crazy.

"Okay, Sam," I say to myself, my voice hoarse. "Keep it together."

As soon as I lie back down, resigned to another endless stretch alone with my thoughts, a second jolt ripples through the floor. This one is much bigger than the first; I can feel it in my very bones. More plaster drifts down from the ceiling. It coats my face and gets in my mouth, bitter and chalky tasting. Moments later, I hear the

378

muffled drumbeat of gunfire.

This isn't a dream at all. I can distantly hear the sounds of a fight from somewhere deep within the base. The floor shakes again—another explosion. As long as I've been here, they've never done any kind of training or drills. Hell, I never hear anything except the echoing footsteps of the guard bringing me my food. And now this sudden action? What could be happening?

For the first time in—days? weeks?—I allow myself to hope. It's the Garde. It has to be. They've come to rescue me.

"This is it, Sam," I tell myself, willing myself to move.

I stand up and move shakily to the door of my cell. My legs feel like jelly. I haven't had much reason to use them since they brought me here. Even crossing the short distance of my cell to the door is enough to make my head swim. I press my forehead to the cool metal of the bars, waiting for the dizziness to pass. I can feel reverberations of the fight below passing through the metal, growing stronger and more intense.

"John!" I shout, my voice hoarse. "Six! Anyone! I'm here! I'm in here!"

Part of me thinks it's silly to cry out, as if the Garde could hear my cries over the massive battle it sounds like they're fighting. It's that same part of me that's wanted to give up, to just curl up in my cell and wait out my ultimate fate. It's the same part of me that thinks the Garde would be stupid to try to rescue me.

It's the part of me that believed Setrákus Ra. I can't give in to that feeling of despair. I have to prove him wrong.

I need to make some noise.

"John!" I scream again. "I'm in here, John!"

Weak as I feel, I pound my fists against the steel bars as hard as I can. The sound echoes throughout the empty block, but there's no way the Garde could hear it above the muffled gunfire coming through the walls. It's hard to tell over the increasing sounds of battle, but I think I hear footsteps rattling across the steel gangway that connects the cells. Too bad I can't see anything beyond the few feet in front of my cell. If there is someone in here with me, I've got to get their attention and just hope it isn't a Mog guard.

I grab my water bucket and dump out what's left of my day's supply. My plan—the best one I've got—is to bang it against the bars of my cell.

When I turn back around, there's a guy standing outside my door.

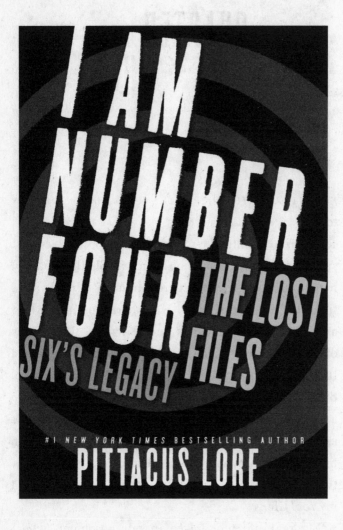

CHAPTER
ONE

KATARINA SAYS THERE IS MORE THAN ONE WAY to hide.

Before we came down here to Mexico, we lived in a suburb of Denver. My name then was Sheila, a name I hate even more than my current name, Kelly. We lived there for two years, and I wore barrettes in my hair and pink rubber bracelets on my wrists, like all the other girls at my school. I had sleepovers with some of them, the girls I called "my friends." I went to school during the school year, and in the summer I went to a swimmers' camp at the YMCA. I liked my friends and the life we had there okay, but I had already been moved around by my Cêpan Katarina enough to know that it wasn't going to be permanent. I knew it wasn't my *real* life.

My real life took place in our basement, where Katarina and I did combat training. By day, it was an ordinary suburban rec room, with a big comfy couch and a TV in one corner and a Ping-Pong table in the other. By night, it was a well-stocked combat training gym, with hanging bags, floor mats, weapons, and even a makeshift pommel horse.

In public, Katarina played the part of my mother, claiming that her "husband" and my "father" had been killed in a car accident when I was an infant. Our names, our lives, our stories were all fictions, identities for me and Katarina to hide behind. But those identities allowed us to live out in the open. Acting normal.

Blending in: that was one way of hiding.

But we slipped up. To this day I can remember our conversation as we drove away from Denver, headed to Mexico for no other reason than we'd never been there, both of us trying to figure out how exactly we'd blown our cover. Something I said to my friend Eliza had contradicted something Katarina had said to Eliza's mother. Before Denver we'd lived in Nova Scotia for a cold, cold winter, but as I remembered it, our story, the lie we'd agreed to tell, was that we'd lived in Boston before Denver. Katarina remembered differently, and claimed Tallahassee as our previous home. Then Eliza told her mother and that's when people started to get suspicious.

It was hardly a calamitous exposure. We had no immediate reason to believe our slip would raise the kind of suspicion that could attract the Mogadorians to our location. But our life had gone sour there, and Katarina figured we'd been there long enough as it was.

So we moved yet again.

The sun is bright and hard in Puerto Blanco, the air impossibly dry. Katarina and I make no attempt to blend in with the other residents, Mexican farmers and their children. Our only regular contact with the locals is our once-a-week trip into town to buy essentials at the small store. We are the only whites for many miles, and though we both speak good Spanish, there's no confusing us for natives of the place. To our neighbors, we are the gringas, strange white recluses.

"Sometimes you can hide just as effectively by sticking out," Katarina says.

She appears to be right. We have been here almost a year and we haven't been bothered once. We lead a lonely but ordered life in a sprawling, single-level shack tucked between two big patches of farmland. We wake up with the sun, and before eating or showering Katarina has me run drills in the backyard: running up and down a small hill, doing calisthenics, and practicing tai chi. We take advantage of the two relatively cool hours of morning.

Morning drills are followed by a light breakfast, then three hours of studies: languages, world history, and whatever other subjects Katarina can dig up from the internet. She says her teaching method and subject matter are "eclectic." I don't know what that word means, but I'm just grateful for the variety. Katarina is a quiet, thoughtful woman, and though she's the closest thing I have to a mother, she's very different from me.

Studies are probably the highlight of her day. I prefer drills.

After studies it's back out into the blazing sun, where the heat makes me dizzy enough that I can almost hallucinate my imagined enemies. I do battle with straw men: shooting them with arrows, stabbing them with knives, or simply pummeling them with my bare fists. But half-blind from the sun, I see them as Mogadorians, and I relish the chance to tear them to pieces. Katarina says even though I am only thirteen years old, I'm so agile and so strong I could easily take down even a well-trained adult.

One of the nice things about living in Puerto Blanco is that I don't have to hide my skills. Back in Denver, whether swimming at the Y or just playing on the street, I always had to hold back, to keep myself from revealing the superior speed and strength that Katarina's training regimen has resulted in. We keep to ourselves out here, away from the eyes of others, so I don't have to hide.

Today is Sunday, so our afternoon drills are short,

only an hour. I am shadowboxing with Katarina in the backyard, and I can feel her eagerness to quit: her moves are halfhearted, she's squinting against the sun, and she looks tired. I love training and could go all day, but out of deference to her I suggest we call it a day.

"Oh, I suppose we could finish early," she says. I grin privately, allowing her to think I'm the tired one. We go inside and Katarina pours us two tall glasses of *agua fresca*, our customary Sunday treat. The fan is blowing full force in our humble shack's living room. Katarina boots up her various computers while I kick off my dirty, sweat-filled fighting boots and collapse to the floor. I stretch my arms to keep them from knotting up, then swing them to the bookshelf in the corner and pull out a tall stack of the board games we keep there. Risk, Stratego, Othello. Katarina has tried to interest me in games like Life and Monopoly, saying it wouldn't hurt to be "well-rounded." But those games never held my interest. Katarina got the hint, and now we only play combat and strategy games.

Risk is my favorite, and since we finished early today I think Katarina will agree to playing it even though it's a longer game than the others.

"Risk?"

Katarina is at her desk chair, pivoting from one screen to the next.

"Risk of what?" she asks absently.

I laugh, then shake the box near her head. She doesn't look up from the screens, but the sound of all those pieces rattling around inside the box is enough for her to get it.

"Oh," she says. "Sure."

I set up the board. Without asking, I divvy up the armies into hers and mine, and begin placing them all across the game's map. We've played this game so much I don't need to ask her which countries she'd like to claim, or which territories she'd like to fortify. She always chooses the U.S. and Asia. I happily place her pieces on those territories, knowing that from my more easily defended territories I will quickly grow armies strong enough to crush hers.

I'm so absorbed in setting up the game I don't even notice Katarina's silence, *her* absorption. It is only when I crack my neck loudly and she neglects to scold me for it—"Please don't," she usually says, squeamish about the sound it makes—that I look up and see her, staring openmouthed at one of her monitors.

"Kat?" I ask.

She's silent.

I get up from the floor, stepping across the game board to join her at her desk. It is only then that I see what has so completely captured her attention. A breaking news item about some kind of explosion on a bus in England.

I groan.

Katarina is always checking the internet and the news for mysterious deaths. Deaths that could be the work of the Mogadorians. Deaths that could mean the second member of the Garde has been defeated. She's been doing it since we came to Earth, and I've grown frustrated with the doom-and-gloom of it.

Besides, it's not like it did us any good the first time.

I was nine years old, living in Nova Scotia with Katarina. Our training room there was in the attic. Katarina had retired from training for the day, but I still had energy to burn, and was doing moores and spindles on the pommel horse alone when I suddenly felt a blast of scorching pain on my ankle. I lost my balance and came crashing down to the mat, clutching my ankle and screaming in pain.

My first scar. It meant that the Mogadorians had killed Number One, the first of the Garde. And for all of Katarina's web scouring, it had caught us both completely unaware.

We waited on pins and needles for weeks after, expecting a second death and a second scar to follow in short order. But it didn't come. I think Katarina is still coiled, anxious, ready to spring. But three years have passed—almost a quarter of my whole life—and it's just not something I think about much.

I step between her and the monitor. "It's Sunday. Game time."

"Please, Kelly." She says my most recent alias with a certain stiffness. I know I will always be Six to her. In my heart, too. These aliases I use are just shells, they're not who I really am. I'm sure back on Lorien I had a name, a real name, not just a number. But that's so far back, and I've had so many names since then, that I can't remember what it was.

Six is my true name. Six is who I am.

Katarina bats me aside, eager to read more details.

We've lost so many game days to news alerts like this. And they never turn out to be anything. They're just ordinary tragedies.

Earth, I've come to discover, has no shortage of tragedies.

"Nope. It's just a bus crash. We're playing a game." I pull at her arms, eager for her to relax. She looks so tired and worried, I know she could use the break.

She holds firm. "It's a bus *explosion*. And apparently," she says, pulling away to read from the screen, "the conflict is ongoing."

"The conflict always is," I say, rolling my eyes. "Come on."

She shakes her head, giving one of her frazzled laughs. "Okay," she says. "Fine."

Katarina pulls herself away from the monitors,

sitting on the floor by the game. It takes all my strength not to lick my chops at her upcoming defeat: I always win at Risk.

I get down beside her, on my knees.

"You're right, Kelly," she says, allowing herself to grin. "I needn't panic over every little thing—"

One of the monitors on Katarina's desk lets out a sudden *ding!* One of her alerts. Her computers are programmed to scan for unusual news reports, blog posts, even notable shifts in global weather—all sifting for possible news of the Garde.

"Oh come on," I say.

But Katarina is already off the floor and back at the desk, scrolling and clicking from link to link once again.

"Fine," I say, annoyed. "But I'm showing no mercy when the game begins."

Suddenly Katarina is silent, stopped cold by something she's found.

I get up off the floor and step over the board, making my way to the monitor.

I look at the screen.

It is not, as I'd imagined, a news report from England. It is a simple, anonymous blog post. Just a few haunting, tantalizing words:

"Nine, now eight. Are the rest of you out there?"

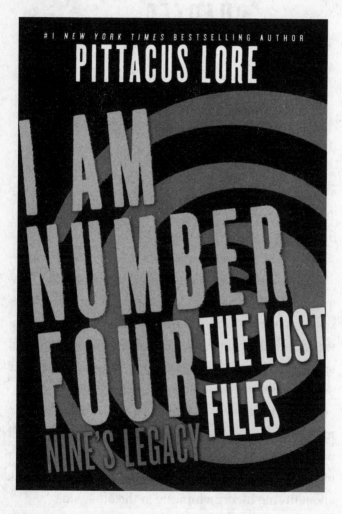

CHAPTER ONE

THERE ARE RULES FOR HIDING IN PLAIN SIGHT. The first rule, or at least the one that Sandor repeats most often, is "Don't be stupid."

I'm about to break that rule by taking off my pants.

Spring in Chicago is my favorite season. The winters are cold and windy, the summers hot and loud, the springs perfect. This morning is sunny, but there's still a forbidding chill in the air, a reminder of winter. Ice-cold spray blows in off Lake Michigan, stinging my cheeks and dampening the pavement under my sneakers.

I jog all eighteen miles of the lakefront path every morning, taking breaks whenever I can, not because I need them, but to admire the choppy gray-blue water of Lake Michigan. Even when it's cold, I always think about diving in, of swimming to the other side.

I fight the urge just like I fight the urge to keep pace with the neon spandex cyclists that zip past. I have to go slow. There are more than two million people in this city and I'm faster than all of them.

Still, I have to jog.

Sometimes, I make the run twice to really work up a sweat. That's another one of Sandor's rules for hiding in plain sight: always appear to be weaker than I actually am. Never push it.

It's dumb to complain. We've been in Chicago for five years thanks to Sandor's rules. Five years of peace and quiet. Five years since the Mogadorians last had a real bead on us.

Five years of steadily increasing boredom.

So when a sudden vibration stirs the iPod strapped to my upper arm, my stomach drops. The device isn't supposed to react unless trouble is near.

I take just a moment to decide on what I do next. I know it's a risk. I know it flies against everything I've been told to do. But I also know that risks are worth it; I know that sometimes you have to ignore your training. So I jog to the side of the runner's path, pretending that I need to work out a cramp. When I'm finished stretching, I unsnap the tear-away track pants I've been rocking every jog since we moved to Chicago and stuff them into my pack. Underneath I'm wearing a pair of mesh shorts, red and white like the St. Louis Cardinals, enemy colors here in Chicago.

But Cards colors in Cubs territory are nothing to

worry about compared to the three scars ringing my ankle. Baseball rivalries and bloody interplanetary vendettas just don't compare.

My low socks and running shoes do little to hide the scars. Anyone nearby could see them, although I doubt my fellow runners are in the habit of checking out each other's ankles. Only the particular runner I'm trying to attract today will really notice.

When I start jogging again, my heart is beating way harder than normal. Excitement. It's been a while since I felt anything like this. I'm breaking Sandor's rule and it's exhilarating. I just hope he isn't watching me through the city's police cameras that he's hacked into. That would be bad.

My iPod rumbles again. It's not actually an iPod. It doesn't play any music and the earbuds are just for show. It's a gadget that Sandor put together in his lab.

It's my Mogadorian detector. I call it my iMog.

The iMog has its limitations. It picks out Mogadorian genetic patterns in the immediate area, but only has a radius of a few blocks and is prone to interference. It's fueled by Mogadorian genetic material, which has a habit of rapidly decaying; so it's no surprise that the iMog can get a little hinky. As Sandor explains it, the device is something we received when we first arrived from Lorien, from a human Loric friend. Sandor has spent considerable time trying to modify it. It was his idea to encase it in an iPod shell as a way to avoid attention. There's no track list or album art on my iMog's screen—just a solitary white dot against a field of black. That's me. I'm the white dot. The last time we tuned it up was after the most recent time we were attacked, scraping Mogadorian ash off our clothes so Sandor could synthesize it or stabilize it or some scientific stuff I only half paid attention to. Our rule is that if the iMog sounds off, we get moving. It's been so long since it's activated itself that I'd started to worry that the thing had gone dead.

And then, during my run a couple days ago, it went off. One solitary red dot trolling the lakefront. I hustled home that day, but I didn't tell Sandor what had happened. At best, there'd be no more runs on the lakefront. At worst, we'd be packing up boxes. And I didn't want either of those things to happen.

Maybe that's when I first broke the "don't be stupid" rule. When I started keeping things from my Cêpan.

The device is now vibrating and beeping because of the red dot that's fallen into step a few yards behind me. Vibrating and beeping in tune with my accelerated heartbeat.

A Mogadorian.

I hazard a glance over my shoulder and have no trouble picking out which jogger is the Mog. He's tall, with black hair shaved close to the scalp, and is wearing a thrift-store Bears sweatshirt and a pair of wraparound sunglasses. He could pass for human if he wasn't so pale, his face not showing any color even in this brisk air.

I pick up my pace but don't bother trying to get away. Why make it easy on him? I want to see whether this Mog can keep up.

By the time I exit the lakefront and head for home, I realize I might have been a little cocky. He's good—better than I expect him to be. But I'm better. Still, as I pick up speed, I feel my heart racing from exertion for the first time in as long as I can remember.

He's gaining on me, and my breaths are getting shorter. I'm okay for now, but I won't be able to keep this up forever. I double-check the iMog. Luckily my stalker hasn't called in backup. It's still just the one red dot. Just us.

Tuning out the noise of the city around us—yuppie couples headed to brunch, happy tourist families cracking jokes about the wind—I focus on the Mog, using my naturally enhanced hearing to listen to his breathing. He's getting winded too; his breathing is ragged now. But his footsteps are still in sync with my own. I listen for anything that sounds like him going for a communicator, ready to break into a sprint if he sends out an alert.

He doesn't. I can feel his eyes boring into my back. He thinks that I haven't noticed him.

Smug, exhausted, and dumb. He's just what I'd been hoping for.

The John Hancock Center rises above us. The sun blinks off the skyscraper's thousand windows. One hundred stories and, at the top, my home.

The Mog hesitates as I breeze through the front door, then follows. He catches up to me as I cross the lobby. Even though I'd been expecting it, I stiffen when I feel the cold barrel of a small Mogadorian blaster pressed between my shoulder blades.

"Keep walking," he hisses.

Although I know he can't hurt me while I'm protected by the Loric charm, I play along. I let him think he's in control.

I smile and wave at the security guards manning the front desk. With the Mog dogging my heels, we climb into the elevator.

Alone at last.

The Mog keeps his gun aimed at me as I hit the button for the 100th floor. I'm more nervous than I thought I'd be. I've never been alone with a Mog before. I remind myself that everything is going just as I planned it. As the elevator begins its ascent, I act as casual as I can.

"Did you have a nice run?"

The Mog grabs me around the throat and slams me against the wall of the elevator. I brace myself to have the wind knocked out of me. Instead, a warm sensation runs down my back and it's the Mog who stumbles backward, gasping.

The Loric charm at work. I'm always surprised at how well it works.

"So you aren't Number Four," he says.

"You're quick."

"Which are you?"

"I *could* tell you." I shrug. "I don't see what it would matter. But I'll let you guess."

He eyes me, sizing me up, trying to intimidate me. I don't know what the rest of the Garde are like, but I don't scare that easy. I take off the iMog, laying it gently on the floor. If the Mog finds this unusual, he doesn't let on. I wonder what the prize is for capturing a Garde. "I may not know your number, but I know you can look forward to a life of captivity while we kill the rest of your friends. Don't worry," he adds, "it won't be long."

"Good story," I reply, glancing up at the elevator panel. We're almost at the top.

I dreamed about this moment last night. Actually, that's not quite right. I couldn't sleep last night, too keyed up for what was to come. I fantasized about this moment.

I make sure to savor my words.

"Here's the thing," I tell him. "You're not making it out of here alive."

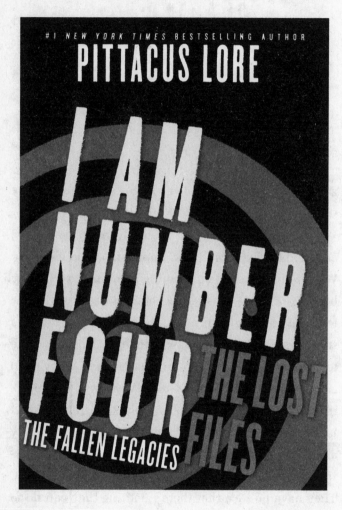

CHAPTER ONE

SOMETIMES I WONDER WHAT THEY WOULD THINK if they knew we were here. Right under their noses.

I'm sitting with my best friend, Ivan, on the grassy, crowded National Mall, the stupid stone obelisk of the Washington Monument looming above us. I've put my homework aside for the moment, and as I watch the tourists studying their maps, the lawyers and officials scurrying obliviously down Independence Avenue to their next meeting, I'm almost amused. They're so caught up with silly fears about UV rays and chemicals in their vegetables and meaningless "terrorist threat levels" and whatever else it is that these people worry about, that it never occurs to them that two kids working on their homework in the grass are the real threat. They have no idea that there's nothing they can do to protect themselves. The true enemy is already here.

"Hey!" I sometimes want to shout, waving my arms.

"I'm your future evil dictator! Tremble before me, jerks!"

Of course I can't do that. Not yet. That time will come. In the meantime, they can all stare right through me as if I'm just another normal face in the crowd. The truth is I'm anything but normal, even if I do my best to look it. On Earth, assimilation protocol demands that I be known as Adam, son of Andrew and Susannah Sutton, citizen of Washington DC. But that's not who I am at all.

I am Adamus Sutekh, son of the great general Andrakkus Sutekh.

I am a Mogadorian. I am who they should be afraid of.

Unfortunately, for now, being an alien conqueror isn't as exciting as it should be. At the moment I'm still stuck doing my homework. My father has promised me that this won't last forever; when the Mogadorians ascend to power on this crappy little planet, I will control the capital city of the United States. Trust me, after spending the last four years in this place, I've got a pretty good idea of some changes I'll make. The first thing I'll do is rename all the streets. None of this Independence, Constitution stuff—this weak, stupid patriotism. When I'm in charge, no one will even be able to remember what the Constitution is. When I'm in charge, my avenues will carry titles of appropriate menace.

"Blood of Warriors Boulevard," I murmur to myself, trying to decide if it has a good ring to it. Hard to say. "Broken Sword Way . . ."

"Huh?" Ivan asks, glancing up from his spot on the grass next to me. He's lying on his stomach, a pencil held across his index finger like a makeshift blaster. While I dream of the day I'll be the ruler of all I survey, Ivan imagines himself as a sniper, picking off Loric enemies as they leave the Lincoln Memorial. "What did you say?"

"Nothing," I reply.

Ivanick Shu-Ra, son of the great warrior Bolog Shu-Ra, shrugs his shoulders. Ivan has never been much for fantasies that don't include some kind of bloody combat. His family claims a distant relation to our Beloved Leader, Setrákus Ra, and if Ivan's size is any indication, I'm inclined to believe them. Ivan's two years younger than me but is already bigger, broad shouldered and thick while I am lithe and agile. He already looks like a warrior and keeps his coarse black hair cropped close, eager for the day when he'll be able to shave it off entirely and take on the ceremonial Mogadorian tattoos.

I still remember the night of the First Great Expansion, when my people conquered Lorien. I was eight years old that night, too old to be crying, but I cried anyway when I was told I'd be staying in orbit above

Lorien with the women and children. My tears only lasted a few seconds until the General slapped some sense into me. Ivan watched my tantrum, dumbly sucking his thumb, maybe too young to realize what was happening. We watched the battle from our ship's observatory with my mother and infant sister. We clapped as flames spread across the planet below us. After the fight was won and the Loric people were destroyed, the General returned to our ship covered in blood. Despite the triumph, his face was serious. Before saying anything to my mother or me, he knelt before Ivan and explained that his father had died in service to our race. A glorious death, befitting a true Mogadorian hero. He rubbed his thumb across Ivan's forehead, leaving a trail of blood. A blessing.

As an afterthought, the General did the same to me.

After that, Ivan, whose mother had died during childbirth, came to live with us and was raised as my brother. My parents are considered lucky to have three trueborn children.

I'm not always sure that my father feels lucky to have me, though. Whenever my test scores or physical evaluations are less than satisfactory, the General jokes that he might have to transfer my inheritance to Ivan.

I'm mostly sure he's joking.

My gaze drifts towards a family of sightseers as they cross the lawn, each of them taking in the world through digital cameras. The father pauses to snap a series of photos of the Monument, and I briefly reconsider my plans to demolish it. Instead, perhaps I could make it taller; maybe install a penthouse for myself in the uppermost floor. Ivan could have the room below mine.

The daughter of the tourist family is probably about thirteen, like me, and she's cute in a shy way, with a mouth full of braces. I catch her looking at me and find myself unconsciously shifting into a more presentable position, sitting up straighter, tilting my chin down to hide the severe angle of my too-large nose. When the girl smiles at me, I look away. Why should I care what some human thinks of me?

We must always remember why we are here.

"Does it ever amaze you how easily they accept us as their own?" I ask Ivan.

"Never underestimate human stupidity," he says, reaching over to tap the blank page of homework sitting next to me. "Are you going to finish this shit or what?"

The homework lying next to me isn't mine—it's Ivan's. He's waiting for me to do it for him. Written assignments have always given him problems, whereas the right answers come easily to me.

I glance down at the assignment. Ivan is supposed to write a short essay on a quote from the Great Book— the book of Mogadorian wisdom and ethics that all of our people must learn and live by—interpreting what Setrákus Ra's writing means to him personally.

"'We do not begrudge the beast for hunting,'" I read aloud, although like most of my people I know the passage by heart. "'It is in the beast's nature to hunt, just as it is in the Mogadorian's nature to expand. Those that would resist the expansion of the Mogadorian Empire, therefore, stand in opposition to nature itself.'"

I look over at Ivan. He's taken aim on the family I was watching before, making high-pitched laser beam noises through gritted teeth. The girl with the braces frowns at him and turns away.

"What does that mean to you?" I ask.

"I don't know," he grunts. "That our race is the most badass, and everyone else should deal with it. Right?"

I shrug my shoulders, sighing. "Close enough."

I pick up my pen and start to scribble something down, but am interrupted by the chime of my cell phone. I figure it's a text message from my mother, asking me to pick up something from the store on my way home. She's really taken to cooking over the last couple years, and, I'll admit it, the food here on Earth blows away what we used to get on Mogadore. What they consider "processed" here would be treasured on my home planet, where food—among other things—is grown in subterranean vats.

The text isn't from Mom, though. The message is from the General.

"Shit," I say, dropping my pen as if the General had just caught me helping Ivan cheat.

My father never sends text messages. The act is beneath him. If the General wants something, we're supposed to anticipate what it is before he even has to ask. Something really important must have happened.

"What is it?" asks Ivan.

The message reads simply: HOME NOW.

"We have to go."

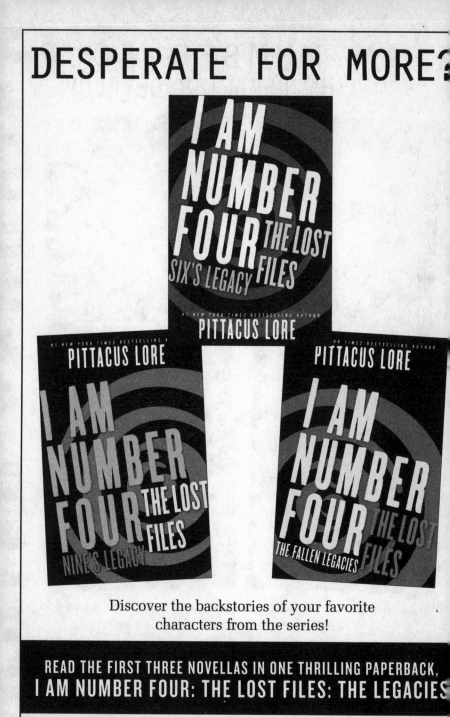